YUKON
MURDERS

Don G. Porter

Don G Porter
10-24-08

McRoy & Blackburn
Publishers

McRoy and Blackburn, Publishers
PO Box 276
Ester, Alaska 99725
www.alaskafiction.com

Elmer E. Rasmuson Library Cataloging in Publication Data:
Porter, Don G.
Yukon murders / Don G. Porter. Ester, Alaska : McRoy & Blackburn,
    c2007.
  p. cm.
ISBN 13: 978-0-9706712-9-5
ISBN 10: 0-9706712-9-6
1. Detective and mystery stories, American—Alaska—Fiction. 2. Alaska—
    Division of State Troopers—Fiction. I. Title.

PS3616.O77 Y85 2007

Book and cover design and layout by Sue and Russ Mitchell, Inkworks.

This book is dedicated to the memory of Alaska State Trooper Timothy Litera. Trooper Litera served the residents of Alaksa in Juneau, Bethel, St. Marys, and Fairbanks. For twenty-five years, he served with exemplary dedication and the highest ideals of the Alaska State Troopers. He retired to Haines, Alaska, as a first sargeant.

He lost only one fight in his life, but it was the big one, with cancer. He succumbed on July 7 in the year of our Lord 2000.

This book is fiction and the character I call Trooper Tom, who bends the law and who marries Minnie from Kiana, is fictitious. However, as I wrote the dialogue and described situations, the memory of Trooper Timothy Litera was always with me. I hope this book conveys the profound respect and affection that I, and thousands of other Alaska residents, had for him.

Tim left a family in Alaska. His wife Rayne lives in Haines, his son Lance, daughter-in-law Jennifer, and grandson Trevor live in Barrow. Tim's daughter Jessica Willis and her husband Rick live in North Pole. Daughter Amber Lynn Busby and her husband Zeke live in Fairbanks.

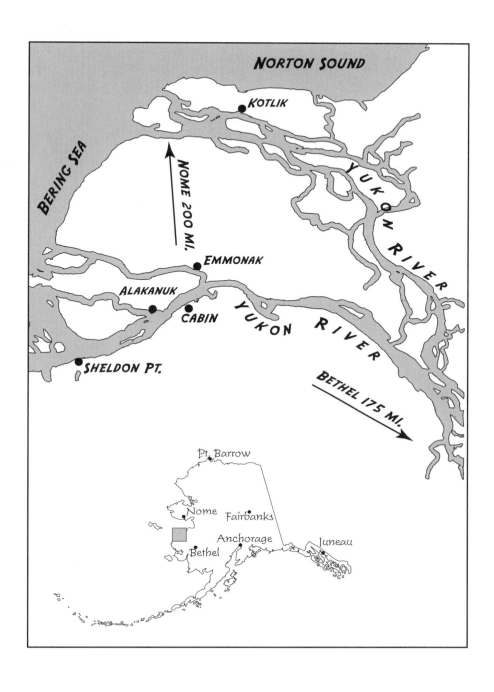

FIRST VISIT
MONDAY MORNING
ALAKANUK, ALASKA

Two men stood in the pool of yellow light from the single bulb hanging above the cash register. Tall and stocky, Demientoff was dressed for inside work in a plaid shirt and jeans. His visitor was shorter, slight, and still wearing his beaver parka but unzipped, hanging open to reveal a blue wool shirt. His matching beaver hat was pushed back on his head; wolf mitts dangled from the lanyard around his neck.

The rest of the store remained dark and eerily quiet, shadows swaying as the light bulb swung in tiny ovals. Demientoff was making a show of moving stacks of bills from the safe to the register, counting each stack. He seemed to be taking a perverse satisfaction in keeping his visitor waiting.

The visitor stood quietly, leaning casually against the counter. He appeared to be subserviently patient, but his mind was churning.

Keep smiling. Pompous ass. He thinks I'm here to talk about the sharing. He did it again this morning: his superior, "Oh, hello, Shorty," as though I was some bum seeking favors. Without me, he'd be the bum, probably scrabbling for subsistence and looking for satisfaction in a whiskey bottle. I gave him this store as a gift, set him up for life, and he never even thanked me. The rest of the world thinks he's a nice guy. Maybe it's because he knows he owes me that he doesn't want to see me. He should be treating me with respect. With his attitude he's going to ruin the plan, and I can't allow that.

Demientoff had started with the twenties, was down to counting out twenty ones, taking his time, turning each bill face up, Washington gazing to the left.

The visitor pushed himself away from the counter, pointed at the glass gun case. "Hey, Demientoff, I need a new .30-06. Let me check one out while you're busy."

"That old blunderbuss of yours finally give up? Remington or Winchester?"

"Bolt action, don't need a scope."

Demientoff stopped counting, shrugged his irritation, but turned to open the locked case with a key on his ring and handed a rifle to the visitor.

"Try this one." He went back to counting money.

"Not bad." The visitor slid the bolt, dry fired it. He aimed at a shadow at the end of the aisle, dry fired it again. "Nice balance. How about a special price for an old friend?"

"No can do. Price barely covers expenses."

There it is again. High and mighty sneer. He's not only forgotten that I'm his benefactor; he isn't even acknowledging me as a friend. The visitor slipped a cartridge into the chamber. A snowmachine coughed to life outside; the driver revved his engine.

Demientoff looked up in shock at the rifle pointed his way. "Hey, be careful where you're pointing that thing."

"I am, very careful." The visitor shot him between the eyes. Demientoff flew back against the wall, brains and blood spattering on the rough boards. He crumpled to the floor, blood spurting and pooling around him. The visitor stepped over the body to reach the polishing rag and the little bottle of gun oil. *He doesn't look so high and mighty now. Still too good for me, Demientoff?* The visitor ejected the shell, pocketed it, poured a few drops of oil down the barrel and wiped the gun clean with the polishing rag. He carefully set the rifle back in its slot in the rack, making sure there was no sign of its having been moved. The key ring still dangled from the lock. He locked the case and bent to stuff the ring into Demientoff's pocket.

You have to plan, think of all the details, he told himself. *Stay calm, don't hurry, don't make mistakes. That's your special genius. You never make mistakes.* He took the bills out of the register to make the killing appear to be a robbery, being careful not to touch anything but the money. He used his handkerchief to open the back door, heard the lock click behind him. At seven-fifteen it was still dark, but a few people were moving in the village, blocked from his view by the silhouette of the store. He could hear snowmachines running, dogs barking for their feeding; somewhere a door slammed. Alakanuk River below him was ghostly white, his snowmachine an indistinct black shadow parked on the trail.

A ridge of unmarked snow covered the edge of the loading dock. He jumped over that, landed a foot short of the hard-packed trail, and sank inches into soft snow on the river ice. All part of his plan; he wanted to leave tracks in the snow.

Just one more detail, the elegant solution. He pulled the wolf-fur cap out of his parka and tossed it up toward the edge of the loading dock. *It's not my fault that big gussak got in my way. I'll smash him. That's what sets me apart from the losers. Nothing stops me. The gussak struts around the village like he owns it. Maybe a few years in jail will put him in his place.*

A hundred yards downstream an engine revved and the headlight of a machine flashed on snow and bumped down onto the river. The visitor started the Arctic Cat and drove up the trail toward the Yukon. He was careful not to drive too fast; he mustn't appear to be running away. Just fast enough to keep out of the light from the machine behind.

CHAPTER 2

10:00 MONDAY MORNING
BETHEL, ALASKA

Vickie's phone ringing at ten on a Monday morning in December sent a groan around the room. The call meant someone had to fly. None of us was particularly eager, but that was why we were there. Vickie answered the phone, wrote an entry on the blank schedule sheet, and pointed at me. She pantomimed a pistol, shooting me with her extended finger and a click of her tongue.

"Trooper Tom needs a ride to Alakanuk in an hour. Expect four or five hours standby. Just two seats; the third passenger will be in a body bag." She went back to reading her book, propping her elbow on her blotter, cupping delicate chin in hand. Her ruby nails disappeared under a honey-blonde tress that swung forward to mask her face, making a personal privacy curtain.

Presiding over the bare wooden waiting room at Bushmaster Air Service, Vickie was an anomaly, but a welcome one, like finding a lush tropical island in the middle of the North Atlantic. In a fuzzy blue sweater, gray skirt, heels and hose, she seemed to be trying to raise the tone of our operation all by herself.

The pilots who were reading magazines or napping around the room were the scruffy lot you would expect in the Alaska Bush, dressed for winter but with zippers open down the fronts and up the legs of their snowsuits. I marked my place in the book I was reading, stood and zipped, pulled a parka on over my snowsuit, grabbed a beaver-fur cap and a pair of wolf mitts from the chair arm, picked up my flight bag, and went out to prepare for Trooper Tom.

When I opened the door to the arctic entry, cold air wafted in and instantly condensed to ice fog. Some wag behind me hollered, "Have a nice day." I looked around, but all I could see was the fog, so I fanned the door a couple of times to share the misery. The "nice day" crack was partly because of the temperature, but also because Vickie had said, ". . . *will be* in a body bag," not ". . . *is* in a body bag." That likely meant that Tom and I would have to do the bagging, so how nice a day it was would depend on the vintage of the body and how many pieces it was in.

When the state troopers called, they asked for me and I chauffeured them if I was available, but not because I'm the best pilot. There's a level of competence beyond which degrees are meaningless.

Richard Bach once wrote a story about a pilot who loved his airplane so much that when the chips were down, the airplane loved him back and made a takeoff in less distance than the manufacturer's specifications. Well, these pilots didn't love their airplanes. In fact, they cursed and swore at them, and they weren't particularly loving or lovable guys. A couple of them were nursing hangovers and hoping to heck they wouldn't get sent out, but to a man, the scruffy pilots sitting around that room knew how to fly.

They made takeoffs and landings that the aircraft manufacturers never dreamed of. They did it routinely, day in, day out. They did it in ice storms, they did it in whiteouts, they did it in pitch-black nights, and they did it with any number of aircraft malfunctions. No, it would be hard to pick a best pilot out of that crew.

The troopers asked for me because I was the one they had conned into getting my private detective's license. If you want one, you can get one, too. Just send a few hundred bucks to the School of Private Investigation. Call me if you want the address. You read a couple of good books, take twenty open-book tests, and get an impressive diploma. You give the diploma and a hundred-dollar bill to the state licensing bureau, and voilà, you're a shamus, a gumshoe, a private dick.

That gives you no official standing whatsoever, and the antipathy between professional police and PIs is legendary. The relationship between Hercule Poirot and Inspector Japp is pure fiction. But normal rules seldom apply in the Bush. It's not that I became a great detective, but I did learn a lot about the law, the rules of evidence, and a lot that I really did not want to know about our courts and the recent history of our police. If I had read the statistics on how few criminals are caught and convicted before I became a charter pilot, I probably would have gone another route.

I took a lot of ribbing from the other pilots while I read the books. They asked if I was learning to pick locks and spy through keyholes. The reality is the opposite. Since the object of most private investigation is to gather evidence that's admissible in court, you have to observe every law against trespass or invasion of privacy. Even jaywalking while you're on a case might get you thrown out of court. In the real world, most of the fictional detectives we grew up with would have gone to jail themselves while their suspects walked free.

It wasn't my detecting expertise the troopers wanted; it was the title. For instance, when a hot gun is submitted into evidence, the chain of custody has to be established. The jurors have to know that the gun the DA is waving in their faces is the same gun the defendant waved at the victim. It sounds better if the troopers can say, "It was signed into the custody of Detective Price," rather than, "I gave it to Alex, the pilot." Notice, I said it *sounds* better. It *isn't* better; many situations are illegal if you insist on getting technical, but in the Bush you do what you have to do.

Bagging and loading bodies was not what I imagined when I decided to fly for a living. I was quoted twenty-five dollars an hour, which was very good in those days, and I pictured myself flying eight hours every day and getting rich by my standards. The catch is that the twenty-five dollars an hour is only for actual flying time. You get half pay when you're on standby. Loading and unloading, changing the oil or even a cylinder on your airplane don't count.

A pilot is required to maintain his plane: gas and oil and such. When it comes to changing a cylinder, that is optional, but if your plane is down, you aren't being paid. Bushmaster, my employer, has a licensed A&P mechanic, but he gets paid the same, fifteen dollars per, whether the plane is repaired today or next week. The result is that if the wind is howling, snow is blowing, and it's getting dark, the pilot is out changing the cylinder and the mechanic is inside the shop with a cup of coffee and his feet on the bench. He has to sign off on the repairs. He might even glance at your work, but he can always keep busy inside a nice warm hangar.

The other reality comes from loading a plane. A load of village mail may be eighteen hundred pounds of small packages. The pilot loads them in Bethel and offloads in the village. That may not fit your idea of a pilot's duties. It didn't fit mine, either. A snowmachine or a portable gold dredge requires two men. The only two people within a hundred miles may be the pilot and the old miner he's moving off a gravel bar. The pilot grabs one end of the load and lifts. He does it because he's a nice guy, but also because his income depends on repeat customers. He wants to be as helpful as possible, partly to save time, sometimes to protect the airplane, and always with an eye to repeat business.

Bagging a body and loading it is a two-man job. If the body is sprawled out on the ice it may take two men and a chain saw, or you may have to skip the bag. You don't bend a frozen corpse, and loading one can be a wrestling match even for two men.

The temperature of thirty below zero and a half-hearted gray daylight were about average. The absence of wind made it a good day. In Bethel at ten o'clock the sun was above the southern horizon, but a cloud cover masked its exact location. Bethel certainly qualifies as arctic because the climate comes from the Bering Sea, but it is below the Arctic Circle so a pale, cold-looking sun does top the horizon in December.

I stomped through the three- and five-inch snowdrifts on the frozen tarmac toward the first Cessna 206 on the flight line, my neoprene soles making squeaks that seemed to be amplified by the cold. Everything was frozen hard and brittle, so it was like walking inside a drum. The tarmac had been plowed, but that was yesterday. Snow in Bethel never stays put.

I'd used 8-4 Zulu, a Cessna 206, on Saturday to haul mail so the four rear seats were already out. Fuel is always topped off before parking a plane to prevent condensation in the tanks. I tossed my flight bag behind the pilot's seat, loosened the straps on the quilted orange cowling cover, and shoved the prop. It turned, so the electric heater that was mounted under the cowling was working, and the engine would probably start. I unplugged the heater and coiled the extension cord back onto its hook in the gas shack. The cord was warm enough to be pliable because of the current that had been passing through it, but if it was left out for a few minutes, the insulation would shatter when you tried to bend it.

A quick check inside the cockpit verified that the magneto switch was off. That doesn't make it safe to pull the prop through an engine cycle, but it makes it safer. If the magneto switch fails, it leaves the magnetos on; if a carburetor linkage falls off, the engine goes to full throttle, not to an idle like a car. The occasional pilot will pull an engine through a cycle, and then jump back in horror while his plane rips down a flight line, mangling other aircraft until it hits something solid enough to stop it.

The walk-around came next, checking for loose control hinges and sloppy or frozen push rods and confirming that no snowmachines had hit the plane overnight. When I pushed the drain cocks, a bright green stream of 100-octane gasoline poured out of each wing tank drain and the fuel pump strainer, confirming there was no ice in the fuel system. The trick is to test the tanks without getting any of the thirty-below-zero gasoline on your fingers. Most pilots make that mistake only once because the sensation and the blisters are exactly like putting your fingers on a hot stove.

A dusting of frost clung to the cowling cover. I brushed it off and stuffed the cover into the passenger compartment so it wouldn't blow away. I pulled the prop through all six cylinders and got good compression, climbed in, hit the electric fuel boost switch and the starter. Half a dozen revolutions and the engine was running. The engine idled while I checked gauges and controls and called flight service for the latest weather. I shut off the engine, jumped out and replaced the insulating cowling cover to let the heat from the engine permeate the lines and oil coolers.

Beyond the tie-down apron, the only thing visible was the two-story wooden FAA headquarters, looming like a yellow ghost. Gray clouds hung low and obscured the horizon, but there was nothing to see, anyway. The bare, flat tundra was unbroken for five miles to the Kuskokwim River and Bethel. Anywhere else, Bethel might be called a village. In western Alaska, it's a regional hub. With five thousand inhabitants, a hospital, a jet airport, a sea-going barge terminal, a trooper headquarters, a bank and hotels, it's the local metropolis. Fifty-seven villages, scattered over an area the size of the state of Oregon, rely on Bethel for transportation and services. They call Bethel a town. What we refer to as villages have none of the amenities.

The frosty planes—Cessna 206s, 207s, 185s, an American Pilgrim, a Howard, a Cessna 310—were all tied down to cables. The granddaddy of our fleet was a remanufactured Ford Tri-motor, called a Bushmaster, and that's where we got the name for the charter service.

The last two machines on the flight line, tightly wrapped and securely tied, looked like a couple of igloos. They were a Bell 47 and a Hughes 500, helicopters that were hibernating until spring. We used them mostly for mountaintop work or supporting the ships that come into Bethel, and occasionally to evacuate a village during spring floods, but those are seasonal things. Helicopters don't work well in winter because they're too exposed, and besides, in winter a Cessna 185 on skis can land almost anywhere, a lot cheaper and faster then a helicopter can.

Waiting for the heat to spread with the cowling cover on is an important arctic survival technique. The electric heater had kept the engine warm, but the heat came from the outside. There could be a few quarts the consistency of Silly Putty floating around inside the oil pan. The noncongealing oil cooler is a joke, almost certainly blocked by congealed oil. The trap for the unwary is that during run-up and taxi the oil pressure is fine, but when you shoot the juice to that three-hundred-horsepower engine for takeoff, every bit of oil has to circulate, fast. If a glob of Silly Putty gets sucked into the oil pump on takeoff, the sudden silence when the engine seizes is the loudest sound you'll ' ever hear.

Trooper Tom's Land Rover emerged from the haze, coming down the road through the flat tundra a mile away. He had his headlights on, which sometimes helps to define the difference between the white road and the white snow berms, but mostly he was visible as a plume of steam rising up ten feet from his exhaust, then freezing and hanging in the air behind him.

Tires squeaked in the dry snow when Tom pulled the Land Rover into the parking spot beside my old International pickup. He tucked a tarp over the hood and the grill and plugged the cord for his circulating engine heater into the outlet that went with every parking spot. His government-issued vehicle was blue with the blue-and-gold Alaska State Troopers shield on the door, one year old and still pristine by Bethel standards.

Tom was around five-eleven and two hundred pounds, with the fat content of a slab of granite. His blond hair and blue eyes screamed Scandinavia, but he struck me as a heartland farm boy, maybe Iowa or Nebraska, the one who was captain of his college football team.

Tom and I came into the Bush at the same time. I was a fully accredited pilot, but my five thousand hours were mostly around Anchorage and Fairbanks, the railbelt and the highways where landings are usually on runways. I blush to admit that I called myself a bush pilot, but that is a common sin. Everyone who has flown a plane in Alaska thinks he's a bush pilot, even if his experience is shooting touch-and-goes in Anchorage.

Tom graduated from the academy at the top of his class, then spent two years working out of trooper headquarters in Juneau. The shock he got moving into the Bush was similar to the one I got, and we learned our survival skills together.

He strode across the tarmac toward the airplane, and the term *squared away* from military jargon described him. His trooper-blue snowsuit with the gold stripes down the sides was sharp and clean, the legs tucked into blue shoepacks making the outfit look almost tailored. The heavy cloth parka matched, except for the wolf ruff. His hat was black fur with earflaps and a collar that could turn down, but now they were up, so his regulation haircut showed. He wore the gold trooper badge on the brim of his hat.

"Mornin', Alex. Ready to fly?"

"Well, remember this is your idea, not mine, but I expect we might survive."

"How's the weather?"

"Stinking, but the coast is no worse than here. Alakanuk called in this morning with a six-hundred-foot ceiling and two miles visibility, same glorious conditions we're basking in now."

When he got close, I could see that Tom looked a little rough. His normally glacier-blue eyes had some serious red in them, and he'd nicked himself shaving. I couldn't resist ragging him a bit.

"You look terrible. Is that what married life does to a man?"

"Nah," Tom gave a dismissive wave. "Marrying Minnie was the best thing I ever did, and if you had an ounce of sense, you'd marry Connie."

"Hey, staying single is Connie's idea, not mine. She thinks I'm unreliable. How does Minnie like your schedule?"

"Touché," Tom chuckled. "Her jaw was a little tense when I came in at four this morning, and when this call came in at nine, she happened to mention that a group of teachers from the high school are heading to Hawaii for the Christmas vacation. You don't suppose she was hinting that I should go back to teaching school?"

"Of course not. Minnie would never stoop to manipulation like that. Four o'clock? Hot poker game?"

Tom sighed and shook his head. "Don't joke about it, Alex. Six high-school kids were coming downriver in a pickup and must have been doing a hundred when they hit a log that was frozen into the ice. Not just lying on the ice, but half submerged, so it nearly tore the pickup in half and never budged the log. Damn it, I took this job to protect kids, not pick them up in baskets."

"Are we cleaning up after an accident this morning?"

"I don't think so. George isn't the greatest on the radio, but I got the impression there's been a murder, or at least I got the impression that George has the impression there's been a murder."

The front door on the 206 is on the pilot's side. Tom climbed in and scooted across while I stowed the engine cover in the back seating area. Bethel doesn't have a control tower, but it does have a twenty-four-hour flight service station. So long as the weather is above visual flight rule minimums, which for Bethel are four hundred feet and half a mile, you don't even have to talk to them if you don't want to.

Usually we want to, because they'll advise us of any other traffic, assuming that the other guy talks to them, too. This morning the airport was all ours. With no wind, I opted to take off from north to south, that is, use runway one-eight in pilot jargon.

We certainly didn't need the whole mile and a half of runway, but because of the temperature, I added power slowly and kept a close eye on the gauges. The engine built up to that deafening roar that means all systems are go. In the cold, dense air and only four hundred feet above sea level, we were off the ground in six hundred feet, but I stayed over the runway to the end before swinging northwest toward the coast and Alakanuk.

The moment the airport dropped behind, we were flying in a circular bubble of visibility, one mile in every direction. I climbed up to eight hundred feet above sea level, four hundred feet above the ground, and stayed there. The floor of our moving bubble was snow-covered tundra, the foot-thick moss that grows on permanently frozen clay. It had features: winding creeks, tiny lakes, occasionally a few willows, but there was nothing to distinguish one lake or creek from the next.

This was a good day because the sky was gray. On a bad day, the sky is the same color as the snow on the ground, and if a few flakes are falling, you don't see anything at all. Tom leaned his seat back, tilted his cap down over his eyes and went to sleep for the hour of sameness.

An hour from Bethel our bubble of visibility was floored by trees where the Yukon River had wandered in the past, thawed the permafrost, and allowed spindly black spruce to take hold. The river was migrating a few feet per year toward the ocean, so the inland side was growing spruce trees; the ocean side, where the villages were, was bare tundra. Ten minutes later, we crossed the mile-wide white stripe of the Yukon River, and the willows of Alakanuk's Yukon mouth were on our left.

At the end of the Delta, the Yukon splits into two major navigable mouths and runs north and south, parallel to the coast. South, the larger portion dumps into the ocean at Sheldon Point. North, the second stream leads toward the seaport of St. Michael, with the mouth at Kotlik. At St. Michael, the seagoing barges from Seattle are offloaded onto smaller river barges for the two-thousand-mile trip up the Yukon. Between Sheldon Point and Kotlik, two significant mouths bring fish, seals, and transportation to Alakanuk and Emmonak.

If you're looking at a map and can't find Emmonak, look for Kwiguk. Forty years ago, the Yukon outlet that we call the Emmonak River changed course one spring. Kwiguk flushed into the Bering Sea, and Emmonak was built on the opposite bank. Not all maps have caught up yet. That was a wild night for the Eskimos who survived, evacuating with waist-high water surging through their village and ice cakes the size of football fields mowing down everything in their path.

Three dozen hardy souls, carrying only what they had on their backs, took to their skin boats, survived a river crossing through the ice, and started over on the opposite bank. The best source for that story is Auntie Vi, the matriarch of Emmonak, who made the trip with a toddler in each arm and lost her second husband in the crossing. She lives in her log house on the riverbank, usually with a horde of great-grandchildren and great-great grandchildren in attendance. She's still bright and active and happy to tell her stories, although no one has any idea how old she is.

We circled Alakanuk: fifty small wooden houses, a school, a store, and a clinic spread out along the Alakanuk River, and an undulating dirt runway paralleling the Yukon with the windsock hanging straight down. I set up the approach at sixty knots with thirty degrees of flaps, kept us in the air with power, and dumped the flaps and power the moment we touched. The problem was that there are serious frost heaves in the dirt runway, places where underground water has frozen, causing hills and valleys. You don't want a hump launching you back into the air.

The second the engine stopped, I jumped out and scrambled for the cowling cover. Here there were no electric outlets, no amenities, just a frozen dirt road with riffles of snow on it, leading through tundra and willows toward the village a quarter mile away. The outside air temperature had sneaked up to twenty-five below, so a tightly covered engine would probably stay warm enough to start for three hours.

Two snowmachines ripped down the road and slid sideways to stop. George, the village cop, was driving a big black Arctic Cat. George was a solid specimen and probably had some Russian ancestors. He looked more European than Eskimo but had the dark Eskimo complexion. He had a way of moving slowly but steadily, giving the impression of an unstoppable bulldozer. His uniform of the day was beaver hat and beaver parka, with a police badge pinned to the hat brim. Tom climbed out of the plane, yawning and stretching, and straddled the seat behind George. Gravel and ice spurted behind the track, some of it pinging off the airplane, and they were gone.

Charlie, the deputy, was driving a little Elan and pulling a wooden sled. He was the same height as George, but half as wide and half as thick. Charlie was resplendent in sealskin hat and parka. I didn't see a badge, but he certainly wouldn't have poked any holes in that hat. I hopped into the sled and the Elan managed to spurt gravel too, this time pinging it against me.

A real Eskimo sled is not the picturesque wooden slats that dog mushers use. The outline is closer to Santa Claus's sleigh, but it's actually a miniature plywood boat with runners. They tow it on twenty feet of line, both features designed to keep their survival gear dry if the snowmachine breaks through the ice or plows into overflow. The down side of the long tow rope and the design is that the sled was whipping back and forth across the road, sometimes sliding sideways, and all I could do was hang on and tell God I'd be good, if I survived.

On the bare spots, the sled made a racket like two washboards being rubbed together in a thunderstorm, and I was taking every bump personally, damning snowmachines to perdition.

Calling an Arctic Cat and an Elan snowmachines when most people call them snowmobiles is an Alaska thing. If you talk to an Alaskan about snowmobiles he'll know what you mean, but when he answers you, he'll call them snowmachines. Maybe that's because Alaskans were building contraptions to drive across snow long before big companies started building snowmobiles. There were motorcycles with a ski in front and a tire-chain on the rear tire, homemade Caterpillar-type tracks on garden tractors, and a number of other ingenious devices.

Bob Gibson, the schoolteacher at Kwethluk, built a wonderful machine with a sleek comfortable cabin for four and an aircraft engine mounted backward like those airboats in the Everglades. Gib could race an airplane on a straight stretch of frozen river. I don't know how he stopped the thing, but it was probably ingenious and it must have worked, because he's still around. Anyhow, those contraptions were called snow machines and the name not only stuck but has become shortened to snowmachines.

The deputy raced and I bumped and slewed, my backside going numb, past the first six houses, each painted green or blue, each built on stilts with three steps up to an unheated wind-blocking arctic entry, and each with a fifty-five-gallon oil drum on a stand beside the door. The houses are up on stilts for a couple of reasons. In the spring there will be a lot of water around, and if an ice jam downstream blocks the Yukon, it will rise up and cover the entire end of the Delta, a couple of thousand square miles, with a lake three feet deep.

The other reason for the stilts isn't so obvious. The stilts are on pads that sit on the permafrost, and the builders want the ground to stay frozen. If they close in the bottom, heat from the house will eventually melt the ice underneath, and the house will sink into the mud, probably forever. Structures like radio towers are built with solar-powered refrigeration in their foundations.

Charlie charged straight toward the clinic, locked up his track and slid to a stop beside the Arctic Cat. The sled and I slid right past them sideways, hit a berm, tilted alarmingly, and dropped back onto the runners. Charlie didn't seem surprised; apparently that was standard procedure for stopping.

My going along to the scene of the crime is one of those Bush things with several reasons, only one of which is that sitting in the airplane for a few hours isn't much fun. In situations where they have the option, police usually work in pairs. Two observers and two memories are better than one. If your job includes mental gymnastics and deductions, it helps to talk things over with someone else who was there. A cop who is working with a partner has that luxury; Canadian Mounties and Alaska State Troopers frequently do not. Discussing police business with a mere civilian isn't exactly legal, but it is expedient.

State police in rural areas do work by themselves, and we usually hear about those when one makes a traffic stop and gets shot. That's another important reason for more than one person at a scene. If an alpha male has an attitude, a fistfight or even a gun battle with one cop may be just what he's looking for. The urban solution to that is to use overwhelming force. A perp faced with a SWAT team and a dozen rifles tends to give up and bloodshed is averted.

If Tom has to walk into a threatening situation, you can bet I'll be behind him with a pistol in my hand. I may not be with the police, but I am *with* the police.

The clinic was brightly lit by fluorescent fixtures that reflected in the white-with-gold-flecks linoleum. It was heated by an oil-fired space heater in the lobby area with ducts across the blue-painted ceiling to make it a central heating plant. Tom and George were in the first exam room checking our passenger, who was laid out on a plastic sheet on an imitation leather examination table. I recognized Demientoff even though he had an entrance wound the size of a dime between his eyes and an exit wound the size of a golf ball at the back of his head. I watched Tom check the forehead for powder burns and conclude that the shot came from at least four feet away because there weren't any.

Sudden violent deaths are common in the Arctic; it's a harsh environment that allows no mistakes. As a charter pilot, I've hauled many a body back to Bethel, some of them close friends, a few of them other pilots, most killed accidentally and too young. However, deliberate murder, as this appeared to be, is rare.

You get used to death, but still, I always think of John Donne's, "never send to know for whom the bell tolls; it tolls for thee." That's particularly true in the Arctic where the Eskimo unit of family, and the larger one of village, are based on every member with a traditional role to play. A village is like a small ecosystem: one priest, one school teacher, one health aide, one cop, one deputy, one storekeeper, one airport maintenance man, and a council of elders.

Demientoff was a bachelor, but he was the storekeeper and a prominent member of the council, so his death would be a blow to the village. He probably wasn't a saint—most people aren't—but he was honest and fair. Bacon and beans in Alakanuk cost the same as in Anchorage, plus thirty cents per pound for the freight. He didn't run his store as a charity, but seasonal credit was available, and he would take a well-sewn pair of wolf mitts or a beaver hide in trade.

There wasn't much blood around, but he was killed somewhere else, and that would be our next stop. First, we had to zip the corpse into the body bag, shoepacks, Levis, flannel shirt, and all. He was pretty stiff, but the locals had done a good job of laying him straight, so he fit into the bag easily. I grabbed shoulders, the deputy grabbed heels, and we hoisted him up like a log. Tom and George slid the unzipped bag under him, we lowered, and Tom zipped, like putting the peel back on a banana.

We found the blood, several quarts of it, behind the counter at the village store. The Alakanuk store is a good-sized operation because it's on the main river-barge line. The entire back of the store is actually a freight dock on the Alakanuk River, and most of the building is warehouse. The sales floor fronts on the dirt path between houses that would be Main Street if villages had streets. Head-high display racks are packed into an area forty feet square with a wastefully high ceiling, but the effect is roomy and classy by Bush standards.

When we stepped through the door only a single bulb was lit over the cash register. George flipped a switch on the wall and light flooded the room. Bare bulbs dangled on cords in an eight-foot grid, so the room would have been bright if the walls and ceiling had been painted. Instead of paint, the boards had the ubiquitous black dusting that comes from years of oil smoke.

George had locked the door to keep the proceedings private. He showed Tom where the body was found, which was pretty obvious from the blood, and another golf-ball-sized hole, head height, right through the rough-cut boards behind the counter.

When you cut your finger, blood doesn't seem to have a smell, but get enough of it and it stinks. It's a sweet smell, but musty, not unlike a butcher shop, and it's automatically unsettling. That must be the association, because most of us think that butcher shops smell good, but there is nothing good about the smell of a murder scene. However, it was good that it was wintertime so there wasn't a cloud of flies and mosquitoes to fight.

The bullet could have come from a .357 magnum revolver, but the way the bullet kept right on going through the wall looked to me like the tracks of a .30-06 hunting rifle. There are a lot of guns around a village, but you don't usually see them unless a hunting party is packing, either boats or snowmachines, for a trip upriver into moose country. Strolling through the village with a rifle, even on a cold Monday morning, should have attracted attention.

"Did anyone hear a gunshot?" Tom asked.

George tipped his hat back so he could scratch his head. "'Course we haven't interviewed everyone, but seems unlikely: no one close, and snowmachines runnin'."

We hadn't seen a soul except the cops since we landed, but you can be sure that every person in the village had seen us, knew where we were and why, and probably what we would do next. Villagers just naturally know what's going on and keep an eye on things. There isn't a lot of distracting entertainment in the villages, and a murderer lurking around discouraged socializing.

The safe and the cash register were both open and empty, so the obvious motive was robbery, but that is unusual in villages. Money doesn't have the same significance there that it has in the larger world. With the store temporarily closed, there was no place in Alakanuk where money could be spent. That doesn't mean people would starve. Every family had its supply of smoked salmon strips, a moose or caribou hanging, and a barrel of *aguduk*. That's the tundra berries that the women pick in the fall and preserve in lard or seal oil so they stay fresh all winter and provide vitamin C. They mix blueberries, cranberries, salmonberries and blackberries into a purple paste. Stirred into clean snow, that treat is sometimes called Eskimo ice cream, and don't knock it until you've tried it. They toss in a little sugar, which they call *sukuluk*, and eating fresh berries in midwinter is both a pleasure and a necessity. However, with the store closed, there would be a lot of twenty-minute snowmachine runs to Emmonak for a pound of salt, a spool of thread, a case of sodas, whatever.

"You say the doors were locked?" Tom asked.

"Yep, locked up tight. Looked like he let someone in before opening time."

Tom checked the front door lock. It was a snap type that locks behind you when the door is closed, so there was no mystery there. He walked back and found the same type of lock on the big double doors at the back.

"Any idea which way the killer left?"

"Not really." George shrugged, "No one saw him, so he probably went out the back, but then no one was watching until after eight this morning. I got a call when Demientoff still hadn't opened at half past eight. Maggie Simeon has company and she ran out of coffee, so she was waiting for him to open. When he was late, she went next door to his cabin and banged on the door. When he didn't answer that, she came and got me. I have a key to the store, in case there's a fire, so I let Maggie in. Demientoff was crumpled up in that pool of blood behind the counter. Maggie pretended not to notice the body, grabbed a can of coffee off the shelf and ran out." George pointed to the shelf of coffee cans lined up behind us where one can of Yuban was missing from the neat stack. "I locked up again and called you. Then Charlie and I lugged the body into the clinic."

It's not standard procedure to move a body before the police arrive, but this was a bit more complicated. Murder is a state crime so the troopers had to be called, but we were in George's jurisdiction, and by his lights the police were already there.

Tom was nodding and checking around on the floor, looking for tracks or bullet casings, but there weren't any. An automatic would have ejected a casing, but a rifle or a revolver wouldn't, and I was still betting on a .30-06 hunting rifle. The cash register was showing "No sale." It looked to me as if Demientoff was just putting the money in for the morning.

I suppose if we'd been in Chicago we might have called forensics to dust for fingerprints, but that wasn't an option, so we relied on common sense. Demientoff had opened the safe and the cash register, whether voluntarily or at gunpoint, so the murderer's prints would only be on the missing money and maybe a door handle that had the prints of every person in the village. We glanced around the room, but saw nothing to indicate that Demientoff hadn't been alone . . . except the bullet hole in his forehead.

We single-filed to the wooden-plank loading dock outside the back door, Tom leading the way. A bare strip a foot wide ran next to the building under the eaves, then four feet of unmarked snow to the edge of the dock and a five-foot drop to the river ice. Tom walked the length of the dock in both directions, keeping to the bare boards next to the building, jumped off the end of the dock, slid down the path to the river, and came back along the snowmachine trail below us.

He stopped opposite the door and bent down. We crowded to the edge of the dock to look, tracking up the snow, but it no longer mattered. A pair of heel marks, six inches deep, showed where someone had jumped from the dock and landed at the edge of the hard-packed trail. The boot marks were made by shoepacks, just like the ones that all four of us, and every other man in the village, were wearing. The packed trail was frozen as hard as concrete, so after the jump, the boots left no more tracks.

Tom looked up at us, then climbed partway up and grabbed a bundle of fur that was almost under the dock. He held up a fur hat and my heart sank to my toes. Sure, we were all wearing fur hats, too, but in the villages every hat is different, lovingly sewn by an Eskimo wife for her man. Everyone on the Lower Yukon knew that hat, made from the faces of two gray timber wolves. Tom looked as shocked as if he'd been shot, and it wouldn't have hit me harder if the hat had belonged to me.

CHAPTER 3

THE SCAR

The presence of that hat at a murder scene had my mind on a roller coaster, and the downhill plunge took me back five years to the spring morning when the river pilot ship *Husky* tied up to the Bethel dock. Erwin Kawalski had climbed over the rail, lugging an old cardboard suitcase and looking around like a space traveler who had just arrived on an alien planet. He had marched past my cabin on the riverbank, headed toward Leen's lodge, and the next time I saw him was several nights later when Tom and I stopped at the lodge for dinner.

A lot of new people come through Bethel, some of them carpetbaggers, phonies, or fugitives, but those get weeded out fast. Bethel is harsh and it's real. The men and women who can meet the challenge are rare. When one comes along that you know is going to stay, you value him or her. Kawalski, or "Ski" as we called him, was one of the best, genuine to the core, the sort of man you're proud to call friend.

Ski spent two years in Bethel working at the cannery before he was promoted and moved to Emmonak, and during those years we spent many long winter nights sharing a bottle in my cabin, or after dinner at the lodge. In the Bush, friendships develop fast and they run deep. Talking, eventually about your innermost feelings and secrets, is the primary winter pastime, and Ski and I did a lot of that. Trooper Tom made it a threesome fairly often in the year after Ski came. Tom had started romancing Minnie that year, but Minnie was Inupiat. She went north to the Kobuk country to spend the winter with her parents, so Tom had a lot of free time on his hands.

The other thing you need to know about Ski is that the left side of his face was all one horrible scar. How he got the scar came out one night in a semidrunken bull session. It was December, a few years ago. Tom and I had stopped at the lodge for steaks and lingered afterward. The rest of the lodgers and Bergie, the proprietress, had gone to bed. Bergie had left one light on in the dining room over the table and one light on in the kitchen so that we could help ourselves to more water and ice.

Tom, Ski, and I had kicked back our chairs at the big wooden dining table. Tom had brought a bottle of Chivas Regal to celebrate the issuance of his new sidearm, a Colt .357 magnum revolver. That Chivas was so smooth and fit the occasion so well that we didn't bother with water. It took a few drinks and some persuasion, but we goaded Ski into telling how he got the scar.

It was either Vietnam or Cambodia, no one was quite sure, but the jungle was steaming and it stank. Artillery shells were crackling overhead, and the platoon was hunkered down in tall elephant grass at the edge of a mangrove swamp. They had come out of the jungle at the bottom of a valley and started to cross a patch of waist-high grass toward the hill ahead.

The Viet Cong, usually called Charlie, was above them on the hill, hidden by the jungle. Charlie had let the platoon wade through the grass for a hundred yards before they opened fire from a dozen rifles. The platoon hit the dirt. Charlie tormented them by firing automatic bursts into their position, just to let them know that he was there and that he knew where the GIs were. Lieutenant Kawalski, *Ski* to his men, had discounted calling in artillery fire or air cover because Charlie was too close. In Vietnam, too many men were killed by friendly fire, and Ski was not going to take that chance.

Tom brought more ice from the freezer and we topped off our glasses, but Ski barely paused. It was fifty below zero outside and the wind was screaming, so neither Tom nor I wanted to leave. The lodge whistled in the wind, flutes and oboes, and occasionally the light would flicker when the power lines swung together. It was a perfect night for telling stories. Ski had been reluctant to start, but once he was into it he was reliving the incident, his eyes flashing, his jaw tense, and I got a vivid picture of the scene he was describing.

❈ ❈ ❈ ❈

Ski looked back down the line of men. Most of his view was of the eighty-pound rucksacks that each carried on his back, but several of the camouflaged helmets were turned toward Ski, and the question "How do we get out of this one?" was implicit in the expressions. Ski wore nothing that would mark him as an officer. His olive-green blouse and trousers were the same as the others wore. His steel helmet, covered with the green camouflage canvas, was standard issue, and he wore the chinstrap cinched up over the brim. Everyone did that, because if concussion from a shell knocked the helmet off, they didn't want their heads taken off with it.

Insignia aside, it would have been easy to pick Ski as the officer in charge. At six feet, one inch, he was taller than most of his men, with the rangy, athletic build you would expect on a basketball court, not a football field. Mostly he was marked by his eyes, with the alertness of the eagle about them, and his expression. The chips were down, but there would have been no panic. His mind was racing, searching for the best solution to the problem.

The swamp behind them was not an escape route. The water might have been waist deep or more, and there was precious little cover beyond the grass. Skirting the swamp, or in fact moving anywhere, seemed suicidal because every time anyone moved the grass waved and a burst of automatic fire from the jungle snickered through. The only option more deadly than moving was to stay put until dark. That's what Charlie wanted them to do, and that would mean certain death without the platoon even seeing their attackers.

Ski was not the type to give up. He grew up fighting for his life on the streets of Chicago's south side, and he wasn't going to stop fighting now. He could see a stand of jungle fifty yards to the right where the swamp apparently ended. He wasn't proud of his plan, but at least it was a plan, and it beat staying hunkered down waiting to die.

They passed the word down the line from man to man. Every man shook his head, "no way," then turned to pass it on. Twenty-five men pulled grenades from their belts. Ski said, "One." Bullets ripped the grass a foot above his head. Ski said, "Two," and rolled to his right. Bullets tore up the spot he'd left, but twenty-five men pulled the pins on their grenades. Ski said, "Three." Twenty-five grenades were tossed toward Charlie, as far as desperate men could throw them.

The entire glade seemed to bend under a barrage of sniper fire. The grenades fell short of Charlie, but Charlie ducked and hesitated. At least the explosions and the smoke masked the whine of bullets. The GIs were up and setting records for the fifty-yard dash. Twenty-three men hit the ground at the edge of the jungle and scrambled on elbows and knees away from the deadly hill. Bullets chewed up the trees, hissing and cracking like angry hornets, but the trees were cover.

Ski took the lead. An open trail through the jungle made by animals and water was inviting, but Ski veered off six feet to his right and plowed through vines and branches. A man on Ski's left took the easy route and was passing Ski. Ski hissed at him to get back in line, but too late. The man tripped a mine and died instantly. Hot shrapnel dug into Ski's left shoulder. Something ripped his cheek, his helmet tore off, bounced on his right shoulder and rolled away, but he didn't stop.

Another mine exploded behind him, but Ski kept crawling and the men lined up single file to follow in his tracks. Twenty-one men crawled out of the jungle into another grass field at the foot of another hill. One of them was known as Sparky, a twenty-year-old black man from Georgia, who was entrusted with the radio. Sparky had the radio concealed between his backpack's aluminum frame and his packsack, but his massive shoulders almost hid the radio. Both Ski and Sparky surveyed the surrounding jungle, looking for snipers, and saw none. They flopped on the ground together, and Sparky handed Ski the microphone. That act marked Ski as the officer, and if a sniper had been there, that was the moment he was waiting for.

Ski pulled a map out of his shirt and ran his finger down a grid. He didn't carry the map in the big pocket that was designed for it, because the outline might have shown, and that, too, would mark him as the officer. Blood dripped on the edge of the map and Ski wiped it off with his sleeve.

"Request five guns, five volleys, twenty-five-meter marching fire at GR-93-24-16-58."

Ski judged Charlie's position by the contour lines and read all the numbers, which would direct the fire with an accuracy of plus or minus ten meters.

The radio replied, "Shot over."

The air above them hissed with a pressure that hurt eardrums, smoke trailed from a shell that plowed into the grass right at the edge of the jungle where Charlie was hiding.

"Splash-out," Ski told the radio.

The men buried their faces in the ground, hands across the backs of their necks. The air turned electric. High explosive rounds shredded the jungle on the hill, ripping it as if a tornado had touched down. The sound was one continuous roar. The ground shook with the detonations. Ski called for another barrage, precautionary, on the hill above them, and for evacuation choppers.

He guessed two stretcher, ten ambulatory, and two killed in action, then added his request to evacuate twelve able-bodied.

The microphone was dripping blood when Ski handed it back to Sparky. He noticed a stinging numbness on the left side of his face. He raised a hand to feel his cheek, and found his left ear missing. Ephraim, or "Eph," the medic, shoved Ski down on his back, pulled the flaps of his cheek together, and taped them there with a big square bandage. Ski saw that the hand applying the bandage was missing the little finger and half the ring finger. Bandages like the one on Ski's cheek were plastered over the fresh amputations.

❋ ❋ ❋ ❋

Ski was shaking his head, remembering Eph, and had completely forgotten Tom and me. Tom had stopped playing with his revolver, and all of our glasses were empty, but Ski was lost in memory, almost in a trance. Tom and I were right with him.

❋ ❋ ❋ ❋

Eph was an old man by platoon standards, into his forties, and once had worked as a delivery boy for a drugstore in New York, which was experience enough to make him a medic in Vietnam. Eph's beard grew coal-black and fast. He had shaved in the morning, as each member of the platoon did. One-third of a cup of water and ninety seconds with a safety razor every morning kept them looking and feeling civilized, but if he was going out to dinner in his native New York that night, maybe at the Russian Tea Room, instead of hunkering down in the jungle to eat cold C rations, he'd need to shave again. Eph's missing fingers would be his ticket home, but right then he had a job to do. Ski later saw to it that Eph got a medal to replace his fingers.

He sat up from Eph's ministrations and surveyed his squad. "I need six volunteers. Anderson, Ramirez, Chung, Peterson, Jimenez, Goldstein, go back and get the guys out of that grass. For God's sake stay off the trail through the minefield, and keep your heads down. Charlie should be gone from the hill, but don't get careless. Not you, Schmitt, if that blood running down your leg is yours, you better just sit down."

Eph shoved Schmitt down, slit his pant leg and the canvas top of his jungle boot with a knife. The brass screen that let the boots breathe, next to the steel reinforced sole that protected against punji sticks, was bent and digging into Schmitt's foot. The medic ripped off the boot, doused the foot with disinfectant, and bandaged. The volunteers dropped their packs and charged back into the jungle. They were back in fifteen minutes, supporting two wounded and carrying two bodies. Ski led his ragtag remnant up the hill.

Half the men were wounded, but the squad secured the hilltop, tramped down a landing area in the grass, and waited. Sunset had begun to streak the western sky and a few of the men were digging in their packs for C rations, when four Hueys came clop-clopping up out of the valley with four Cobra gunships buzzing around providing cover.

The radio came to life. "Delta four-six, this is evac four-niner-three, pop smoke." Ski tossed a smoke grenade into their clearing and yellow smoke billowed.

"Tally yellow, that you?" The radio crackled.

"Roger, four-niner-three. The landing zone is cold, so come get us already." The evacuation Hueys lined up to pick up the wounded, then two slicks, unarmed except for machine guns at the doors, dropped down for the able bodied. The Cobras raced around the perimeter, blasting machine-gun fire or rockets at any leaf that twitched within five hundred yards of the landing zone. Ski was the last man aboard the evac chopper. He suddenly noticed that he felt very tired; he realized that he had lost a lot of blood, and maybe that was why the earth was starting to spin. He needed to close his eyes for just a moment.

❄ ❄ ❄ ❄

Tom and I did, too. I felt as if I had just had a religious experience, and Tom didn't say a word. We split the last of the bottle three ways, stood and toasted each other. Ski stumbled up the stairs toward his room, Tom and I pulled on parkas and went out to our idling cars.

Ski's life has taken some twists and turns in the years since he told us that story. His rapid advancement from forklift driver to engineer at the cannery is an Alaska thing, and a darn good reason for young men to head north. If you have a skill, or even can learn one fast, you are needed and shoved along in a way that would never happen in a more settled area with a larger and more experienced labor pool. His transfer to Emmonak where he was in charge of the mechanical operation came too fast and scared him, but he met the challenge. His marriage to Punik could be called beauty and the beast. Neither could have found a better mate on the planet, but that, too, was more apt to happen in the Bush than in Los Angeles. Neither Punik's beauty nor Ski's scar were important to them; they were both looking for deeper values.

My mind was churning. There had to be an explanation for Ski's hat at the murder scene. Detective School 101, lesson one, states unequivocally that there are no such things as coincidences, but Ski involved in a murder simply would not compute in my brain. Regardless of the gyrations his life had taken, I couldn't imagine Ski anything but arrow straight.

CHAPTER 4

THE FOX

It was around two in the afternoon when Tom and I lugged Demientoff's body down the stairs and propped it up in the deputy's sled. Tom was carrying Ski's hat inside his snowsuit, and both of us were struggling to understand how the hat got to the murder scene. The solid overcast was getting lower and darker, with a pregnant look to it as if it might snow at any moment. I stood up in the sled, straddling the body and holding onto the plywood sides. Apparently out of respect for the dead—certainly not out of respect for me—we set out at a more sedate pace. George rode beside the sled and Tom reached out a mittened hand to hold us steady.

We loaded the body bag. I laced it down with the seat belts for the rear seats and tossed the engine cover in on top of it. Tom climbed in, I leaned in the door to check the switches and walked around front to pull the engine through a few revolutions. The first couple of turns were stiff, but then it loosened up. I jumped in and the engine started.

The engine idled while we buckled our belts and wiped the frost off the inside of the windshield. This time there was no worry about congealed oil inside the engine because this time the inside had been warm, and the cold came from the outside. The oil temperature came up, a little too high, then dropped back when the noncongealing cooler decongealed. We took off, skimming under the overcast, and headed up the river.

The log cabin that Ski and Punik had built was across the river from, and halfway between, the villages of Alakanuk and Emmonak. Ski had found an old abandoned log cabin on a little rise above the river. When the cannery closed in the fall, Ski's second year in Emmonak, he and Punik moved into the derelict structure and started building the magnificent log cabin that was now attached to it.

Don't picture a cabin built of the spindly spruce that grow along the lower Yukon. This cabin was precut to Ski's specifications from peeled and varnished fir in Seattle and shipped by barge. It stood on pads with three-foot pilings. The idea was not to keep it permanently level, but to make it easy for Ski to crawl under and bang in wedges when one of the pads settled. The original derelict became a pantry and utility room three steps down from the back porch.

My part in building the cabin had been sneaking miscellaneous materials onto charter flights: a keg of nails here, plumbing fixtures there. When I came to Emmonak or Alakanuk with an empty plane to take passengers back, I left Bethel an hour early and dropped off sheets of plywood, a deep-well water pump, or a two-thousand-watt generator. It wasn't charity. Punik baked the most hellacious blueberry pies on the Delta, and during the two years of construction, I probably put on as much weight as Ski and Punik lost.

Tom and I circled the cabin, and I found a smooth patch on the ice that was six or seven hundred feet long. Rivers don't freeze all at once, so at first the ice is pretty rough. Slow and shallow spots freeze, then the river rises an inch, or the temperature rises a degree, and the chunks of ice roar downriver and bunch up. They grind together and make pressure ridges, or climb on top of each other, pretty much the way geologists tell us that the tectonic plates move and make the mountain ranges.

In a few weeks, the ice gets smoother. Wind wears down the peaks, and moisture fills in the hollows, and before spring you could ice-skate for two thousand miles. In December, I was happy to find a smooth stretch six hundred feet long and thirty feet wide. I set the main gear on the first smooth foot in a full-stall landing, racked the flaps all the way down for air brakes, and held my breath while we slid to a stop. With a few inches of loose snow over ice, there was no braking and precious little steering from the wheels, but we stopped a hundred feet from the end of the ice sheet.

Ski came bounding down the trail from the cabin. He seemed to look younger every year. He was wearing his wolf parka, the one that matched the hat, and shoepacks. Punik stood in the doorway, keeping warm, wearing jeans and a sweater, making the silhouette that every man dreams of finding at home.

The trail from the cabin was thirty yards long, with an open area on the left so the view of the cabin wasn't blocked, but with a good stand of black spruce that smelled like Christmas trees on the right. The knoll the cabin sat on was only ten or twelve feet higher than the riverbank, but in that flat country it looked like a hill, and it put the cabin above the flood line.

"Alex, Tom, this is great. Come in, come in. What's the special occasion?"

Ski had his hand out for shaking for the last ten feet of his charge, and we both rushed to shake his paw. He had a lot more calluses than he had when he left Bethel.

Tom tried to look official with that special set of his chin, his mouth a straight line, but Ski's exuberance got him, or maybe it was the sight of Punik waiting on the porch, undoubtedly the prettiest girl on the Delta, with a cascade of coal-black hair down her back. In any case, it was the friendliest official look I ever saw.

"Can we go inside?" Tom asked, but he needn't have. Ski was already dragging us up the steps. We each collected our hug and cheek kiss from Punik and sat on the couch that I had smuggled up the time I brought the freight-hauling Pilgrim up empty to take back a load of fur. Punik went to the kitchen and brought us each a big mug of hot coffee.

Ski and Punik sat on opposite arms of an easy chair, not touching each other physically, but mentally and spiritually I think they were hugging. When two people are really in love and proud of each other, it shows. They always seemed to be glowing.

The chair and couch sat at right angles, so Tom and I were almost facing Ski and Punik, but also facing the stone fireplace that covered half the end of the room. Fireplaces are usual up river where there are mountains with rocks, but at this end of the Delta it was a rare luxury. I don't mean it was frivolous. It had the heat vents and radiators built in that made it a good alternative way of heating the house if the oil supply failed. What I mean is that those stones were shipped from Seattle along with the logs.

There are no stones on the Delta. As I said, it's an area the size of the state of Oregon, but it's composed entirely of silt from the Yukon and Kuskokwim rivers. If you thawed out the dirt and dried it, it would all go through a flour sifter. When the Alaska Department of Transportation finally built some runways at a few villages, they imported gravel. Schoolteachers took their classes out to watch the barges unload gravel because the kids had never seen a rock before.

Tom had settled in to drink coffee and visit, but then he remembered we were on a murder investigation.

"What do you know about the manager of the Alakanuk store?" Tom asked.

Ski frowned. "Not much. We usually go to Emmonak because Punik's cousins are there, but the few times I've dealt with him he seemed nice enough. When Alex dropped our water pump off at Alakanuk instead of Emmonak, I borrowed a skiff from Demientoff and he was really helpful about that."

Tom pulled the wolf-fur cap out of his suit and held it out. Ski recognized it, and his face lit up like a five-year-old on Christmas morning.

"Oh, my gosh, thank heaven. I thought it was gone forever and I was sick over that. It was Punik's wedding present to me, you know. Where did you find it?"

We both nodded. We both knew, and so did everyone on the river who wasn't both deaf and blind.

"Where did you lose it?" Tom countered, still trying to be official.

"I was cutting driftwood for the fireplace a couple of miles upriver, about a week ago. It was cold in the morning, but it warmed up later, so I took the hat off and set it on a stump. When I was ready to leave, I went for it and it was gone. I thought a fox got it."

"Some fox," Tom said. "The fox that stole your hat shot Demientoff in his store. I don't suppose you happened to be in Alakanuk around seven-thirty this morning?"

"Are you kidding? I was here in bed where I belong on cold mornings." Ski reached out and patted Punik's shoulder. She blushed prettily, and it certainly looked sincere to me.

Tom stood up and tossed the hat to Ski. I guessed we were leaving. That was good, because I'd forgotten to cover the engine.

"You've got to help me on this one, Ski. It's too late for us to go up there before dark, and I don't want to make this official, so would you go up there in the morning and see if you can find out anything from any fox tracks that happen to be around?"

"You bet I will, Tom. If there's anything there I'll find it, but don't expect much. We had a nasty windstorm a few days ago that probably wiped everything away. You think someone stole my hat and then lost it again this morning?"

Tom was nodding, but his expression had that veiled look that means he isn't saying everything he's thinking. "Looks that way, Ski. We'll keep in touch and let me know if you find anything." Tom stood and zipped his parka.

Ski stood for our handshakes and Punik pecked our cheeks, but the two of them seemed to huddle together. The idyllic world they had built for themselves was threatened. They weren't about to crumple, would pull together and fight, but a dark cloud had just drifted over them without warning.

Ski was telling the truth about the windstorm. It was the Thursday before to be exact, and I'd had to land on the lake sideways at Sheldon Point. The lake at Sheldon is nine hundred feet long, but only two hundred feet wide. When the wind is blowing 50 or more, you can point a 206 straight into it, approach at 55 mph airspeed, and touch down at 5 mph ground speed. That day, I had come straight down, landed at a dead stop, kept the engine running to hold the plane on the ground while my passengers scrambled in, and taken off straight up.

The engine started; I slid us around on the end of the smooth spot, held the brakes and shot the juice to her. When we started to slide I released the brakes. Four hundred feet later we were indicating forty-five knots. I racked down twenty degrees of flaps and raised the left wheel to cut the drag from loose snow. We were clear of the snow in five hundred feet. I was busy for one minute, climbing, stowing flaps, setting up the cruise, but Tom was about to burst.

"Did he do it?" Tom asked

"For my money, no; he did not. Ski isn't a killer, and he doesn't need money. Why would he?"

"He killed a good many people in Vietnam, and who knows why people need money, or think they do. Or, maybe the money had nothing to do with the killing; maybe it was a red herring."

"Yeah, and maybe the hat had been there in the snow for a week and has nothing to do with the murder."

"Sorry, that hat had been there for six hours, max, definitely not overnight. How about this? There's a drifter in the area, stole Ski's hat last week, Demientoff's money this week, thinks he's so far out in the Bush that there is no law."

"I like that. If Demientoff saw Ski's hat at the door, he would have opened up, no matter who was wearing it."

Tom tilted his hat down and pretended to sleep, but he wasn't fooling either one of us. He had a real problem between being a good cop and being a good friend, and I couldn't help him any.

We were still fifty miles out when the last of the cloud-diffused sunset faded. For fifteen minutes we saw only the green glow of the instruments, then the Bethel beacon cut through the clouds ahead. From the air at night, especially after flying in total darkness for a while, Bethel looks like a real city. It's always a disappointment to come down and see what's actually there.

I parked by the gas pumps and helped Tom carry the body bag to his Land Rover. I gassed up the plane, put it to bed, filled out a flight ticket, and tooled my old pickup into town, thinking I'd listen to some Vivaldi and hoping there was some Captain Morgan's rum left in the bottle.

Tom stopped at the Public Health Service hospital that doubles as our morgue, dropped off the body, and went back to the station to write his report. He included finding the hat, but neglected to mention whose it was or where it went. He must have been sleepy; he shouldn't have done that.

The oil stove in my cabin had been on low all day so the cabin was nippy. I left my snowsuit on while I poured the rum and Coke, but then I wasn't in the mood for Vivaldi. The possibility of Ski as a murderer was blowing my little mind. I thought I knew him better than that. Still, when a serial killer is caught, his neighbors always say he was a nice quiet guy and they can't believe he'd hurt a fly. I was getting right along with the rum and took off the snowsuit when the cabin warmed up, but my mind was going back to a day in spring, four years before, when Ski told me the rest of his story. At first I was searching for any false note, any hint that he was not what he seemed, but eventually that day was running through my head like a movie.

CHAPTER 5

BREAKUP

My mental movie took me back a few years to the end of May, when spring had arrived in Bethel. The river was breaking up and rising. Great chunks of ice were racing downstream, grinding and crashing together. The road to the airport was under water and dirt runways in the villages had turned to slippery mud six inches deep, so I had the day off unless a real emergency came up.

Annual breakup is a thrill you don't want to miss. The power and grandeur of nature on a rampage puts man's achievements in perspective. Chunks of ice weighing hundreds of tons spin and crash together, climbing on top of each other, and you just have to watch and listen. Imagine all of the noise and ruckus of a busy construction site and multiply it by a hundred.

Ski and I were wearing rubber boots, walking up the riverbank past the edge of town, exploring the sloughs and the ancient derelicts, the skeletons of wooden barges and steamships that were rotting in the willows. We were stopping every couple of minutes just to watch the river, and Ski was introspecting, maybe trying to understand why he was in Bethel himself and worried about what was coming next. As he talked I had the impression that he was baring his soul to both of us.

❋ ❋ ❋ ❋

When he got out of the veteran's hospital in Honolulu, he had returned to Chicago, but Chicago wasn't the same city that Ski remembered. The streets were narrower and dirtier, the people meaner and more petty. Traffic seemed a perpetual, purposeless chaos. It appeared that everything that could be vandalized had been. Half the people Ski met on the streets turned around to stare at the scar running from his hairline to his chin and the little stub of ear that was left. Ski smiled at a toddler on the dusty sidewalk. The kid screamed and grabbed his mother, the mother glared, then gasped and hurried away.

He reported back to work at Roberts Sash and Door on South Halsted Street, but the cubic block of warehouse was suffocating. Ski had a new, maybe pathological, need to see the sky.

He could not see the point of climbing around the warehouse all day, list in his hand, picking out the frames and doors and carrying them down to the loading dock. Other employees disappeared when Ski came onto the dock. His scar gave the left side of his face a permanent scowl. When he tried to smile with the right side, people scurried away even faster. By the time he picked up his paycheck, four hundred dollars for two weeks, he had given up smiling. He felt trapped, needing to escape from Chicago, from his face, maybe from life.

His paycheck bought him a bus ticket to Seattle and two weeks' rent on a room in a flophouse by the Ballard docks. Seattle wasn't much better than Chicago, warmer but wetter, and he seemed to be meeting the same people on the streets. He spent his days climbing up and down hills, usually on wet, slippery sidewalks.

He was down to his last fifty bucks, tromping through a light mist in Ballard. The canal beside him was lined with dark, silent boats, a black cliff across the canal blocking out the lights of the city. It had been another long, fruitless day of job hunting, and he was hating the thought of going back to his bare little room.

Music and laughter spilled out of a dark doorway. Ski leaned against a light pole and considered the gulf that separated him from the happy people inside. He was shocked to realize that he had actually been considering suicide. That struck him as cowardly, and one thing he was not was a coward. He was still Erwin Kawalski, still a man, and a damned good one. He hadn't asked to have his face blown away. If it bothered people, that was their problem.

He decided to spend two of his last dollars on a drink in the little bar named the King's Alley. The bar was nestled under the sky-scraping span of the Aurora Bridge, and had the feel of a cave that might be safe.

Ski found a seat in a dark corner and sat with his left side toward the wall. The pretty blonde waitress in short skirt and nylons took his order and smiled at him. His guts churned with a longing and the knowledge that if he faced her, her smile would turn to horror. He leaned farther, almost pressing his left cheek against the wall. When she brought his drink, he tried a smile with his right half, but it didn't work and the waitress hurried away.

A dozen tables in intimate twilight stretched between Ski and the brightly lit stage. A festive buzz of conversation, clinking glasses, and laughter made a background for the music. A Norwegian extrovert, fifty years old, short but stocky and wearing a plaid shirt and chinos, was singing with the band, belting out a good tenor and having a wonderful time. The singer finished a number, scooped his drink off the end of the bar, collected a hug from the waitress and a kiss from the next singer, and wandered past the tables, shaking hands, cracking jokes, but zeroing in on Ski's corner.

"Hi, can I buy you a drink?"

Ski turned his mangled face toward the happy smile, and to his amazement the smile didn't fade. The singer pulled out a chair, plunked down next to Ski and waved to the waitress for another round.

"Looking for work, by any chance?" The singer already knew the answer. He extended a hand for a good solid handshake.

The singer turned out to be Captain Sumstad of the *Husky*, who was leaving in the morning, bound for his annual stint as the river pilot on the Kuskokwim. He had the contract to set the buoys and escort the ships that came into Bethel, and he needed a deckhand. The captain had been waiting in the bar for a likely candidate to come in. *Kuskokwim* didn't mean anything to Ski. Even *Alaska* conjured only a vague image of Eskimos living in igloos and hunting polar bears with harpoons, but it didn't matter. Ski and the captain closed the bar at midnight. Ski found himself feeling warm, and even laughing, for the first time since 'Nam.

At one o'clock in the morning, Ski lugged his battered old suitcase into his cabin on the *Husky*. The room contained bunk beds and two tiny closets, but he had the room to himself. He stretched out on the lower bunk and reached clear across the little compartment to click off the light. The bunk was subliminally moving, just a hint that he was not on land. The smell of rope, tar, and the ocean was pleasant. A steady thrum of generators somewhere below him lulled him to sleep.

At six bells, Ski stood on the rain-slicked dock. The diesels rumbled to life, disturbing a flotilla of ducks that was majestically patrolling between ships, and Ski learned to cast off lines. He jumped aboard, and the ship eased out of her berth into the canal. The *Husky* slipped through the Ballard locks and headed up Puget Sound toward the Inside Passage, passing timber-covered islands and occasional small towns.

Ski learned his duties fast. He helped Paula, the no-nonsense, middle-aged cook, washed the pots and pans, and fetched whatever she needed from the pantry. He spent an hour a day with Jimmy, the engineer, who looked like a blond college kid in overalls. Ski oiled and wiped, getting familiar with the diesels and the generators. He swept the decks, did a quick load of laundry, and hurried out onto the afterdeck to stare at the mountains and forests streaming past, more spectacular than anything he had ever imagined.

Gray whales played and spouted around the ship; deer and bear stood along the banks to watch them pass. Eagles by the dozen wheeled around tall spruce that leaned out over the water. The world had turned clean and green, with snow-covered mountains for a backdrop. Ski had forgotten his scar, forgotten his face, and knew that he would never again travel south.

They tied up briefly to a rickety wooden dock at Hoonah. A dozen shacks that lined a dirt lane up the hill were dwarfed by a round, wooden water tank at the top. The *Husky* took on a fresh supply of soft pure rainwater to top off her tanks and headed straight across the Gulf of Alaska. The gulf, or more properly the North Pacific, was a different experience from the Inside Passage. The *Husky*, for all of her eighty tons' displacement, ninety-foot length, and thirty-foot beam, wallowed and plunged like a rowboat in the huge swells. By the time they reached False Pass to slip through the Aleutian Chain, Ski had decided: Alaska, yes; sailing, no.

The Aleutians were a welcome sight, but only because they were land. They looked dark, lonely, somehow mournful. The mile-high peaks, usually shrouded in mist, with little snow and no trees, appeared hostile. Gray rock cliffs hundreds of feet tall jutted up out of the water. The captain lined up with the entrance to False Pass between two mountains, but the *Husky* was struggling to hold her own in the current.

The two bodies of water, Pacific Ocean on the south, the Bering Sea ten miles through the pass, were out of sync. The tide was running out on the Pacific side but in on the Bering side, and the resulting current through the pass was like a mountain cataract. The *Husky* strained and bucked but seemed to be stuck at the mouth. Seventy-five miles west, at the other end of Unimak Island, Unimak Pass was twenty miles wide, but that meant sailing west, directly away from their destination, for six hours and then east for six, and that wasn't the captain's style.

The tide slackened and the *Husky* slipped into the half-mile-wide gap between mountains. They rounded a bend and the village of False Pass went by. It seemed to be all one big green wooden cannery and dock squeezed between the water and the mountains, right at water level. A few houses were connected to the cannery by wooden walkways over marshes.

Ski heard the roar behind them and looked back. A bore tide was rushing from the Pacific back toward the Bering Sea. The *Husky's* tail rose up on a six-foot wall of water and rode it like a surfer on a wave. Mountains rushed by, almost close enough to touch. Around the next bend, a swirling blanket of white fog blocked the pass. Ski climbed up to the bridge, he thought maybe just to get as far as possible from the cold, roiling water.

Captain Sumstad stood at the wheel, a cup of coffee in his right hand, the left hand on the wheel holding a cigarette. The captain watched the radar screen on the console, ignoring the white wall ahead. The *Husky* plowed into the fog. The radar screen showed two solid green walls and a black gap that looked no wider than a city street. The captain switched hands to take a drag from the cigarette, then switched back for a sip of the coffee. The air got colder; it reminded Ski of the chill people report in haunted houses. Ski noticed steam rising from the captain's cup.

The clear path on the radar widened and the solid walls dropped away. Only a few bright green stars on the screen showed where islands, really just rocks, broke the surface. Ski climbed back down to the deck and tried to get used to the new rhythm of the waves, shorter but rougher than the Pacific. Two nights later, they anchored in a calm bay and waited for daylight.

❈ ❈ ❈ ❈

Ski interrupted his story while we crashed through willows to go around a rust-pocked steam engine and the remains of a boiler that sat at the edge of the slough. The wooden ship that had carried them was completely rotted away, leaving only the metal parts.

We continued our walk, came to the end of Steamboat Slough, and started north along the bank of the main river. Water was running fast, even with the banks, spilling over into low spots. Between the rushing freight trains of ice, occasional clear patches of water looked black and angry. The sound was like a busy freeway, a steady hiss accented by guttural grinds and crashes. We had walked and waded four miles, but the river and the movement were pulling us on. I suspect the near-euphoria we were feeling was akin to being released from prison. For seven months, the river had been motionless and dead, the world a static thing, and our spirits were being released from winter's bondage just as the river was. We stopped to watch a flight of geese, majestic in their V, their honking just audible over the river's racket.

You never forget your first sight of Bethel. I had long ago told Ski my story of getting off a jet on Mother's Day, fresh from the beginnings of spring in Anchorage, to find Bethel buried under dirty snow, the river still frozen. If I'd had the price of a return ticket, I might have gone back, but I didn't. All I had in this world was the promise of a job flying for Bushmaster.

Ski was reminiscing, partly because he had decided to leave Bethel. A job as the engineer had opened at the cannery in Emmonak. Ski was offered the job, which was a nice promotion, and he couldn't turn it down. We weren't saying goodbye, and that is one of the perks of flying. I could expect to be in Emmonak every week or two, so our friendship would continue, but it would be a big change for Ski.

The breeze picked up and it was cold, but there was a moistness to it, the smell of water and vegetation. We hunched our shoulders, stuck out hands in our pockets, and continued walking. Ski went back to his story.

※ ※ ※ ※

Daylight from the deck of the *Husky* showed mudflats, miles of ugly gray mud, with a line of flat black shore just visible on the horizons. They were anchored in a river that meandered through the mud. Ski stood on the foredeck beside the anchor winch and shivered, partly from the cold, partly from the sheer drabness of the surroundings.

Tiny waves began to lap over the mud behind them. The captain signaled from the bridge, and Ski raised the anchor. The *Husky* plowed a crooked trail up the sluggish river through the mud. The rising tide caught and passed them, mud became a lake; the *Husky* continued to twist and turn up the now invisible river. The flat shoreline came closer, separated to become the banks of the Kuskokwim River, and Ski got his first close look at tundra.

Eight-foot crumbling banks of black mud were topped by green moss a foot thick that stretched, flat as a pool table, to the horizons. The sun came up ahead of them and lightened the green tundra but didn't change the chocolate brown water. There was seldom more than half a mile of river visible at a time.

The river wound, and the sun swung back and forth across the sky, sometimes almost behind them.

Late in the afternoon, the *Husky* paused to tread water. An outboard skiff planed out of a tiny opening in the riverbank. The captain said they were at Tuntutuliak, but all Ski saw was the twenty-foot gap in the tundra. The skiff idled alongside and the relief river pilot scrambled up a rope ladder. The skiff pulled away, raced across the river and disappeared, apparently right into the bank. At five-foot-nine, the new crewman was tall and lean for an Eskimo. Ski was impressed by his air of quiet competence and his acceptance of Ski's scar without a second glance.

Darkness came slowly, the twilight lingering for hours while the sun raced along sideways, just below the northwestern horizon. Powerful spotlights were switched on and the *Husky* continued to plow its crooked course up the river. Sandbars reared up right beside them and the ship slewed from bank to bank to follow the channel. Ski began to see campfires on the little islands they passed, and long, flat outboard boats beached on mud. They passed two tiny villages, Napakiak nestled below a bluff on the left bank, then Napaskiak at river level on the right. Each consisted of a couple dozen houses, mostly log, with bare poles sticking up to support radio antennas.

It was daylight, the sun teasing the northeastern horizon, when Ski got his first glimpse of Bethel. They rounded a bend, the bank dropped down, almost to the water, and was lined with hundreds of junked cars, dumped into the river every which way to form a home-grown, erosion-controlling seawall. Beyond the seawall, a scruffy parade of one- and two-story wooden buildings lined the riverbank. Most buildings had been painted either white or green, but none of them recently.

The *Husky* tied up between river tugs next to the city dock, shore power was snaked aboard and plugged in, and the diesels shut down for the first time since Ballard. Ski had had enough of the seafaring life, and in Bethel experienced deckhands looking for work were climbing aboard the moment they docked. The captain shook hands with Ski and handed him a check for a thousand dollars.

Ski felt the pay was pretty good, considering that his two weeks' work included room and board and probably the most spectacular cruise available on the planet, but he wondered how he was going to cash the check here at the end of the world, with only his Illinois driver's license for identification.

He wandered down the dirt road along the riverbank, suitcase in hand. He passed a salmon cannery, the main building a green wooden structure a block square on the inland side of the road, with docks and sheds lining the riverbank across from it. A tiny log cabin, precariously perched next to the water, had a hand-lettered sign: *Dentist*. More cabins, one or two rooms each, lined the bank with admirable optimism. On the inland side, a one-story wooden building that had once been green had a sign reading *Consolidated Freight Line, offices*. An ancient two-story clapboard building, nominally white, with a definite list to it, struggled to hold up a sign proclaiming *Leen's Lodge*. Next to the lodge, the first concrete block building he'd seen since Seattle was painted yellow and labeled *First National Bank of Anchorage, Kuskokwim Branch*.

Ski thought that maybe if he opened a checking account and deposited the check, the bank might honor it. He tromped up the wooden stairs and shoved through the glass door. The lobby was deserted, three cashier's windows unattended. He strode across the tile floor to the first window and laid the check on the counter. An attractive young woman, dressed for business in white blouse and dark skirt, got up from a desk and came into the cashier's cage. With long black hair and large almond-colored eyes in a smooth round face, she was a pleasant introduction to Yup'ik Eskimos. She was five feet tall, but stepped up onto a platform and looked Ski right in the eyes with a friendly smile. She picked up the check, glanced at it, turned it over for endorsement, and counted out ten one-hundred-dollar bills. That gesture finally told Ski just how far he had come from Chicago.

With the roll of bills in his pocket, he marched next door to the lodge, standing straighter and wearing his version of a smile. He asked for a room. The matronly bundle of energy who bustled out of the kitchen wiped her hands on her apron, swiped a few errant gray strands back under her hair net, and introduced herself as Bergie Leen. So, the lodge was not named for its physical impairment.

She opened a loose-leaf notebook and picked up a pen from the desk. "And you are?"

"Erwin Kawalski, please call me Ski."

Bergie nodded, wrote *Ski* next to *Blue Door*. "Come on and see the room."

She scurried up the stairs like a teenager and opened a blue door that was two doors down the hall from the bathroom. She relieved him of one of his hundred-dollar bills.

"That's the weekly rate, $375 if you take it by the month. Price includes breakfast between six and seven-thirty. We put on a spread here in the evenings and that's extra. Holler if you need anything." She bounded back down the stairs. Ski noticed that he hadn't been asked to sign anything.

He closed the door of his new room and saw that there wasn't any lock. The room was ten feet square and had a single bed, a dresser, a tiny closet, and a chair. Sheetrock walls were painted yellow. The floor was carpeted, brown at one time, but bare threads showed the paths to the bed and the window. From his second-story perch, he could see over the Consolidated Freight office to the river and across the river to a stand of willows. A range of snow-covered mountains pricked the eastern horizon, he guessed eighty miles away.

He wandered down the hall to the bathroom. The carpeted floor in the hallway had humps and sags to it. The bathroom consisted of commode, lavatory, and steel shower; no tub. He wondered if the term for the lodge was *primitive* or *basic*, but he noticed that he already felt right at home.

Downstairs again, he followed the path worn in the carpet toward the front door, past the doorless entrance to the kitchen on the left, thirty-foot-long dining table with wooden chairs on the right. He had just passed the kitchen entrance when Bergie hollered, "Hey, Ski."

He backed up and stepped into the kitchen. An eight-foot by four-foot black-iron stove was roaring with a fan-fed oil fire. Bergie had a tiny smudge of flour on her cheek. The oven door yawned open and Bergie was shoveling cookies off a sheet onto a platter with a spatula.

"Have a cookie. Dinner at six, steaks tonight." She flashed Ski a quick smile and turned back to the oven for another tray. Ski grabbed a cookie and had to juggle it to keep from burning his fingers. Outside, he turned left on the dirt road and walked along the riverbank back toward the dock. The river was half a mile wide, the same chocolate brown color as the road, and racing along at a good clip with mini whirlpools here and there. The far bank seemed to be willow-covered islands, no higher than the water.

He paused in front of the cannery to watch some men shoving open the big double doors. The men all wore gray coveralls and hair near shoulder length. One, who seemed to be in charge, reminded Ski of Indians he had seen in Seattle. He appeared disjointed, like a puppet, his arms and legs larger and more muscular than nature had intended. His face was swarthy and slender, sporting that beak that Ski had noted on Indians in Seattle. The foreman turned around and hollered.

"Hey, gussak, know how to operate a forklift?"

"No, but I'm a fast learner."

"Fair enough. Got a name?"

"Kawalski, call me Ski."

"I'm Hank. Practice on that green one; fifteen dollars an hour if you can make it sing." Hank turned to follow the group into the cannery.

In twenty minutes, Ski understood what Hank had meant by making the forklift sing. He had the knack of backing up while turning, simultaneously raising and tilting the forks, both hands and both feet busy like an organist or a helicopter pilot.

Big Red, the mother of all forks, was parked next to the little green fork. Red had elevator tracks the size of bridge girders, two stories tall, cables an inch in diameter, and looked capable of lifting a boxcar off a railroad track. Ski climbed up and checked the controls. They seemed to be the same as the little green one. He fired up Big Red, scooped up the green forklift, and set it twenty feet up on top of two stacked container vans. He was starting to lift it down when Hank came out of the cannery.

"Hey, I told you to practice with the green one."

"I am practicing with the green one." Ski lifted the green fork down and set it six inches from Hank's feet. "And what the heck is a gussak, anyway?"

"Gussak is the Eskimo name for a gringo, a honky, a tenderfoot, a green-horn, or 'cheechako,' as we call them. The first white men the Eskimos saw were Russian Cossacks, so all white men became Cossacks or Gussaks. Want to start work this afternoon or wait until morning?"

❆ ❆ ❆ ❆

We came to the banks of a small river that was rushing to join the Kuskokwim, blocking our path. A rise beside us was snow free so we climbed up and sat on the tundra. Behind us, the black line that was Bethel looked out of place on the unmarked natural horizon. A flight of swans went over, a couple thousand feet above us, looking like tiny white stars in the sunlight. Ski was laughing at himself for the way he'd been rambling on, but I was enjoying his tale and the quiet camaraderie. He looked the question, I nodded the answer, and he continued.

❆ ❆ ❆ ❆

The bank was open late on Friday night, so Ski dropped in and endorsed his first week's check from Kemp Fisheries. He was handed six more hundred-dollar bills with the same friendly smile. He returned the smile, rolled the bills into his pocket and hurried back to the lodge to wash up for dinner. It was steak night, but that was an understatement. It was a rib steak that covered his platter so that Ski had to put the home fries on top of it, and it seemed to be another in the string of the best meals he'd ever eaten. He was getting to know the other boarders, and noticed that several of them were missing some body parts from accidents, from freezing, from fights. The only one who seemed to notice Ski's scar was Jack McGuire, who described himself as a gambler, and looked the part, possibly transplanted straight from the old Mississippi riverboats. Ski guessed that Jack was old enough for that, but it was hard to tell because he didn't show the usual ravages of weather and dissipation that should have gone with his age. Jack, Ski would learn, always wore silk shirts, a string tie, and a sports jacket over slacks. His hair, almost red, but going gray, was razor cut with a natural wave. He nodded toward Ski's cheek, said, "'Nam?" Ski nodded, and that was the end of it.

When stuffed diners pushed their plates away and poured a second glass of wine, one old-timer, definitely Indian with hawk eyes and the appropriate beak, who had introduced himself as Dummy, explained why his left wrist ended at the cuff of his plaid shirt sleeve.

"Well, ya see, that's why they call me Dummy. Any greenhorn *cheechako* with a week in Alaska shoulda known better. Me, I been runnin' snowmachines since they was invented, and dog teams before that, so my only excuse is just dumbness."

Bergie left the table to carry platters into the kitchen. Dummy sneaked a third glass of wine and continued.

"I was twenty miles up the Piamute Slough and I got a rock stuck in my snowmachine tread. Well, I reached in, dumb as you please, engine idling, and pulled out the rock. Machine jumps forward a foot, and there's my hand, caught in the tread and the rear idler gear sticking an inch-square tooth right through my palm." Dummy sneaked a peek, but Bergie was coming back so he covered his glass with his right hand.

"Well, I was stuck good. I couldn't reach to shut off the engine, so I'm pulling back and the engine is pulling forward, and there we sat. It commenced to gettin' dark, and I'm getting' cold and hungry for dinner. I took off my belt, wrapped up my left wrist so it wouldn't bleed, and cut off my stupid hand with my hunting knife. Took me two hours to ride home with only one hand, and I was about starved to death."

Bergie was back in the kitchen. Dummy emptied the rest of the wine into his glass.

❄ ❄ ❄ ❄

Ski smiled at the memory. "I guess it was the next day that you and Tom came in. You'd been upriver somewhere so you smelled like spruce trees and you were laughing and talking in a way that reminded me of my old college buddies. When you sat down, introduced yourselves, and pulled me into the conversation, I knew I was finally home."

We stood, brushed the wet moss off of our fannies, and turned back toward Bethel.

❄ ❄ ❄ ❄

My mental movie ended. Ski's declaration of solidarity, his sharing of moments of weakness, were so open, so trusting, so intimate, I could not believe he was other than he seemed. I finished my drink and fell into bed, but not to sleep. My mind was churning, and if I was worried, I could imagine what Ski and Punik were going through.

CHAPTER 6

SECOND VISIT
TUESDAY EVENING
EMMONAK, ALASKA

ood old Jesse. Everyone loves Jesse. Pilots and bigwigs hang around in the daytime, women sneak into his cabin at night. So busy, busy. No time for old friends, can't be bothered. Oh, he consented to have a nightcap with me, since I brought the whiskey. Good night for it, snow falling a couple of inches an hour and the wind whipping it around. Won't be any snuggle bunnies surprising us.

The visitor plunked a pint of Old Granddad on the table. Jesse brought two glasses from his cupboard and the ice tray from his refrigerator. The two men poured bourbon over ice cubes, saluted each other with glasses, and drank, savoring the smoky flavor and the bite of alcohol. The old log cabin shuddered in the wind, the light bulb swinging on its cord. The visitor watched Jesse's shadow moving back and forth on the wall behind him, back and forth, back and forth, like the pendulum on a clock, measuring his final hour.

"Here's to February twenty-sixth." Jesse saluted with his glass again.

"To February twenty-sixth," the visitor echoed. "We agreed on ten years, and the time is up. The case is cold, no one remembers the incident, and it's finally safe to share. Have you thought about where you'd like to go?"

"Might take me a vacation in Hawaii if I can get someone to take care of the runway." Jesse drank and checked to be sure the bottle was still within reach.

"I wasn't thinking of a vacation, I meant where would you like to move permanently. You know we can't stay here. We have to move away one at

47

a time, cut the old ties. If we don't, someone will slip up, and if one of us is caught, we'll all be."

Jesse didn't answer. He buried his nose in his glass, took a healthy sip, and glanced at the snow that was pelting the window, avoiding eye contact.

The visitor sighed and reached to top off Jesse's glass. A gust of wind rattled the windowpanes and a blast of cold air came under the front door to set the light bulb swinging again. Jesse heaved himself up and shuffled across the room, his slippers making scraping sounds on the bare wooden floor. He used his foot to shove a blanket tighter against the crack under the door.

"Look, Jesse, that was always our plan. We all agreed. In two months you can move anywhere in the world and live like a king for the rest of your life, no danger."

Jesse returned to his seat, took another sip from the glass. "I don't want to go nowhere. It would be like running away."

"Not running away, running to a new life. You could buy a hacienda on the Gulf Coast of Mexico. Golden beaches, year-round sunshine, beautiful women, you can have anything you want. We'll claim it's for your health, no one will blame you."

Jesse drew circles on the oilcloth with his glass, then took a drink and met his visitor's eyes. "Look, it's different for you. You don't have roots here like I have."

The visitor winced. That was a low blow. Jessie forged ahead. "My whole life, everything I know is here. Sure, you helped me buy the equipment, and I thank you, but that does not give you the right to dictate the rest of my life." Jesse drained his glass; the visitor refilled it. Wind vibrated the stovepipe, making a mournful, lonely sound, a low note on a flute. A smatter of heavy wet snow slammed the window and stuck.

"Jesse, it's not just for you. It's for all of the partners. After we share, if one stays, someone will notice. I really can't let you do that."

Bad choice of words. Jesse flared. "You don't let me, or not let me do nuthin'. You don't own me. You just do the share out. What I do is none of your damn business." Jesse drained his glass. The visitor poured the last few drops from the bottle into it and reached for his parka pocket. The bottle had been wrapped in a dishtowel. The object he removed was again wrapped in a dishtowel.

Jesse had barely registered that the new object was not another bottle. It was a .45 automatic. The visitor flipped the cloth off the barrel, but still held the grip in the cloth when he blew Jesse's brains out.

So long, good old Jesse. Maybe heaven is in the Bahamas. The visitor carried his glass to the sink, dipped water from the barrel to wash it, and replaced it behind the group of six still in the cupboard. He wiped his place at the table, pocketed the empty bottle, and looked around the room. Bare boards, sparse furnishings, no sign that he had been there. The automatic was still in his pocket with fingerprints on it, but not his.

Stupid trooper didn't arrest the gussak. Maybe the gussak had an alibi, maybe the trooper was too slow to connect the hat with the murder, but this time there can be no mistake. The visitor opened the door. A blast of snow-laden wind slapped his face. He stepped out into six inches of heavy wet snow, the wind stinging but fresh and clean. He pulled the door closed, but the draft-blocking blanket was caught, the door didn't latch. No problem, snow would cover his tracks in minutes.

CHAPTER 7

WEDNESDAY AFTERNOON
BETHEL, ALASKA

I spent the next two days after we lugged Demientoff's body back to Bethel hanging around the single-sideband radio whenever I wasn't flying. I kept hoping to hear Ski on the radio with a cryptic message about finding a calling card in a fox track, but the call didn't come. There weren't many passengers that week. They would flood us the next week when the University of Alaska closed for Christmas break and the students all wanted to go back to their villages at once.

Mail was feeling the pre-Christmas avalanche coming, though, and I was letting it stack up until Vickie started giving me the stink eye and I flew a few loads. My problem was that I couldn't get Ski and Punik out of my mind, and nothing else seemed important. I should have been feeling like Santa Claus.

I had just dropped off fifteen hundred pounds of packages at Tuluksak, half of them gift wrapped, but I couldn't shake the sense of foreboding. Tuluksak is twenty-five minutes, sixty-five miles, up the Kuskokwim, getting close to the Kilbuck Mountains. It has forty-foot spruce trees, and the Tuluksak River is clear water, so it's a pleasant change from Bethel.

Fifteen hundred pounds of mail is five pounds for every man, woman, and child in the village, and the half of the mail that wasn't gift wrapped was cases of Carnation condensed milk and cases of soda pop with stamps stuck on them. For various reasons of supply, demand, and quality, drinking water is not normal on the Delta. The Kuskokwim is muddy and loaded with mercury from Barometer Mountain. The Tuluksak River is often host to the giardia parasites excreted by animals upstream and life-threatening to humans. The only reliably potable water in the village comes from the 300-foot-deep well at the school. Villagers were welcome to collect bucketsful, but they seldom drank it. Instead, we hauled entire planeloads of sodas destined for very small villages.

When I taxied up to the fuel pumps in Bethel and saw Tom's Rover in the lot, I knew it was bad news; I just hadn't imagined how bad. I was still topping off the right tank when Tom came out and climbed into the passenger seat.

All he said was, "Emmonak," and he either pretended to or actually did go to sleep while I was still talking to flight service. The Emmonak airport hadn't been plowed, and it should have been. The weather was warmer and eight inches of heavy snow had fallen overnight. I landed halfway down the strip because the snow stopped us pretty fast and it took a lot of power to taxi off the runway.

The Emmonak airport starts out in the tundra and ends right beside the village, cannery on the left, wooden bridge over a slough to the village on the right, river at the end of the strip. The village cop met us on the bridge. This cop was named Joe, and he was small for a policeman, but I doubt anyone he had to face down ever noticed that. He stood five-foot six inches tall, with a slender wiry build, but he had the bantam-rooster swagger that many small men affect. He wore a tightly trimmed mustache that gave him an ominous cast.

Some of Joe's attitude was probably because he was a half-breed; his father was a Chamorro from Guam. That's not as unlikely as it sounds because young folk come from all over the Pacific to work in the Alaska canneries. In the fall, most go back to Hawaii, Guam, Saipan, and Seattle, but Joe's father stayed and married a local girl. He lasted a few years, turned into the village drunk, and eventually disappeared, either back to Guam or to the bottom of the river.

Being left fatherless young and with a sick mother had made Joe grow up too fast, and I think it also soured him on life. He's not a guy you can get to know, and I don't remember him ever smiling. His expression of daring us to cross him was his usual. However, Joe was wearing a holstered .38 outside his beaver parka, and that was not a usual thing.

Village cops can get a gun in a hurry if they need one, but they don't usually wear them. Their normal duties are digging drunks out of snowbanks and helping them home when someone smuggles booze into the village, or maybe arbitrating a squabble at the nightly bingo games. Their other job is dealing with domestic violence. Villages have more than their share, mostly in January and February, but the last thing anybody wants in those cases is to have a handgun in the melee.

Joe led us across the bridge and turned right, away from the river, on the path beside the slough. The first house was a long, low structure made from driftwood logs. It belonged to Jesse, who was the local ticket agent, radio operator, weather observer, and airport maintenance man. The village snow-plow is a front-end loader fitted with a blade, and it sat behind the house with inches of snow on it. Jesse's front door was wide open and snow had drifted in and across the room. Jesse didn't mind; he was sitting in a wooden chair at his kitchen table with an empty glass that smelled like whiskey in his right hand and a bullet hole in his forehead.

I may be blasé about death, but that one hurt me. Jesse not only ran the airport and manned the radios, he kept open house for any pilot who hap-pened to land. Pilots spend a lot of time on standby, waiting for passengers, and they have to be instantly available when passengers return. Usually, that means sitting in the airplane, but with Jesse's cabin located right across the slough from the airport apron, it was safe to visit, drink coffee, swap philoso-phies, sometimes play a little poker or cribbage, and generally enjoy Jesse's company and the standby time in Emmonak.

He was wearing a flannel shirt and jeans, with wool socks and slippers on his feet. His shaggy gray-streaked hair was mussed, as if he'd just gotten out of bed. His great, bushy dark eyebrows were drawn up in a surprised expression, but that may have been caused by the bullet, rather than preceding it. The hole in his forehead was made by a .45 automatic.

There was an exit wound, but the bullet was smashed against the log wall behind him. Tom knelt and retrieved an empty cartridge from the floor under the stove. He dropped it into an evidence bag. There was a clincher. Joe took a dishtowel out of his pocket, unwrapped the weapon, and dropped it on the red-checkered oilcloth. It sat there gleaming a soft, black, metallic, oiled sheen.

"Found it in the snow outside." Joe was a man of few words.

My feeling of foreboding went away. The disaster had struck. I knew who that automatic belonged to. Tom knew who that automatic belonged to. Joe knew who that automatic belonged to. Even Jesse would have known that that automatic was a present. It was mailed to Ski in Chicago from one of the guys he had led out of the elephant grass in 'Nam. Ski's former landlady in Chicago had forwarded it the year before when Ski sent her a Christmas card.

Jesse wasn't going to lie down for the body bag. Not only had rigor set in, but with the door open, it was well below freezing in the cabin. Since he wouldn't conform to the bag we had to make the heavy leather bag conform to him, and when we finally got him zipped in, he still fit in the chair. His right arm was extended, fingers wrapped around a glass. Tom pried the glass loose, but the arm would not bend. We zipped the bag up as far as the arm and down as far as the arm, but Jesse still seemed to be reaching for a glass. If I'd had seats in the plane, I would have put him in one, but we laid him in back where he made a letter Z.

Tom took a notebook and a pencil out of his pockets (pens don't work well in the Arctic), and started through the village to ask questions. I fired up the snowplow loader and made four passes down the center of the runway. That made a twelve-foot-wide strip, and even a Cherokee Six needs only seven feet.

I parked the loader and went back to the plane to keep Jesse company. He was "signed into the custody of Detective Price," and all that. I had custody of the automatic, too, and I took it out of my parka pocket and stuffed it into the map case. I wasn't about to unwrap it because there just might be fingerprints on it.

Tom came trudging across the bridge at four o'clock. It was already nearly dark, but no one else walks quite like Tom. When he got close enough that I could see his face, he did not look happy.

"Any luck?" I asked.

"None. Nobody saw anything, and that's the truth. If anyone had an idea, they would have told me. There are no strangers in the village. The only good news is that no one has seen Ski for a few days. Can we land at the cabin?"

"Sure, no problem there, just don't ask if we can take off again." We flew across the river and circled past the cabin. The big picture windows in the cabin's living room gave off a warm friendly glow and made bright yellow trails in the snow outside. You see pictures like that on Christmas cards.

The glow meant that Ski was running the generator. He usually ran it a couple of hours every evening. That kept the frost out of the generator shack, charged the batteries for the single-sideband radio, pumped up the pressure tank from the well, and ran the fan on the cook stove. It ran the freezer chest on the back porch, too, usually not necessary, but it didn't hurt, and the generator powered nice bright lights to cook dinner by.

The downriver end of my smooth strip was next to the cabin, so I used the cabin for a marker and tried to judge how far out I should be. I slowed us down to sixty knots, dropped thirty degrees of flaps, and kept us above the snow with power until the landing lights showed my smooth spot. I chopped the power, and we stopped as if the brakes were locked up, but it was the snow that stopped us.

It took full power to turn us around and plow our way back next to the cabin. Ski came out and Tom went to meet him, but I took a minute to pull the cowling cover off Jesse and cover the engine. I followed them inside.

My first thought when Punik handed me coffee was that she didn't look so good. Not that she wasn't still the most beautiful girl on the Delta, maybe in the world, but her usual sparkle was gone. I joined Tom on the couch; Ski sat on the chair arm, but Punik stayed busy in the kitchen.

Tom got right to the point. "Where's that .45 automatic of yours?" he asked.

"It's in the gun cabinet." Ski got up and took a key ring out of his pocket while he walked toward the cabinet on the wall. He started to insert a key in the lock and stopped.

"That's funny, I thought I locked it."

Tom went over to have a look. Ski opened the cabinet. Three pegs that were meant to hold the .45 were empty. Ski stared in shock. Tom reached into the cabinet and pulled out Ski's .30-06. He sniffed the breech.

"Fired this lately?" Tom asked.

"Couple of days ago. Don't tell me you're moonlighting for the Fish and Game?"

"Nah," Tom put the rifle back in its slot. "Moose?"

Ski nodded, and we went back to our seats. Ski was looking pretty worried. So was I, but I guess his reasons were better.

Tom had a thoughtful expression that told me his mind was racing, but I wasn't reading it.

"You should run down to Alakanuk and report the stolen automatic to George."

"Tom," Ski said, "I have an awful feeling that you know where my .45 is."

Tom nodded. "I'm sorry, Ski, it's in an evidence bag. It was used to shoot Jesse last night."

Punik screamed and we all jumped up, but she wasn't being killed; she was standing in the kitchen doorway listening. She covered her face with her hands and ran for the bedroom. Ski was poised, ready to follow her, but not sure he was excused.

"Tom, do you need to see the moose I shot?"

"Of course not, Ski. You said you shot a moose, so you shot a moose. Go take care of Punik."

Ski ran for the bedroom, but I hollered, "Hey, Ski, can I use your snowmachine?"

He didn't answer; he tossed me his key ring.

Ski's Polaris was hooked to a sled, gussak fashion, with a trailer hitch and a tow bar. I unhooked the sled and made three passes up our ice cake and back, packing down the snow, but the big machine had a wide track for floating on soft snow and it wasn't packing much. I parked the machine, rehooked the sled, and put the keys back inside on the coffee table. Punik's sobbing and Ski's soothing sounds were coming from the open bedroom door. Like the coward that I am, I ran.

Tom had already uncovered the engine and climbed in. I lined the airplane up with the snowmachine tracks. We were nearing fifty knots when our landing lights showed an ice ridge at the end of our smooth patch. I'd been holding the yoke back to keep the nose wheel out of the snow. At the end of the smooth ice, I jammed down twenty degrees of flaps and jerked the yoke all the way back to get the nose as high as possible. The main gear hit an ice cake with a bang. We bounced into the air, almost stayed there, came down for one more bounce, and flew away.

The nose wheel on a 206 is mounted on an oleo strut, and a good whack can tear it off, but the main gears are mounted on spring-steel legs. The only problem with whacking a main gear is that you might blow a tire: inconvenient but not dangerous. If you're nearly flying, you can change it when you get home. We skimmed low over the ice in ground effect and I slowly bled off flaps until we hit seventy. I pulled the nose up and let those three hundred horses bore a hole into the velvet black night. At a thousand feet we turned toward Bethel, retracted the remaining flaps and set up a cruise.

"What in the devil was wrong with Punik?" Tom asked.

"You mean, why was she upset when you practically accused her husband of murder?"

"No, when we first got there. Something just wasn't right. She was nervous, kind of distant, maybe pale. That girl has something heavy on her mind."

"Can we forgive her for being a little upset over Demientoff's killing? Maybe she hasn't recovered from that one yet . . . then you show up looking all official. Anyone would be scared."

"Yeah, I hope that's all it was, but Jesse's killing is downright strange. I doubt he owned anything worth stealing, and if he did, he'd give it to you if you asked. This was a planned killing, almost an execution. Someone is really working at framing Ski, and who would have a grudge against Jesse or Ski?"

That was a good question. I couldn't imagine anyone wanting Jesse dead. I reached for a motive. "Maybe he did have some money stashed. I'm pretty sure that he owns that village snowplow, probably some of the radios, and he leases them to the state. I think a rig like that must cost thirty thousand bucks, so maybe he had a cigar box full of cash and someone wanted it."

"Yeah, maybe, but the real problem is that both murders are linked to Ski. Punik spent some early years in Emmonak. Maybe Jesse raped her, something like that, and she got her revenge."

"That's impossible!" I blurted.

Tom was shaking his head, but not very adamantly. "Not impossible, *improbable*. Sherlock Holmes said, 'Eliminate the impossible, and whatever is left must be true, no matter how improbable.' Of course I don't believe Punik would murder, for any reason, but two people had easy access to the hat and the automatic. Maybe we're dealing with a touch of insanity here, justified or not."

"Nuts. I can't believe you're saying this. Next week someone from the area will call for a charter to Anchorage, pay for it with cash, and you can pick him up in a Fourth Avenue bar throwing twenty-dollar bills around that belonged to Demientoff and Jesse."

"Alex, I really hope you're right." Tom tipped his hat down to sleep mode, which ended the conversation. Twenty minutes later a glow on the horizon turned into Bethel.

We sat Jessie up in the front seat of the Rover and Tom buckled him in nice and safe. He was still reaching out of the bag for his glass. I put the plane to bed, filled out a flight ticket, and locked up the office.

When I got back to my little two-room mansion on the riverbank, I turned the oil-fired cook/heating stove up high so there would be some hot water for a shower. It doesn't take much water for me to shower because water in Bethel is delivered by a tank truck and costs six cents a gallon. My cabin is perched right on the riverbank, and some spring the flood will take it downriver, but in the meantime it's comfortable enough.

Next to the black-iron woodstove, converted to burn oil, is a sink with hot and cold running water, and cupboards above it. A refrigerator stands in the corner. I have a wooden table and two wooden chairs: matching, by the way. I can sit in my chair at the table, and without getting up, reach the refrigerator, the sink, and with just a little stretch, the stove.

Off the living room is a hallway that has the water barrel, pump on top, and the hot water tank. Squeeze past those, and the end of the hallway is blocked off to make a bathroom with honey-bucket style commode, lavatory, and steel shower. My bedroom opens off the hallway. There isn't any door, because all of the heat comes from the kitchen, but the doorway is at the side of the hallway, so if you're in the kitchen, you don't see directly into the bedroom.

I didn't feel like listening to Vivaldi, but I had a fresh bottle of Captain Morgan in the cupboard. I grabbed that and a glass, some ice and a Coke from the refrigerator, and sat at the table to make a serious dent in the bottle. Mostly I sat there wondering if it would help to bang my head against the wall. I knew Tom was just thinking out loud, trying to cover the bases, but the suggestion that Punik could even harbor a grudge was outrageous. I've known her family since she was in grade school and there isn't a vindictive or dishonest gene in the lot of them.

CHAPTER 8

THE MISSION

Since she married Ski, I considered her a sister-in-law and would have loved her in any case, but Punik was very much more than a sister-in-law. I know her brother Evan who runs the engine repair shop in Marshall, her brother Charlie who has a small store in Mountain Village, and her sister Rose who is raising babies in Pitka's Point. Her parents, Evan and Ella, are very special friends who live at St. Marys and are the generation that bridged the gap between the traditional Eskimo lifestyle and the present. I've spent enough evenings, and drunk enough tea with her family, that I know exactly what Punik's story is.

It must have been better than a dozen years ago that I was ferrying reindeer meat from the Stebbins herd to St. Michael. Villagers were butchering at Hunting Point, miles from the airport. We had a Howard on floats, and that old workhorse could lift a ton of meat off a choppy sea and deliver it to the freezers in St. Michael in fifteen minutes. The problem came when the fall tides ran a little extreme and left the Howard high on the beach. You don't move a plane the size of the Howard by hand; it has to float. The low tide of the day was in the morning, the high one late evening, so I had to use the evening tide to get off the mudflats.

That put me halfway to Bethel in the dark when the engine blew a jug. That's not terribly uncommon for those old nine-cylinder radials. A cylinder head will crack, or blow right off, and they keep on flying. Eight cylinders is no problem, even seven would keep it in the air, but the one that blew was on the left side and it was shooting out a stream of fire like a flamethrower, right past my window. That made me want to set it down, and the first opportunity was at St. Marys on the Andreafsky River.

There were enough lights on shore to show me the river, and I got down fine with landing lights, but when I tried to taxi to shore I hit a submerged piling and poked a hole in the float. The plane settled down onto mud, jumping distance from shore, and I was stuck. It was Evan who strolled down the path and invited me to join the family for dinner.

That would not have happened during my first year or two in the Bush. I would have been sleeping in the airplane and eating hardtack. When you first arrive, Natives are civil, but hardly cordial. They don't expect you to stay, so they don't waste time on you. If you survive a couple of years with no problems, they pull you in and treat you like family. For that first year, I had begun to notice that there never seemed to be any women in the villages. It wasn't until they decided I was there for honorable reasons that women began to appear and the mix of genders I saw reached normal proportions.

Eskimos survive by sharing, but it's not quite the open-handed society that the early historians described. When they witnessed the meat from a hunt being distributed, they didn't realize that each person or family was receiving a preordained portion, based on their participation in the hunt, the butchering, or facilitating village life. Still, your credit is good. A favor now may be repaid later. It wasn't that Evan was expecting payment; he was genuinely being hospitable. Evan and his wife Ella were parents to the world, but he did know that I wouldn't forget the favor.

Don't be fooled by the gussak names. There was nothing gussak or modern about Evan and Ella's early lives. In the 1860s, missionaries did a census of the Alaska Eskimos. Since the missionaries could neither pronounce nor spell the Eskimo names, they gave each Eskimo an English name. The Eskimos were proud of the new names and passed them down to later generations.

Dinner was boiled beaver and cabbage, a little gamy, but boiled tender, rich and good. It was cooked without spices, but every Eskimo table has a saltshaker, a little bottle of seal oil, and a bottle of Tabasco, and we kept those circulating. Seven of us sat around a kitchen table under a Coleman lantern: me, Evan, Ella, and four beautiful children. The atmosphere was relaxed and friendly, but no chatter. The Eskimos take eating very seriously, and as each kid finished eating he or she grabbed a book and slipped away.

The conversation started when Ella served tundra tea, or *ayuq,* to the three adults.

Drinking *ayuq*, also called Labrador tea, is a ritual that invites conversation and intimacy. It's made from a little plant on the tundra that looks like a six-inch hemlock tree, reddish-brown and pungent. Historically it was used for both medicinal and religious purposes and served sometimes to the accompaniment of the Tarvaq Eskimo dance. I've been told that the ritual was important at funerals to drive away bad spirits. Now, it's usually brought out as a social occasion, and that's how we were using it. Evan and Ella took turns with the story of their lives, a very great honor for me and a pleasant evening for them. Truth is, I knew most of the story already, because they were legends even then, but I listened with rapt attention.

The story started in Ingrihak, which sat on a bluff above the Yukon River. Sod huts with log bases were scattered through the trees. The view across the river was of flat tundra, reaching to the horizon. On the left, the Yukon had been flowing south, following the mountains, and the mountains made a ninety-degree turn to the west. The river spewed straight ahead through the tundra for several miles, then turned around in a sharp bend and came right back to the mountains.

The bend, called Ohogamute, or Devil's Elbow, was laddered with old channels and sloughs, many sloughs blocked on both ends to form oxbows. The beavers that had blocked the sloughs with their dams provided pond homes for muskrat and thousands of ducks and geese. Food was plentiful in the summertime for those hunters who survived the trip across the river in their skin boats and back again, but in the winter, with ice four feet thick on the river and sloughs and the birds gone to warmer climates, food was a different matter.

Punik, their youngest, was born on a moose hide in a one-room sod house. Ella raised the hem of her robe above her knees and squatted down. Her eyes were squeezed tight shut, fists clenched, her round face a mask of concentration. Long black hair was matted with perspiration. She leaned against Evan's arm and knew that she was safe. The arm that supported her was as strong and as steady as a tree limb, and she knew that Evan was favored by the gods. Just taller than Ella, but with shoulders that seemed massive to her, Evan was as weathered and tough as the logs that drifted down the river, and yet was the kindest and gentlest of men.

Ella felt the head emerge, took a deep breath and pushed, gently, lovingly. She reached down between her legs, pulled out the baby and handed her to Evan. Baby Punik met the world with a healthy squall. Evan leaned Ella back against a pile of furs. He ceremoniously tied the cord with leather thongs, bit it in two with his teeth, and handed the baby to Ella. He sat back on his heels to embrace his other three children. Ella was exhausted and pale, but she smiled and cuddled her fourth baby.

❄ ❄ ❄ ❄

Ella told most of that story. She worshiped Evan and wanted me to understand. She had no qualms about discussing the birth. Eskimos know where babies come from. They assume that you do, too, and they view the entire process as wonderful and social. Ella topped off our teacups and Evan took over.

❄ ❄ ❄ ❄

Evan stood and led his two boys outside, leaving his three-year-old daughter, Rose, with her mother. Cleaning up was women's work, and as soon as Evan left the hut, Ella's sisters slipped in and took charge. Evan loved his children and loved his wife, although he couldn't have told you that. His language didn't include that concept, but he felt it, and the feeling drove him to be one of the first Yup'ik speakers to learn English because he wanted to understand the priests who visited Ingrihak each summer.

Evan patted the two tousled heads and turned the boys toward their cousins who were hiding behind the corner of a house, peeking out, waiting for news. Evan had to leave the village, find a fresh patch of snow to cleanse himself, and give thanks to the Earth Goddess and the River God for this new baby. His first three were now old enough that he expected them to live, if there were no accidents, so even if the gods took this new one back, they had been generous.

The supreme being in Evan's cosmos was Ellagpiim Yua, the spirit of peace. Ellagpiim Yua kept the world in balance through harmony in nature and in the spiritual realm, but Evan addressed his immediate concerns to the lesser gods. His relationship with them was more personal and they would have more time for him.

The gods had been very good to Evan in many ways, always putting an animal in his traps or a fish on his line, so his family ate almost every day. The few times that the gods tested him, he thanked them anyway, never complained, and stayed with his hunting or fishing for a day, two days, whatever it required, until the gods relented.

Now he was concerned, because there was a new God, the god of wealth and immortality. Evan was very interested in this new God, but needed permission from the old ones. He decided that it was okay to learn about this new God because surely the gods all knew each other, and Earth Goddess and River God were kind to the new priests.

The priests told strange stories of lands where it never snowed, of people who raised edible plants and all sorts of strange animals and never had to hunt for food. Evan supposed those lands were the heaven referred to in the sermons.

It was hard to believe some of their stories, like the ones about machines that went faster than dog sleds, cities with thousands of people in them, and hard-packed trails that were longer than the Yukon, but then those might be part of the heaven the priests talked about, too. Evan didn't know how many a thousand might be, but he guessed it was lots more than the inhabitants of Ingrihak.

One subject that was undeniably true was their talk of immortality. Evan was an old man, somewhere in his thirties, with not many winters left ahead of him. Ella had been a young and beautiful fourteen years old when he married her, but now, almost ten years later, Ella was getting old and tired. Some of the priests and nuns who visited the villages were sixty, sometimes even seventy years old, and yet they looked younger than Evan and Ella.

The priests from St. Marys Mission seemed to know a great many very strange things, and that knowledge made them rich beyond imagination and made them immortal. Evan determined that his children should attend the school at the mission in St. Marys. Late that fateful fall, he captured floating logs and lashed together a driftwood raft.

He didn't mention his plan to Ella, because it really didn't concern her. Ella was a good wife. Each day she boiled the fish or beaver, squirrel, or rabbit that Evan brought home and scraped the furs and sewed them into garments. She bore and nurtured his children and did what she was told. When it was time to get on the raft, he would tell her to get on, and she would do it. There was no need for discussion.

Ella watched the building of the raft and said goodbye to her sisters. It was neither a happy nor a sad occasion. She knew that she would never see them again, but life was like that. Men went out hunting or fishing and did not come back. Children went down to the river for a skin full of water and never returned. Women went into labor. Sometimes they had babies, sometimes they died; that was life.

Evan packed his raft with a supply of salmon strips, his fishing tackle, Ella's wooden bowls, and the family's fur blankets. He told Ella to climb aboard. With little Rose clinging to the hem of her summer parka, her two sons marching at her sides, and Punik in her arms, Ella crossed the mud and sat down in the center of the raft. Evan pushed the raft out into the Yukon River and jumped on. No one waved goodbye and no one looked back.

The raft picked up speed until they were fairly flying along the bank, faster than a man could run, faster than any of them had ever moved before. They gradually drifted toward the center of the river where they moved at the same speed as the water around them, so it didn't seem so fast, but the mountains on the right bank marched steadily past.

Evan planned to land at Fortuna Ledge, the place the gussaks call Marshall, because it was closer to St. Marys and cousins could give directions, but the current was too strong. He missed Fortuna Ledge and they continued on down the river. The familiar mountains on the right bank became unfamiliar, but the flat tundra on the left bank remained always the same. The day after they passed Fortuna Ledge, the little raft came around a broad bend and was suddenly caught in whirlpools that spun and tossed it, threatening to tear it apart, but the family clung to the raft, and Ella clung to six-month-old Punik.

Another river had slammed into the Yukon, and old Evan was terrified when he realized he could see right through the water. He'd never seen a river that wasn't brown before, and he wasn't sure the strange, clear water would hold up the raft. The Andreafsky River, boiling straight down from the mountains, not only held up the raft but spun it violently across the current and slammed it into the bank, smashing it to pieces on the mountain side of the Yukon.

The family scrambled out of the wreckage and huddled on the gravel riverbank. Their bowls and furs were gone, but they saved the remaining salmon strips and the fishing tackle. They solemnly ate their next-to-last meal of one salmon strip each. Punik's mother nursed her and cradled her in strong arms. The family continued their quest, trudging beside the river against the unfamiliar hills.

They walked until evening, sometimes on a narrow gravel strip beside the water, but sometimes climbing over mounds of dirt that had slid down from the hills above. When their trail was blocked, Evan would hold Punik while Ella scrambled over, then hand each of the kids over, and finally the bundle of salmon strips and fishing tackle. When it got too dark to see, they huddled together for warmth and slept in a dry wash that rain had carved from the hillside. They continued their journey at first light without eating. Evan was saving their last five salmon strips until they got hungry. They had walked most of their second day, little Rose hitchhiking on Evan's broad back, when they heard dogs barking and came to a valley between hills. The village of Pitka's Point nestled on a bluff above them. They were taken into a sod house, fed, washed in seal oil, and given caribou furs next to the fire where they gratefully slept.

The village elders held a solemn council, deciding how to tell Evan that he was heading in the wrong direction, because no Eskimo wants to tell another that he has made a mistake. No one had told Evan that St. Marys was not on the Yukon, but seven miles up the Andreafsky River. It had never occurred to Evan that there were other rivers besides the Yukon.

The elders solved the problem by leading the family up onto the hilltops and pointing them along the barely visible track across the tundra that was left by the winter dogsled trail. It wasn't really obvious that they were heading back up the river. With a fresh supply of salmon strips and a blanket made from three caribou hides that was big enough to wrap all six of them, they set off in high spirits for the three-day trek overland.

❄ ❄ ❄ ❄

Evan roared with laughter when he described the elders' predicament. He had understood what was happening, and would have done the same, but there is nothing wrong with a good joke on an Eskimo, so long as the Eskimo is telling it himself. Ella served more tea and Evan continued.

❄ ❄ ❄ ❄

They topped the final hill, and the valley below them held fifty driftwood and sod houses perched on the bank of the Andreafsky River. The left end of the village was a collection of white wooden buildings larger than Evan had ever imagined, clustered around a church. This, he knew, was the seat of wealth and power, St. Marys Mission.

Evan was a hustler. He gathered driftwood for a frame and built a sod house. He caught dozens of strange white fish out of the clear Andreafsky. He traded fish for a pot so that Ella could boil their meals. He joined a hunting party that was going upriver after caribou. This hunting party had a rifle;

Evan's job was to be a strong paddler against the current, and that he did with skill and dedication. His share of the hunt was half a caribou and a hide. The family settled in for the winter, as rich as they had ever been in Ingrihak.

Evan trapped for furs and food and fished through holes in the ice, but spent every spare minute working on his plan, which was to make himself indispensable to the priests at the mission. Eventually the priests gave him the gussak name of Janitor and he was allowed to work in the mission every day. At the end of each month, they gave him a little paper certificate of appreciation, a handsomely printed form signed in ink by one of the priests. Evan was proud of his certificates, which apparently meant that it was all right for him to continue cleaning and helping out wherever he could.

He took the certificates home to show Ella. Her heart nearly burst with pride in the man who had braved the perils of the unknown world and was now mastering the strange new culture. Ella saved the little certificates in a box to show the children when they were old enough to understand.

When the days began to lengthen, Evan borrowed a handsaw from the mission and explored downriver until he found two logs, as thick as his waist. He cut them off at three times his height and rolled them up the bank, out of reach of spring floods. He gathered poles and willows and stashed them with his logs. The villages up river from Ingrihak were Athabaskan Indian villages, and Evan had watched and memorized the wonderful way that the Athabaskans caught salmon.

When the winter ice was gone and the spring flood subsided, Ella traded two pairs of muskrat-fur mittens for a coil of rope, and Evan lashed together and secured his logs to make a fish wheel. His wheel floated, using the logs for pontoons, and had four spokes. Two of the spokes were baskets woven from willows, two were paddles between the baskets, so that there was always either a basket or a paddle in the water. The river turned the wheel and the baskets dipped down into the water and up again. When the river seemed to be boiling with uncountable salmon, the baskets scooped up many of them. The salmon rose high in the air, slid down toward the center of the wheel, and out a chute at the side into a box.

He built a second sod hut, smaller than their living quarters, with many poles crisscrossing just higher than his head. Each evening when Evan finished his duties at the mission, he trudged down the riverbank to his wheel. The king salmon came first. Evan would hoist a thirty or forty-pound fish onto each shoulder and march back to the village. He laid the fish on Ella's cutting bench and went back for more, working long after he was so weary he could barely see the trail, navigating by memory.

Ella used her *ulu*, the crescent-shaped bit of steel that was sharpened and fitted with a bone handle, to cut the fish into strips. Ella's ulu was made by her father, her dowry when she married Evan, and Ella kept it always with her, in her pocket or in her hand. The boys, Evan Evan and Charlie Evan, gathered the driftwood that fed the constant fire to smoke the fish. Little Rose fussed and tried to help Ella, being more bother than help but learning to be a good Eskimo wife and solemnly carrying armloads of strips into the smokehouse where Ella hung them.

When their oldest son, Evan Evan, was nine winters, the family tested Evan's plan. Evan Evan was a solid, serious boy, who stood patiently while Ella scrubbed him clean and plastered his hair down with her fingers. He marched down the hill to the mission and was welcomed into the mission school. He came home bubbling with excitement, proudly produced a tooth-brush from his pocket, and taught the family how to use it.

Ella hung the toothbrush in a position of honor beside the washbasin, and each member of the family brushed religiously. The brush was nearly worn out a year later when Charlie Evan entered the school. Charlie was slender, compared to his brother, with the touch of a gamin in him and a tendency to figure angles, a budding entrepreneur. He came home with six brushes, one for each of the family, and announced that the red one was his and only to be used by him.

Each evening Evan rushed home from his job at the school to grab a couple of salmon strips and his gear. In summer he fished, in winter he tromped across the tundra to tend his traps. He brought home beaver, muskrat, often the ground squirrels, called *sik-sik-puk* or parky squirrels, not because the squirrels appear to wear parkas, but because so many parkas are made from the squirrels. Evan's trapping also brought home foxes, beaver, muskrat, once a lynx and twice a wolf. The family ate, and Ella sewed the furs into garments.

Ella was amazed when she discovered that the gussak man at the store would trade beautiful warm cloth snowsuits for each of her children in exchange for a single muskrat parka. The storekeeper was very old, and he never smiled, but Ella thought he was always fair. Ella sewed and traded, the family ate and prospered, and the little certificates of appreciation piled up in Ella's box.

Evan studied the garden at the mission until he understood how it worked. He scraped the moss off little plots of tundra and used the moss to make windbreaks around the patches of ice he uncovered. The second summer after the ice was bared, it was mud six inches deep. Ella traded a beaver hat for seeds, and by fall she was boiling cabbages, lettuce, and spinach in the pot with their beaver meat. The kids complained, but they ate the green stuff. When a plot reached its fifth year and was thawed a foot deep, Evan planted potatoes.

It was the year that Rose Evan started the third grade. The first barge that came up the river unloaded a great pile of very strange lumber at the village store. Evan stared in disbelief at the boards they called plywood, unable to imagine how big the ply trees they came from must have been. Evan thought that if he could get one of those plywood boards and a 2x4, he could build a platform for the family to sleep on.

Now in his forties, Evan had developed a new appreciation for Ella and considered her almost a partner. He told her his dream of obtaining a plywood board. It was Ella's idea that he take the box of certificates to the store to show what a faithful worker he was. The storeowner might let him work to earn a plywood board and a 2x4.

The storeowner stared at the box of certificates, shaking his shaggy gray head, and began writing a column of numbers on a sheet of paper. He showed Evan where to make an X mark on the back of each certificate, then took him out to the lumber yard and put X marks on stacks of plywood, pallets of 2x4s, pallets of 2x8s, and a pallet of the most amazing pink blankets with tinfoil backing.

Old Evan and young Evan found books on house building in the school library. Old Evan memorized the pictures; young Evan read most of the words. They found a level spot just outside the village and carried their lumber, board by board, Charlie doggedly plodding behind them dragging the 2x4s, to begin building a house just like the ones the priests lived in.

When little Punik was seven, she was welcomed into the school as the youngest daughter of their janitor, his fourth child to enter the school. Punik was as bright as she was beautiful. Her older sister Rose had taught Punik to read when Punik was five, and Evan's chief delight in life came to be watching his little daughters devouring books at the kitchen table in their new gussak-style house.

❊ ❊ ❊ ❊

Ella brought me a blanket and ushered me to the couch. It took three days to get that airplane repaired. By the second evening, the kids were talking to me and I was blown away by their simple openness and bright intelligence. I gave Ella two twenty-dollar bills for room and board, which was all the cash I had with me. I'm not sure if she knew what they were, but she solemnly put them in the box with Evan's certificates.

When I finally flew away, it was like leaving family. If I ever have kids, I want them to be just like the Evan children. It's been a number of years since that first meeting, but I visited every chance I got. The kids have grown up and moved away, spread up and down the river, but we remain fast friends.

CHAPTER 9

THE DEVIL

"Tom wants to what?" Vickie had already done the shooting thing with her finger and now she was enjoying my incredulity.

"He says you need to exorcise a devil. Get cracking, he'll be here in twenty minutes."

"Can I borrow your bell, book, and candle? I seem to have misplaced mine."

"I think Tom is bringing those, and he says to put a couple of back seats in the plane. He may bring the devil back with him. You're taking the 185 on skis. Old Lucifer is hanging out on the river south of Kotlik." Vickie went back to reading her book. I checked, but it wasn't by Stephen King.

I had the 185 ready to travel when Tom pulled into the lot. It was only ten below zero, and the sun was showing through the clouds, but Tom covered his hood and plugged in his heater anyway. Maybe it was a Boy Scout thing— be prepared— and he was right. If we were out for more than a few hours, it could turn thirty below.

He strode across the tarmac, but he wasn't carrying a black satchel with an exorcism kit, he was carrying his rifle.

"What the devil are you getting me into, so to speak?"

"Let's go. I'll explain on the way." Tom walked around to the passenger side. The 185 has doors on both sides, so no need to scoot across.

We cleared the control zone and turned northwest. Tom had leaned the rifle against the back seat, but he was staying awake for a change.

"You may elucidate at your convenience." I tuned in the nondirectional beacon at St. Marys and headed toward it; it was between us and Kotlik.

"Call from the village cop at Kotlik. The devil has been raiding the village, killing dogs and robbing caches. They tracked him out of the village. Had to be him, he's camping on the riverbank in the snow with no fire. Wassilie says the footprints are bigger than his shoepacks, and Wassilie is a good-sized man."

"Maybe we'll finally learn the truth about Big Foot, or Sasquatch, or Yeti, or whatever you want to call him, but maybe it's a drifter. He's going the right direction, Alakanuk, Emmonak, now Kotlik."

"Whatever, the important thing is that he's outside the village jurisdiction so he's our problem. Wassilie didn't sound too unhappy about that."

"He didn't need to. I'm unhappy enough for both of us." I had climbed up to two thousand feet to nice smooth air. The mountains along the Yukon were coming up on our right.

I was mentally wrestling with the cultural differences that triggered this expedition. The term *Eskimo* is an umbrella name, like *American Indian*, made up of numerous and disparate tribes, not necessarily friendly with each other. Esquimau is an Algonquin Indian term, denoting their neighbors to the north. I've heard that it's mildly derogatory and means eaters of fish. We anglicized it to denote a race of people, as differentiated from Irish or Chinese.

Precontact Eskimos had no such concept. Before the first square-rigger wallowed over the horizon, they didn't know there were other people on the planet. What they did do was name all of the animals, and along the north coast their name for a biped that walked upright and had opposable thumbs was Inupiaq, as differentiated from *oogruks* and *sik-sik-puks*.

Inupiat, or Inuit, live along the coast and the Seward Peninsula. Bordering them to the south is the Yup'ik nation. Yup'iks will tell you that the term *Yup'ik* means the *real* people, implying a level of civilization that they do not concede to their northern neighbors. Yup'iks occupy five hundred miles of coastline, the entire Yukon–Kuskokwim Delta, and reach up the rivers a couple of hundred miles to the borders with the Athabaskan Indians. To the south, they border the Aleuts. They have the Yup'ik language in common, and they share loyalty to Chief Eddy Hoffman. Our base in Bethel is the center of the Yup'ik nation.

Tom had been watching the mountains when we crossed them below St. Marys. He pointed out a pack of six gray wolves and we circled them. The wolves stopped their trot and looked up, as interested in us as we were in them. Tom turned back toward me with a quizzical expression. Apparently his thoughts had been running parallel with mine.

"So, why do you think the average Eskimo has an IQ in the stratosphere and still believes in devils? Is our culture screwing them up? Is it an experiential problem?"

"Yeah, I've been wondering the same, but there are still Yup'iks who have never been more than a day's travel by snowmachine from the village of their birth. Last summer I picked up a planeload of Catholic elders from the village of Tununak on Nelson Island and took them to Bethel for a conference. These were men in their fifties and sixties, and several had never seen a tree. We made a detour upriver to Tuluksak just to correct that oversight. Remember, when we talk about Eskimos and lifestyle, we are not talking about the race, we're talking about a relatively small geographical area and a culture that is rapidly assimilating and modernizing."

Tom nodded. "Yeah, I know there are cultural things we'll never understand, and many villagers do believe in a very real devil."

My turn to nod. "Why not? Preachers have been describing him for years, always lurking and ready to cause trouble. If the villagers believe them, I'm not sure which party to call superstitious. The villagers are not overly gullible. They're in a tough position, still attached to the ancient gods and struggling to fit what they know to be true with what the missionaries are preaching."

The coastline was just visible ahead. I judged where Kotlik should be by the notch the river made, turned left a couple of degrees, and got back to our conversation. "Villagers who travel back and forth and try to make sense of it all probably find the ancient gods an island of sanity. You've heard about the little people? Apparently like Irish Leprechauns or Hawaiian Menihune?"

Tom gave me his skeptical sneer. "You're kidding, or exaggerating."

"Not a bit. Do you know Dave and Gary who work for the Department of Transportation? Every spring they descend on the Delta like a couple of storm troopers and work on various airports until freeze-up. They're a cross between civil engineers and a construction battalion, at home with blueprints, but artists with heavy equipment. In a typical summer, I move them to half a dozen villages."

"Yeah, I've run into them here and there. Don't tell me . . ."

"Not exactly, but one memorable year, Dave and Gary were grading a new airport at Kotlik that was set quite a distance out in the tundra. One evening some villagers asked if they ever saw the little people out there. The guys thought it was a joke, so they said, 'Oh, sure, we see them all the time.' That was a mistake. The villagers were deadly serious, believed them, and it was too late to back out. When I picked them up a week later to move to Chevak, they were very glad to be leaving."

That Tom believed. "And that's exactly how those beliefs get perpetuated. I've heard people say that before the arrival of Christianity, the Eskimos worshiped the devil. What's your erudite take on that, professor?" Tom was teasing, making fun of my reading habits, but I do usually have a book or two in the airplane. If I catch four or five hours of standby, well, I've read a heck of a lot more on this job than I ever did in college. I've also spent many hours absorbing culture from some very astute and knowledgeable Natives.

"Always happy to share a little learning. The missionaries who blanketed the world in the 1800s considered anything different from their home congregations to be devil worship. They called everything from the Eskimo reverence for elders to the Hawaiian hula devil worship and set about stamping it out. In Bethel the Moravians saved their students from devil worship by beating the Yup'ik language out of them with canes. Obviously the Eskimos had never heard of the devil before contact. He's a Judeo-Christian concept."

Tom wasn't letting me off easy. "I thought their culture was ruled by shamans, like African witch doctors. Are you saying they were good?"

"There were bad shamans who took advantage, and there were good shamans doing their best, probably in about the same ratio as any institution. As in all nonscientific cultures, many natural phenomena were attributed to supernatural sources, and mistakes were made. But your question is about the devil. What we try to forget is that the Salem witch trials and the enslavement and murders of California Indians were done in the name of Christianity. The good Christians of Salem really believed that the devil was hanging out in the woods and fornicating with their young girls. The concept the missionaries have foisted on the Eskimos is similar."

"Okay, and I hope this devil we're after is purely imaginary. Look, Alex, I've got to sleep. I was up over half the night, and no, it was not a poker game. One of the Hawley boys from Napakiak was riding around the hospital shooting out lights in the parking lot. When I got there he took off and I had to chase him halfway home. Do not chase a snowmachine with a Land Rover. It ruins your kidneys."

"You caught him, of course. Did he finally lose his tentative grasp on reality?"

"Nah, he just found a bottle of Seagram's Seven. He's sleeping it off now, so he'll be back to normal by tonight."

"Too bad. Exactly where are we heading?"

"Yukon, couple of miles south of Kotlik. I really hope it isn't the devil. I'd like to think we have a drifter working his way north and doing some killing on the way. Wake me up when you find the tracks."

Tom leaned back, tilted his hat down, and immediately emitted a loud snore. He sniffed and hacked a couple of times and stopped snoring, but he was sound asleep.

We hit the Yukon a mile below Kotlik. Snowmachines had turned around at that point and gone back to the village, but a trail of footprints continued on down the river. I reduced power and circled down. Tom woke up, rubbing his eyes, and we followed the tracks to an area where several sloughs had made small islands and a mishmash of scrub alders, willows, and spruce were fighting for dominance. The tracks left the river and disappeared into the trees.

"Let's land and have a look." Tom reached behind the seat and held onto his rifle for the landing. I cut the engine and drifted down, almost silently, to land in the middle of the river. The snow was pretty deep so the skis floated over the rough spots. I covered the engine while Tom climbed out and checked the load in his rifle. I dug my .357 out of the survival bag and stuck it in my belt.

When we got to the tracks, we saw that the devil was barefoot. We recognized the tracks and knew that the marauder was a grizzly and apparently a darned big one, but we didn't fault the Yup'iks for not knowing that. The bear was a long way out of his territory, and that's probably why he was raiding the village. Athabaskan Indians, two hundred miles upstream, know all about grizzly bears but might not know a seal from a walrus. The Inupiat on the north coast know polar bears, and polar bears would be out and about in December, but on the Arctic Ocean ice pack.

Tom measured a footprint by placing both hands in it lengthwise. The print was longer. "You know, Alex, it's not that we have a vendetta against bears, but since this one has raided the village and killed dogs, he will go back again. He really has little choice for food, and something has gone seriously wrong with his inner chemistry. In December, he should be sleeping in a cave two hundred miles upriver. Something is keeping him awake, very possibly a toothache or some other pain. Animals in pain tend to be suicidal, or at least nasty tempered. He would likely make no distinction between killing dogs and killing people, so he does have to be put down. Pretty unusual finding a bear this far from the mountains."

"Thank you for the natural history lesson, Doctor Tom." I had to counter Tom's sermon. "But I don't know. I landed at Scammon Bay one time and was met by an excited herd of youngsters. Someone had shot a bear in the mountains between Scammon and Cape Romanzoff. They were butchering and preparing for a feast, and I was just in time. I joined the feast, and it was good, big chunks of tender meat roasted over an open fire, but the bear's head was still attached to the hide, and it had a pair of muskox horns."

"Muskox at Scammon Bay? Keep your stories believable."

"Right, the muskoxen herd never leaves Nelson Island, although for half a year they could just walk across the ice. But the old bulls that can no longer keep up with the herd do wander off by themselves. This guy had made it halfway back to the high Arctic where he belonged. Natives at Scammon had never seen a bear or a muskox, so *bear* was as good a guess as any. They just knew a good source of meat when they saw one. Or maybe I have that all wrong. Since muskox are federally protected, and bears are fair game, if you shoot a big shaggy animal it might be smart to call it a bear."

Tom was looking at the tracks and shaking his head. "Alex, with the power vested in me by the size of those bear tracks, you are hereby deputized. Does that peashooter of yours really work?"

I nodded and spun the cylinder to check the load in the .357.

Walking across the river was rougher than landing. Ice under the snow had some ridges, so it was step-carefully time, and that through a foot and a half of snow. We slogged across to the mouth of a small slough where the tracks left the ice. The tracks did look very much like a barefoot man. A bear's front feet are paws like a dog, except the size of a dinner plate, but his hind feet are uncannily human, and he tends to put his hind feet on top his front tracks.

Tom reached up, caught a willow branch, and pulled himself up the bank. I scrabbled up behind him. The trail led into the brush for fifty feet, and then led everywhere. That animal had stomped all over the area. Tom motioned with the rifle for me to go left while he angled off to the right.

I got my pistol in my hand and followed tracks left, but splitting up was an extremely dangerous thing to do. At that point you're trusting your partner with your life. You have to know that he's not going to panic and shoot something moving through the trees, because it might be you. We spread out a hundred feet and were moving parallel to each other, mostly out of sight, but occasionally I got a glimpse of Tom's blue parka through thin spots in the brush. We were trying to be quiet, and the bear was there, I could smell him, like a wet dog, and fresh spoor was scattered around. We kept walking, and I was following the pistol.

Hunting bears with a pistol is not recommended, but if you are going to do it, use a .357 magnum. Mine was loaded with 146-grain Speer copper clads. Speer loads them up with eight and a half grains of Uniq powder, and the six-and-a-half-inch barrel gives you a muzzle velocity of thirteen-hundred-plus feet per second. Not quite a rifle, but darn close, and it's extremely accurate.

Thinking about pistols and shooting had me stalking through the woods, expecting to be jumped by a grizzly at any second, but remembering my father. Dad grew up on a cattle ranch in the Idaho desert, half English, half Scottish, and half bulldozer. The Idaho ranch went with the Great Depression, so I was raised on what we called a stump farm outside Seattle, but we still kept livestock. Dad routinely swung a two-hundred-pound bale of hay onto his shoulder and walked with it. I struggled to tip a bale into a wheelbarrow.

I was always a disappointment to Dad when he tried to teach me manly things. Half my genes were from an Irish mother, and I never measured up to Dad's expectations until the day he taught me to shoot. That I could do, first up to his expectations, then to his amazement and delight. It was my first taste of parental approval. I ate it up and kept practicing.

Alder scrub thinned and gave way to spruce. I could see Tom, a hundred feet to my right. He nodded, and we both stepped into the spruce. The next second there was a roar like the end of the world. It came from Tom's direction. I jumped back out of the trees to see Tom pin-wheeling over backward, trying to get his rifle up, but a bear the size of a small horse flew out of those trees in one bound and landed on top of him.

Tom had disappeared under the snow, and his rifle with him. That bear gave one more roar and opened a mouth the size of an alligator's. I dropped to my right knee, rested my left elbow on my left knee, gun butt on left palm. You don't shoot a bear in the head because his skull is too thick and has too many angles. A bullet is apt to glance off. I put the bullet into the bear's spine right behind the skull. He dropped like a sack of potatoes.

I waded through the snow, trying to hurry. The bear was obviously dead; he had a bloody gash across his neck with splinters of vertebrae sticking out, but he still seemed to be moving.

"Damn it, Alex, are you trying to kill me? Get me out of here." That muffled plea came from under the bear. I grabbed a front paw and heaved, but the body barely wiggled; it must have weighed four hundred pounds. I did notice some serious blood on the claws.

"How bad are you hurt?"

"I don't know, my chest is on fire, but the main danger is smothering."

"I don't suppose you can help me lift this monster?"

"Don't you think I'm trying?"

"Okay, wait right there, don't go anywhere. There's some rope in the airplane."

"Me about to be crushed and you a damn comedian? Will you *move it*?"

I ran. I keep four half-inch nylon tie-down ropes in the plane. I grabbed those and the hand axe from the emergency kit, and ran back to the scene of the crime. The bear had stopped moving.

"You still down there?" I asked.

"Yeah, I'm getting to like it here, nice and warm."

"Good, but maybe I won't stop for lunch."

I whacked down a four-inch-diameter spruce, cut it off at four feet and hacked and ripped off the branches. I looped the bear's paw with the rope, went around the first solid tree, and brought the rope back to the paw. I got my back into it, pulled the paw up as far as it would go, and tied it there with the other end of my rope. That made two parallel ropes from the paw to the tree. The pole goes between them, and turning the pole puts a twist in the rope. It's slow, but that is the point: you have a leverage of hundreds to one. I've heard that method called a Polish windlass, and it works. I turned the pole, the rope twisted and shortened, the paw came up, and the body started to roll.

It was halfway over before Tom came scrambling out, hacking and coughing up bear hair. He had serious rips on both sides of his parka and he was leaking blood, so the blood on the bear's claws was Tom's. He kicked through the snow, found his rifle, and used the barrel like a lever to free it.

"Did you have a nice lunch?" Tom asked. "It sure took you long enough."

"Well, I did skip dessert. Anything broken?"

"Most damage is to my pride, I think. That guy was fast, and he jumped up so close I had to step back to get the rifle on him. That would have worked if I hadn't tripped. Lord, he needs a toothbrush. Halitosis like a flamethrower."

"Might want to step back, there's some serious energy stored in this rope." Tom backed away and I released my lever and jumped behind the tree. The pole spun like a propeller, the paw dropped to the ground, and the rope was loose. I collected it and we trudged back toward the river.

"I think we'd better get you to a clinic. You're going to drip blood in the airplane."

"Well, not Kotlik. Let's leave the devil question alone for a while."

"How about Pitka's Point? It's right on the way home and on skis we can land on the river right below the clinic."

"Can we make Pitka's Point in half an hour? I think I can live that long."

"Can do. Speaking of raw meat, don't we have to salvage the bear for the children's home or something?"

"Nah, Fish and Game can do that. There's a little interdepartmental tension over devils, but once it becomes a dead bear, it's definitely theirs. Hey, you don't suppose that bear was rabid?"

"I didn't notice any sign of it. Rabid animals are supposed to be crazy, but as far as I could see, the bear was the most sensible animal in the woods today."

CHAPTER 10

THE EXODUS

Punik's sister Rose was the health aide at Pitka's Point. That made a lot of sense because she had four rambunctious boys, so she would have been tending scrapes and scratches anyway. We got Tom stripped to the waist and Rose went to work with disinfectants and bandages. His chest had some ugly scratches, but none deep. He was in pain, but wasn't going to miss any work because of it.

When she pronounced Tom sanitary, Rose went to the closet and brought out one of her husband David's shirts and a jacket. Tom put them on, and, with the preliminaries out of the way, we sat down for a glass of tundra tea. Rose had matured into a gorgeous younger version of Ella, competent, self-assured, almost regal, but warm and comfortable as a favorite mitten. I could still see the bright-eyed, eager twelve-year-old who had first enchanted me. Visiting with any member of the Evan family is always a delight, and I've been following their progress since the first time Ella fed me.

Their stories were gleaned over time. I got bits and pieces visiting with Charlie Evan at his store in Mountain Village one slow afternoon. More came from chatting with young Evan Evan and his lovely wife Donica in Marshall. Evan was repairing a portable generator that belonged to my passengers, and Donica kept us supplied with coffee, carrying the baby Ella in a sling on her back. A good bit of family history was from Ski and Punik. Some was related while we worked on the house, Ski and I guiding logs into position while Punik scurried back and forth mortaring joints, a little smudge of white mortar on her nose, and chattering a mile a minute.

❋ ❋ ❋ ❋

Evan Evan was seventeen, taller than his father, and as strong as a plywood board, the spring that he finished high school. For the last half of the school year, he found himself thinking only of Donica, the half-Yup'ik, half-Russian daughter of the postmaster from Marshall. Donica, with silky black hair, heart-shaped face, long black lashes over almond eyes, and coffee-with-cream complexion, was so beautiful she took his breath away and drained every ounce of his courage. He longed to talk to her, dreamed of touching her, but in her presence he was unable to speak at all or even raise his eyes to meet hers.

Donica was aware of the tall, silent boy who stared at her longingly and dropped his eyes to her feet whenever she glanced at him. She noticed that each afternoon he went straight from the school to the back door of the village store. One spring day, Donica gathered girlfriends for a walk down to the river and passed the back of the store. Evan Evan had shockingly removed his shirt and stood at a long bench, his back to the girls. He had a red outboard motor on the bench, a bewildering collection of small parts strung out beside it.

Donica watched the way his smooth muscles rippled beneath his skin, and the serious intensity with which he studied the parts on his bench. She thought that surely no human could ever put that engine together again, but the next afternoon when the girls giggled past his workbench, the red motor was attached inside a wooden barrel of water, chuckling happily, and he had a blue one spread on the bench.

He had removed his shirt again and had a tiny smear of grease on one shoulder. Donica felt an almost irrepressible urge to run over to him and wipe off the grease. Her body flushed with an inexplicable warmth, and she hurried to join her girlfriends.

When the first spring barges came from St. Michael, Donica waved good-bye to her girlfriends and boarded the wooden paddle steamer *Nenana* for the trip upriver to Marshall. She looked for her silent admirer, but he was not on the dock.

Evan Evan kissed his mother and sisters, hugged his father and brother, and pushed out into the river in the skiff he had built from scrap lumber after the house was finished. He had worked many evenings at the store to earn the five-horse Johnson outboard that pushed him up the river. He hadn't been able to speak to Donica, but he was equally unable to let her go. His little skiff carried a sackful of salmon strips, his winter furs rolled into a bundle in the bow, four extra cans of gasoline, and a certificate that his father had signed with his X.

The *Nenana* plowed steadily up the river, pushing her four barges, her great wooden paddle wheel, powered by two steam engines, making a wake that spread to both shores. Hour after hour, all through the day and the following night, Donica leaned against the rail above the paddle wheel and watched Evan Evan doggedly fighting the current in the steamer's wake.

The following spring it was Charlie Evan who boarded the *Nenana* as a deckhand. He was gone for four weeks, then back for one hour while the *Nenana* took on wood and water. Charlie had been all the way to Fort Yukon, and couldn't begin to describe his adventures or how far he had gone. He danced around the house, grabbing each family member and hugging them, over and over. He delighted them with the report of his twenty-minute visit in Marshall with Evan, Donica, and their little daughter Ella.

The *Nenana* blew her whistle and Charlie ran for the ship. On his way out, Ella shoved a bag of salmon strips into his hands. The family stood on their porch and watched the great ship back out into the Andreafsky and swing her barges downriver toward the Yukon. When the *Nenana's* smoke-stacks disappeared behind the hills, Punik brought a geography book to the table and showed Evan and Ella where Fort Yukon was, and where Charlie was headed now, down the river to Kotlik, and then right out into the Bering Sea to St. Michael.

Evan measured the family's trip from Ingrihak to St. Marys by making marks on a piece of paper, and then laid his strip over and over and over, measuring the voyage that Charlie was on. He found that he could not comprehend such distances, and yet one of his own boys was making that trip. He decided that the earth must be very large indeed.

Charlie made three trips up and down the river, dashing to the house for an hour on the trips up, half an hour on the trips down. On his final trip, when the willow leaves had turned to gold, the tundra to reds and russets, and the new young ice was running in the river, he sat his parents and his sisters down at the table to announce that he was not getting off the ship. He was staying aboard downriver to Mountain Village, where he intended to marry a teacher's aide who had attended St. Marys school.

He hugged Ella long and hard and promised to bring his new bride, and maybe a grandchild too, to visit after a couple of winters, when he had his own dog team. Evan hugged his son, handed him a certificate signed with an X, and the *Nenana* blew her whistle.

Ella was concerned about Rose, who stayed through her seventeenth year to finish high school, unmarried, and not even pregnant. It was a great relief when Rose announced that she would be moving to Pitka's Point with David at the end of the term.

The wedding was held in the mission chapel the day after graduation. Evan was satisfied with Rose's choice. David was a strong lad who would be a good fisherman and trapper, and Evan felt that David would be kind to Rose.

Evan and Ella sat in the front seats in the chapel. Evan was brushed and combed, wearing his best clean shirt, and thinking back on his own marriage to Ella. Rose's marriage seemed to be taking forever to get started. Rose and David stood before the priest with Punik and some other young people beside them, and the priest was droning on and on.

Evan's marriage to Ella had been performed by Ella's father. That patriarch had taken Ella's hand, put it in Evan's, and pronounced that they were now married. Evan expected to do the same for Rose. He kept waiting for the priest to call him up to perform the marriage, but the priest didn't call him. Finally, the young couple turned and marched down the aisle, followed by their attendants. The congregation worked their way out; Evan and Ella, completely bewildered, followed the young people up the hill to the house.

Rose, Punik, and David stood at the kitchen table, drinking lemonade, happy and laughing, but they sobered instantly when they saw the scowl on Evan's face. He took Rose's hand, placed it in David's, and solemnly announced, "You are now married." He poured a glass of the lemonade for Ella, another for himself, and the happy laughter resumed.

The newlyweds shouldered Rose's dowry of blankets and bowls and set off over the hills for the three-day walk to Pitka's Point. Ella handed them a bag of salmon strips for the journey, and was sorry when her mother's intuition told her that Rose was still not pregnant. Evan handed a certificate with an X to his new son-in-law, and the three remaining family members stood on the porch to watch David and Rose walk up over the hill and out of sight. Ella would have been pleased to know that Rose was properly pregnant before the young couple reached Pitka's Point.

Punik was so beautiful it made Evan's heart hurt to look at her; she was brilliant beyond her parent's comprehension, but she was a terrible disappointment. Punik herself felt as if she were being pulled apart on a rack. When

Evan Evan and Donica came for a visit, baby Ella would run to Punik with outstretched arms. Punik would scoop the child up into a desperate hug, feeling Ella's tiny heart beating against her own. Punik was consumed by a longing that made her knees weak, but when Rose and David brought their boys to the house, Punik knew that she could not live her sister's life.

The boys were great. Punik loved and played with them, and Rose and David were obviously happy, but then Punik would look at David. He was a big, solid lad, as dependable as the seasons, and he was handsome enough, but Punik saw no fire in him. He would be content to live the rest of his life just as he was now, and that thought filled Punik with a panicky claustrophobia.

Punik buried her despair in the school library. The local boys wouldn't even look at her. They had been dismayed when she squandered her eligible years in the library instead of cooking and sewing. They had seen the way she walked and talked with nuns and even priests, as though she were one of them, when the sensible girls were sneaking out onto the tundra to cuddle under blankets. Now it was too late; Punik, at eighteen, was past her prime.

Evan felt a terrible weight in his chest for his unmarried daughter. If something were to happen to him, and Punik was left with no man to hunt and fish for her, she would starve to death. He was no longer worried about Ella because now Ella could move in with Rose, become a full-time nanny, and earn her keep, but Punik had no such option.

He began inviting the widowers in the village to drop by for tea. Punik was terrified. If one of those men wanted her, Evan would perform the marriage, and Punik would have no choice. She would go with the man, cook his meals and warm his bed because she was a dutiful daughter. It would never occur to Punik to question Evan's judgment, and she knew that his motivation was his great love for her, but the thought made her skin crawl.

Men came, sat at the table, and sipped tea. Punik knew that proper decorum was for her to sit quietly while the men looked her over and made their decision, but she couldn't do that. Punik would sit at the table with the men, polite and modest, but she managed to tell each one about the book she was reading. She was hoping, almost praying, that one of the men would mention reading a book himself, but none did.

Each of the suitors left in disgust. They thought the girl with the strange opinions and the funny ideas was probably crazy. Furthermore, she joined their conversations, just as if she were a man. No good could come of that.

In the spring of Punik's nineteenth year, Evan and Ella sadly gave up. There was only one option left. Punik must go downriver to her cousin in Emmonak. In Emmonak, she could work in the cannery and support herself in her spinsterhood. They put Punik on one of the new diesel-powered tugboats and sent her down the river. Evan gave his beautiful daughter what he supposed would be their last hug, and pressed a certificate into her hand.

Evan and Ella stood on the dock while the steel tugboat *Tanana* whipped the river to a froth with a bellow of diesel power and bore Punik down the river. Evan and Ella held hands and trudged up the hill to their empty nest. Punik clutched her bag of salmon strips and blinked back tears while the hills of St. Marys disappeared behind.

In Emmonak, Punik was met by her cousin Stella. Punik had read of towns and cities, but never imagined that a village could be so big, and the cannery loomed beside it, covering more ground than all of St. Marys. Stella was older than Punik and looked like Punik's sister Rose, but Punik thought that she was too thin. Her speech was faster and louder than Punik was used to hearing. Punik wondered if Stella was nervous about the new living arrangement.

Stella had a wooden house, built by a government agency, as big as the house Punik's father and brothers had built, but it wasn't nearly as warm or comfortable. The house had an extra bedroom with a cot, a chair, and a desk, and that room was to be Punik's.

Punik gave Stella's husband Marvin the certificate from her father to pay for her first three months' rent. Marvin didn't speak and hardly seemed to notice Punik's presence. He was wrapped up in his own world, apparently thinking, but not about the present. Punik began to wonder if Stella was just lonely. The following morning, along with Stella, she reported to the cannery for work. There was always work at the cannery for those who wanted it: floors to be swept, endless belts to be scrubbed, roe boxes to be stacked beside the belts. Punik worked and marveled at the building. Some rooms were bigger than the entire mission at St. Marys, with ceilings higher than the roofs of houses. Room after room was filled with machinery.

The Alaska Department of Fish and Game was charged with the duty of ensuring the escape of enough salmon to sustain the stock. They did that by monitoring the runs and setting commercial fishing periods, skewed to favor the fish. The length of the commercial periods, determined by the estimated escapement, was sometimes nine hours, sometimes six, occasionally only three. When a fishing period, an opener, was declared, usually starting at midnight or noon, a hundred boats set out from Sheldon Point, Alakanuk, and Emmonak.

On Punik's fourth night in the village, a nine-hour opener was declared, starting at midnight. At eleven-thirty, Marvin loaded his net into his boat, grabbed a thermos of coffee, and shoved out into the river. His boat was flat-bottomed, twenty-four feet long and six feet wide, made for sliding over sand-bars, and pushed by a pair of fifty-horse Evinrudes. His net was a hundred feet long, eight feet deep, with cork floats on top, and lead weights on the bottom.

The next day, Marvin broke his silence to brag about his fishing success to Stella and Punik. Stella was delighted and plied them with coffee while Marvin described his night. Sunset colors had streaked the northern sky and made enough light for him to see the banks. He skimmed out of the Emmonak River into the Yukon and headed upstream. He had located a sandbar ten feet below the surface: no hazard to navigation, but it would steer the fish to-ward the right bank. He beached his boat next to the natural funnel to claim the spot and waited for midnight. He could see other boats, both upstream and down, riding with a single white light, so the river looked like a sparsely lighted runway. He saw his brother pull up and anchor a hundred yards far-ther upstream. Marvin watched the lit dial of his Casio wristwatch until the numbers blinked twelve. All up and down the river, motors roared to life. He shoved straight out, forty feet from shore, and began feeding his net over the side of the boat.

With the engines at a dead slow idle, he worked straight across the river, feeding out net as he went. When the entire net was in the water, he motored back near the center of the net and killed his engines. The boat drifted silently down the river, following the net, the only sound the occasional swishing of branches in the water or the slap of a beaver that was disturbed by the human activity.

Marvin felt the boat speed up when it entered the funnel. Cork floats be-gan to bob below the water, then the entire net seemed to be alive, threatening to go upstream and wrap around his boat. He fired one engine, idled to the end of the net, and began pulling it up. The net was filled with fighting, wrig-gling, silver salmon. He dispatched each with a quick thrust of his knife to the base of the skull, and piled the fish in the bottom of the boat.

The boat filled up fast, salmon stacked to the gunwales, only inches of freeboard left before the boat would take on water, and still there were twenty feet of net to pull. He took a police whistle from his pocket and blew one long blast, three short ones. The sound echoed away up the silent river. He heard his brother's motor start. The brother raced around the end of his own net, and stopped next to Marvin. They worked the net over the bow of the empty boat and stacked the rest of the salmon into that one.

The brother turned back upstream to follow his own net. Marvin started downstream, very slowly and carefully, toward the cannery. He guessed that he had three thousand pounds of fish on board, and if he didn't swamp the boat, he had earned three hundred dollars in an hour.

At midnight, Punik and Stella had reported to the cannery and donned rubber aprons, boots, and gloves that reached to the elbows. The building had been a great silent vault, reminding Punik of stories of cathedrals. Now it was screaming with activity, lit brighter than daylight. Belts and machinery were running and rumbling. Hundreds of people were milling and lining up beside the belts. Punik and Stella took their places on the sliming line where they would clean and dress the fish. A trap door at the end of the belt burst open and a solid stream of silver salmon flowed onto the line.

The salmon were washed by spray. People at the head of the line slit the fish from gullet to anus, the next ones ripped out guts and dropped them down a chute to become fertilizer. Roe was carefully removed from the females and packed in wooden crates. The crates of pale orange fish eggs would be shipped to Japan, where they were worth their weight in gold.

The fish were thoroughly washed and inspected, then disappeared into the next room. The journey down the belts would take the salmon through flash freezers, then into baths of sugar water to form a glaze, then more freezers. At the end of the belt, two hundred yards from the room where Punik and Stella were sliming, the fish were packed in white cardboard boxes and whisked into freezers to wait for ships to carry them to Seattle or Japan.

Around four in the morning there was a snap and a crash from the loading dock. A belt had broken and the crane dropped a load of fish on the deck. The fish stopped coming and Stella and Punik gratefully sank down onto a bench.

"These fish are so beautiful and so fat." Punik was amazed.

Stella, eyes closed and aching arms resting on the bench, explained, "These silver salmon have been in the ocean for two years, storing up fat. When they enter the freshwater river, they stop eating and live off the stored fat. Some of these guys are headed for Canada, twenty-five hundred miles, and have enough fat stored to make it. The fish your daddy catches at St. Marys have been out of the ocean for a week, but the ones here have been out of the ocean just a few hours. You should have seen the king salmon two weeks ago. They had been in the ocean for five years, weighed forty to sixty pounds each, and were so beautiful that you wanted to take a bite out of every one of them."

Salmon were coming down the belt again, and Stella and Punik jumped back to their stations. At nine in the morning, when the fishing period closed, Punik glanced out the window. Thirty boats were tied side by side, mounded with fish, waiting their turns to unload, and more outboards were screaming down the river toward the queue.

It was past noon when Punik and Stella stripped and stumbled into the showers. They inspected each other for cuts, because a cut from a salmon fin could lead to salmon fever and often resulted in the loss of the infected limb. Fourteen hours after the season started, Punik fell into bed, her arms and legs numb from exhaustion. But she felt a flush of satisfaction; she had earned a month's rent.

The silver salmon left, then the chums. The cannery was closed, cleaned, and put to bed until spring. Punik watched the days get shorter, watched the river freeze and the snows come. She visited the grade school and sometimes got called to teach a class. Evenings were long, and she read in her room, finishing every book the store had in stock and trading with neighbors. She felt like a hibernating bear by the time the days began to lengthen.

Sunlight was back and temperatures were above zero when the river ice began to heave and crack. Water was pouring down from spring runoff in the Canadian mountains, and the river was rising, straining to rip the ice. In May, there seemed to be thunder coming down the river and suddenly the ice was bulging up, making cracks like explosions, and moving, hissing, tinkling, grinding, then rushing downriver. Huge chunks like islands came roaring past, some with trees and even parts of cabins on them.

The water rose to the top of the riverbanks, then spilled over into the village. Children, some of them not so young, marched through the village in rubber boots, laughing and celebrating. Then the flood was gone, the river ran ice-free, and planes from Bethel brought men who shouldered their duffel bags and moved into the cannery.

When the big strange gussak came to be the engineer at the cannery, Punik noticed his eyes and the way they always seemed alive, actually looking at things. She barely noticed the scar. Her brother Charlie had a scar almost as bad from a flying fish hook, and anyway, beauty was not what she looked for in a man.

They noticed each other at the bookrack in the store after each barge came in, but only as peripheral presences. A large white hand, or a small brown one, would come into their range of vision to pluck the best of the new books off the rack. This day, Punik, with an uncharacteristic bravery that took her breath away, turned and looked directly at the man beside her.

She saw the crisp clean lines of his profile, the power in his shoulders, his quick intelligent eyes, strong hands twice the size of her own. There was the self-assurance of competence about him that reminded her of her father. She saw in him the answer to every question and the goal of every romantic dream she'd ever had. Her body began to tremble and she dropped her books.

Ski stooped to pick up her books, and when he stood he faced the most beautiful girl he had ever seen. Her smile was shy, but frank and honest. He couldn't know that the high color in her cheeks was caused by a racing heart. She was a head shorter than Ski with a neat, compact little figure and raven hair she could sit on. She had the round smooth face that Ski associated with china dolls. Her eyes were kind and gentle, but he saw the depth and the bright spark of intelligence behind them. He had meant to hand her her books, but he took her hand and held it instead.

CHAPTER 11

MISSING HAT

To keep from thinking about murders, I concentrated on hauling mail. The temperature was up around zero, so it was possible to start the Pilgrim. Our Pilgrim is all white and looks like the ghost of an oversized Piper Cub, but the engine is a very serious, four-hundred-fifty-horse radial.

Air-cooled engines are loose and sloppy when they're cold and tighten up when they're hot. That old nine-cylinder radial is probably the best aircraft engine ever made before jets, but on a radial engine, two of the cylinders are upside down. When it gets cold, oil from the crankcase seeps past the rings and pools in the lower cylinder heads. If the engine ever fires with oil in the combustion chamber, it will blow the head right off the cylinder because oil does not compress.

You heat the bottom cylinders and tug on the prop to pull the cylinders through two cycles very slowly. The oil gets squeezed back up past the rings or out the exhaust port. Once it's running, that old Pilgrim is a wonderful flying machine. One of the best things about it is that it's a tail dragger. That is, it has main gear and a tail wheel like the 185s instead of a tricycle gear like the Cessna 206. That means that the cargo door is only sixteen inches from the ground, so you can load in pallets with a forklift and then shove them out by hand in the villages.

In the Pilgrim, I had to put my flight bag back in the cabin because there wasn't room for it in the cockpit. The Pilgrim was an airliner in its day, so it has a big cabin. We regularly hauled nine drums of fuel oil, standing on end. There's a bulkhead between the cabin and the cockpit with only a one-foot-square hole between, just right for passing coffee cups to the pilot.

In front of the bulkhead, the top of the fuselage narrows and the cockpit is the same size as the front seat in a Super Cub. The pilot climbs up steps on the outside, past the bulge the engine makes, opens the cockpit door, and has a window against each shoulder when the door closes.

I really hated to put the flight bag in back, but I barely had room to wear my parka in the cockpit. The flight bag is a canvas duffel with straps that make it a pack sack, if you wish. A pilot carries it with him from plane to plane, pretty much the way a woman carries a purse. You don't even think about it; you just always have it.

Flying is the safest mode of transportation ever devised by man. In terms of miles per fatality, airplanes beat the heck out of Conestoga wagons. They're even safer than walking. However, airplanes do go down. Having your flight bag with you makes the difference between an inconvenient camping trip and possible death, especially in the Arctic. My bag contains a compass, a hand ax, a collapsible spade, sleeping bag and two space blankets, dry socks, a first aid kit, water purification tablets, a buddy burner, a mess kit, matches, beef jerky, chocolate, and a .357 magnum revolver with a box of shells.

I liked having that bag within reach for the same reason that we wore all of our arctic gear while flying. It's not that the planes don't have heaters. Not long ago, a crew of surveyors was picked off a cold job in the evening by a Bell Jet Ranger. The ranger cabin was comfy. The surveyors shed their wet awkward parkas and snowsuits, tossed the pile behind the back seat, and relaxed in comfort in the warm cabin.

When the engine blew, fire blossomed through the cabin roof. The pilot auto-rotated straight down to the tundra in ten seconds, and they all piled out with flames licking their tails. They stood in pants and shirtsleeves, up to their knees in snow at ten below zero, and watched all of their Arctic clothing burn up. They were lucky. They were picked up in half an hour, but you'd better not count on that.

I did feel a little like Santa in a sleigh, bumping along at a hundred and twenty miles an hour, and I was dumping off Christmas cheer, thirty-six hundred pounds at a whack. I did my "Ho ho ho" at Mekoryuk on Nunivak Island, and as usual, came home in the dark, but it was a glorious star-filled dark. When I walked into the office, Vickie was slipping on her parka. Hers was rabbit fur, mostly white with a black pattern, and a very nice wolf ruff.

Vickie smoothed her hair back behind her ears, flopped her hood up, and was ready for the Arctic. She wore a heavy wool skirt, and her parka covered her to the hips. Over her shoes she wore a kind of overshoe that showed she was wearing heels, with fur ruffs around the ankles. Between those ruffs and her skirt was sheer nylon, which showed that Vickie had very nice legs. I'm all in favor of the nylon, but I've sure never been tempted to cross dress.

"There's a note for you on the desk." Vickie pointed and walked out to her car. I could hear her car, already idling so it would be warm and her legs wouldn't freeze.

I called Tom at home, per the note.

"Detective Price?" he answered the phone. Not a good sign.

"We have a little chain-of-custody problem with a certain wolf-fur hat. The captain wants that hat. I was way out of line, giving the hat back to Ski. It was evidence and should have been submitted. We knew Ski was innocent, the evidence either planted or coincidental, but if I had turned it in, Ski would probably have been arrested. With just one isolated murder, there wouldn't have been a problem.

"Now, with two murders, and both pointing at Ski, things are getting out of hand. The second murder got the captain interested. He's trying to trace the owner of the automatic, and the fingerprints that are all over it. Worse, he read my report about Alakanuk. As far as I know, that's the first report he's ever read. He wants the hat, real bad, and you know, Alex, I've gotten sort of used to being a trooper. I'd like to keep at it a while, and that depends on producing that hat."

"How about I stop by the Alaska Commercial Company and buy the captain a nice new one?"

"That's Plan B. Plan A is for you to beg Ski for the loan of his hat next time you're up that way. Do you happen to know the penalty for obstructing justice, or aiding and abetting a murder suspect?"

"Was that in the detective course I read?"

"I doubt it. I think it's too horrible to contemplate. Alex, if I thought this would hurt Ski, I wouldn't ask, I'd just face the music. But the captain is going to trace the gun in a couple of days. It won't do Ski any good to have you and me in jail with him. We know he's innocent, and his best bet is for us to prove it, outside of jail."

"Yeah, I see what you mean. By a strange coincidence, I was just ready to take off for Emmonak; I only stopped to return your call. I think that hat was probably left in the airplane. I can be pretty careless sometimes."

"Thanks, Alex. Alex, I know Ski's innocent, but I'd like a second opinion."

"SKI IS INNOCENT!" I hung up the phone.

CHAPTER 12

FUGITIVE

Actually, I'd been planning to stop by Leen's Lodge for one of Bergie's steaks, and then head home to bed, but suddenly I wasn't feeling hungry or tired. A Cessna 185 on wheel-skis hadn't been flown for a couple of days, so I was doing the company a favor by checking it out. I threw my flight bag behind the pilot's seat and cranked up the 185. The Bethel airport was plowed and bare, and I didn't want to drag the ski tails on the pavement, so I asked for, and was cheerfully granted, permission to take off on the taxiway.

The weather had turned cold, but this time it was clear, crystal, sparkling, breathtakingly clear. When the airport lights dropped away, I was met by a cloud of Milky Way and a solid dome of stars from horizon to horizon. I was so mesmerized by the stars that I forgot to stop climbing until I was at ten thousand feet. If there had been a moon, it would have stolen the show, but the moon had the good taste to be absent.

If I'd been headed for Anchorage on the other side of the Alaska Range, I'd have gone to twelve thousand, and then to fifteen over the mountains, but for the hour and twenty minutes across the Delta, climbing was just for the view. Flying from Bethel to the coast, you do cross a continental divide. You start out with streams flowing south into the Kuskokwim, and then suddenly they are flowing north into the Yukon, but that divide is five hundred feet above sea level. Sometimes there will be two streams, side by side, meandering in opposite directions.

95

From my lofty perch I could see a green aurora flickering on the northern horizon. We do get northern lights overhead in Bethel. The most spectacularly colored display I've ever seen was over Anchorage at the same latitude, but that doesn't happen often. Twenty minutes out of Bethel, I could see a little patch of lights off to my right that was Marshall on the Yukon, and then make out the dark outline of the mountains behind the village.

The Big Dipper and the North Star were to the right of my course, and shining bright, but don't conjure up images of beacons. The bright stars up there were Sirius and Rigel with old red Betelgeuse and Aldebaran looking like streetlights, and Jupiter twice as bright as any of them. Polaris, the North Star, was in my windshield but is actually a second-magnitude star, important only because of its location over the pole. It doesn't move, and the rest of the sky appears to wheel around it when the earth turns.

Smudges of light ahead were St. Marys and Mountain Village where the mountains and the Yukon make a dip to the west, then the four glows ahead of me were Kotlik, Emmonak, Alakanuk, and Sheldon Point. It's sixty-five miles from Kotlik to Sheldon, but I was seeing two hundred miles, and with no other lights anywhere, they looked clustered. I cut the power, tilted the nose down, and let the speed build to two hundred knots for the last fifteen minutes. White tundra below me was bordered by the black stand of timber along the river.

I had stayed up enjoying the view too long and was still fifteen hundred feet up when I crossed the Yukon. I circled over Alakanuk and checked the windsock, which was a black silhouette in the starlight. It was lackadaisically indicating a north wind, so I circled south and headed into the wind to zero in on the smooth spot in front of Ski's cabin. The starlight reflecting on the snow showed the unbroken smooth patch with darker ridges around it.

There wasn't any glow from the cabin, but it was getting close to nine in the evening, so I wasn't surprised. I used landing lights, mostly to show my altitude, and plunked the skis onto the snow with thirty degrees of flaps and the nose as high as I could pull it. The plane rattled and banged like the wreck of the *Hesperus*, but that's normal for a metal airplane on skis. I slid a couple of hundred feet past the cabin, horsed the plane around with power, taxied back, and put the cowling cover on.

All of that took a few minutes, and I was surprised that I didn't see Ski coming down with a flashlight. I started to reach into the jockey box for my own flashlight, but realized that I really didn't need it. I could see the white trail past the dark trees, and the steps up to the porch by starlight. Still no glad-handing Ski dashed out.

I crunched and squeaked up the trail and had started to climb the steps when I noticed that the cabin door was open. Then I saw starlight glint on the barrel of Ski's .30-06, sticking out the door and pointed straight at my belly. I froze, without being asked.

"Ski?"

No answer. I suddenly realized that I was in an unfamiliar airplane, and walking up without a light might look suspicious.

"Ski, it's Alex. Will you put down that cannon?"

"Alex!" It was almost a scream, but it wasn't Ski. It was Punik. She dropped the rifle on the porch and jumped into my startled arms. I caught her with her feet off the ground, and she was hanging on as if her life depended on it. I scooped up her legs and carried her up the steps and into the cabin. She was belting out tears, a quart a minute, and that's not a good thing to do outside in the cold.

I peeled her loose, set her in the easy chair that she and Ski usually shared, and turned on the battery-operated lamp on the coffee table. I retrieved the rifle from the porch and closed the door, went back and knelt down to resume the hug. I was brotherly about it; I wasn't forgetting whose wife she was, but she needed a shoulder and I was happy to lend her one.

When the storm passed, I slipped off my parka, unzipped my snowsuit, and dug a handkerchief, fortuitously clean, out of my back pocket. She almost laughed at my contortions, getting to my back pocket with the snowsuit on. She accepted the handkerchief and started mopping up.

She wasn't the mess that a gussak girl might have been because she didn't wear makeup. She didn't need any. When she got the hair unstuck from her cheeks, she looked pretty normal, but she kept the handkerchief ready.

"Where is Ski?" That seemed to be the operative question.

"He's gone."

"Yes, I figured that out. Where has he gone?"

That brought a fresh fit of wailing, this time with the handkerchief staunching the flow but getting damp, and I think she said, "I don't know."

I took the lamp and went into the kitchen. The oil stove was on low and the big enamelware coffeepot was sitting on the warmest spot. I took a couple of mugs from the cupboard, filled them, and carried them back with the lamp. That made things more normal, except this time it was me handing a mug to Punik.

I sipped and waited; she sipped and composed herself. Coffee is almost a ritual in Alaska, maybe because it's both warm and liquid, and both are rare and precious commodities in the winter. I didn't have to ask again.

"Ski figured that Tom would have to come up and arrest him. He thought Tom should have arrested him as soon as the gun was found, especially with his hat being found the way it was. Ski said it would rip Tom's heart out to do it, and that Ski couldn't stand to be in jail, even for a single night."

I was nodding. She was right on all counts.

"Punik, be very clear on this point. Both Tom and I know that Ski didn't kill anyone, and that is why Tom didn't arrest him. Apparently someone is trying to frame Ski for the murders and we've got to figure out who and why. However, Ski is also right. Tom is in serious hot water for giving back the hat. He hasn't told anyone who the hat belonged to or why he doesn't have it. He also hasn't admitted that he knows who the gun belongs to. The problem is that Tom's captain is having the gun and the fingerprints traced, and Ski's prints will be on file because he was in the service.

"Tom figures that Ski's best chance is for Tom to find the real murderer, and he's planning to bluff it out and play dumb when the captain comes up with Ski's name. The problem is that the cop in Alakanuk, and probably everyone else on the river, knows that Tom had the hat. Now, if Ski has it, it will be hard for Tom to claim he didn't know whose it was."

I felt scuzzy telling Tom's problems to Punik when she had worse ones, but she understood.

"Ski is wearing his hat, but you can take mine. It's smaller, but otherwise the two are very much alike. I was trying to make them a matched pair."

Punik went into the bedroom and came back with a hat that could have fooled me. For a second, I wondered if maybe Ski wasn't really gone, but a glance back at Punik killed that idea. With Tom's problem solved, except we'd probably get the electric chair if we were caught actually switching hats, we got back to Punik's problem.

"When did Ski leave?"

"Last night. He moped around for two days, expecting you guys to come back for him, and he couldn't stand it anymore. He had to run, and he wouldn't tell me where because he knew that I'd tell you."

I was nodding. I could picture Ski's problem pretty clearly.

"How did he go?"

"He took his Polaris, but not the sled because that would make unusual tracks."

"Punik, would you like me to take you to St. Marys to your mother's?"

"No, thanks, Alex. When Ski comes back, he's going to find me right here with the home fires burning, but I would appreciate it if you brought Mama here in seven months."

"Seven months?" I asked.

That brought a geyser that finished the handkerchief.

"Oh, Alex, I'm pregnant and Ski doesn't even know he's going to be a father. I couldn't tell him when he was so worried. It would only have made things worse."

CHAPTER 13

MERRY CHRISTMAS

I presented myself at the troopers' office in the morning, hat in hand, so to speak, but the hat was in a clear plastic evidence bag. Captain Danker scowled his way over to the counter and extended a big official hand while I spluttered about a dark cold night and being busy with Christmas mail, and finding the hat but forgetting that it was in the truck. He snatched the bag and stalked back to his office. He slammed the office door, but I didn't mind; I was already running out and letting the front door bang behind me. I'm sure you know this, but just in case, you don't have to worry about fingerprints on soft things like cloth and fur. Fingerprints are on hard smooth things, like Ski's automatic, for instance.

Tom and I needed to talk, so we bumped into each other by accident at the restaurant in the Kuskokwim Inn for lunch. We took a table by the window, looking north across the tundra, and watched a hundred ravens wheeling above the garbage dump half a mile away.

I brought Tom up to speed, including the true ownership of the hat. He winced as if he'd been shot but didn't offer any better suggestions. For a planning session, or maybe it was a war council, there was a lot of silence.

❄ ❄ ❄ ❄

The jet from Anchorage was dropping off fifty students every evening and we were shuttling them out to their villages. I made sure I got the trips to the mouth of the Yukon and scanned the trees for a camp on every trip, but Ski was far too savvy to be seen from the air.

By afternoon on Christmas Eve, the rush was over. Tom and his wife Minnie brought a cooked turkey and the fixin's out to the airport. Spending Christmas Eve with Punik seemed like a good idea. Tom's wife Minnie was a real Inupiat princess from the Kobuk country, and except for the five hundred miles between birthplaces and different tribes that once killed each other, she and Punik could have been sisters. Minnie's maiden name was Kiana, and she was from the village of Kiana, and I'm not kidding about her being a princess.

We teased her about the Kobuk River's producing two kinds of art: jade and beautiful women. Jade Mountain, between the villages of Kobuk and Kiana, is the source of the brownish-green jade that Alaskan Natives carve. Minnie's eyes were dark Kahlua brown, as Eskimo eyes should be, but they had definite flecks of jade green in them. Go figure.

We took the Cessna 185 on skis, and I tossed in a catalytic heater that might keep the plane startable overnight. I put in two of the back seats and set the turkey on the floor behind them. Tom stayed awake for a change and turned around in his seat to give Minnie a steady travelogue. Those of us who fly out of Bethel see trees, mountains, and oceans on a daily basis. It's easy to forget that if you stay in Bethel, you see nothing but tundra every day.

Tom and I shoved the plane backward to the edge of the ice strip that was becoming my airport. Tom and Minnie carried the goodies inside while I made a couple of arctic tie-downs. You chip a hole a foot deep in the ice with your hatchet. You tie a knot in the end of your rope and put the end in the hole. You scrape the loose ice and snow back into the depression on top of the knot and fill up the hole with the gallon jug of water you brought with you for that purpose.

When you tie the plane down, you have to be careful not to pull the ropes out of the holes, but an hour later you couldn't pull them out without breaking the rope. I got the catalytic heater going with a nice red glow, stuffed it up through a cowling vent and closed the vents, then wrapped up the nose like a Christmas present and went in to join the party.

As Christmas parties go, it was a quiet one. I ran the generator for a while and built a nice cheery fire in the fireplace, but it didn't cheer anyone much. The picture from Ski and Punik's wedding was on the mantel, but that didn't have its usual cheerful effect either. The wedding had been in St. Marys. The picture showed Ski and Punik, flanked by Evan and Ella.

Ella and Punik looked like sisters in frilly white dresses. Ski and Evan wore sport coats and neckties, probably Evan's first. At that wedding, Punik had explained the facts of life to the priest. When the priest had finished his spiel, he invited Evan to come up and perform the marriage. Evan solemnly did that. I could see that he wasn't too sure about his new son-in-law. Ski didn't look like much of a hunter or a fisherman to Evan, but Punik seemed happy, and Evan probably figured that she was lucky to find any husband at all.

I was sitting directly behind Evan and Ella. When Evan came back to his seat, he whispered to Ella, "Don't worry. If they get hungry, I'll teach him to hunt and fish." In the meantime, he presented Ski with a certificate to help them get started.

Funny about Evan. He stood next to Ski, not quite as tall as Ski's shoulder and fifty or sixty pounds lighter than Ski, but Evan had a presence that made them seem the same size.

Remember that line from Kipling's "Ballad of East and West"? "There is no east nor west, border nor place nor birth, when two strong men stand face to face, though they come from the ends of the earth." I think of that line every time I see that picture.

I'm in the picture, too, standing behind them, looking as glum as Punik looked tonight, but that was because Ski had bought a case of Dom Perignon. Everyone, including the priests, was toasting away, but I had to fly Ski and Punik and the cousins to Emmonak in a couple of hours, so I couldn't drink.

Punik and Minnie had a lot to talk about. Tom and I spent some time out on the porch, watching moonlight make shadows on the river, smelling the spruce trees, and pretending that we enjoyed cigars. One or the other of us went inside once in a while for more of the Korbel Brut that Tom and Minnie had brought. We ate moose steaks and coleslaw. We gave up early. Tom and Minnie got the spare room, Punik went to bed, I shut off the generator and sacked out in pants and shirt on the couch in the living room.

You have never heard silence until you spend a night in a cabin on the Yukon in the wintertime. You find yourself actually listening to the silence, and it's a strange experience. I think we have become so used to sensory stimulation that we need it to keep us operating, the way we need a cup of coffee in the morning. When there's nothing to hear, we strain to hear something.

When a shoepack squeaked on the porch, I heard it like a thunderclap. I jumped up and was standing behind the door before it opened, the fireplace poker in my hand. I grabbed the intruder from behind, ready to brain him, before I recognized Ski. I dropped the poker and hugged him pretty much the way Punik had hugged me.

Ski charged into the bedroom, came out swinging a laughing and crying, nightgown-clad Punik in his arms, and made straight for the kitchen. He was still holding Punik in one arm while he raided the refrigerator with the other. Tom and Minnie came into the kitchen, and suddenly we were having a real Christmas party.

Santa didn't come, but we didn't need him. We gathered in the kitchen for a late breakfast and a planning session. We didn't have a lot to plan, but we did establish that Ski and Punik should keep the radio on. If they heard either Tom or me on the radio asking about a house fire in Emmonak, Ski was to disappear. If they heard us ask someone about snow conditions, there was a friendly visit coming up.

Tom had a bit of good news. The fingerprints on the automatic that shot Jesse had been traced to one Erwin Kawalski, last known address on Maypole Street in Chicago. Tom had held his breath when the name came in, but the captain didn't recognize Erwin Kawalski. If the report had said "Ski," the captain would have put it together, but he wouldn't have known where Ski had moved. Ski's ex-landlady told the Chicago police that she hadn't heard from Kawalski in years and thought he might have moved to Mexico.

Ski was nodding. "Yep, that's Maude. She wouldn't steer a cop toward an exit if the building was on fire."

Ski confided that if he wasn't at the cabin and I needed to find him, I might get lucky if I circled twice around the second slough upriver above the bend and then landed on the slough. The ice on the slough was nice and smooth, and there were no snowmachine tracks on it.

Tom, Minnie, and I developed urgent needs to get back to Bethel. We left the turkey and split. We didn't think that Ski and Punik needed company when she told him about his impending fatherhood.

I wish I could tell you that we all spent a merry Christmas at home, but we didn't.

For my part, my little cabin was looking pretty bare. Tom and Minnie left the airport with their arms around each other. It was best if I didn't even imagine what Ski and Punik were up to. I sat at the table looking at Captain Morgan in his red hat and red coat, blue cape flying. He had one boot up on a keg of rum, and he balanced himself with a magnificent gleaming sword. The captain had a big friendly smile, but he still struck me as lousy company for Christmas.

Maybe if I'd had a dog, I could have petted him, but animals are out because I don't have a schedule. All Vickie had to do was point a ruby-tipped finger at me, make her "Khhe" sound, and I'd be gone to Nome or Kodiak for three or four days. If I got even a goldfish, I'd probably come home to find that the fire had gone out and the fish was frozen.

Tom and Minnie's togetherness had started me thinking about Connie and wondering how she was spending Christmas. Connie is the legal secretary in the DA's office, and we've had a few laughs together. She'd fled from a nasty divorce in Missouri a couple of years before and ended up in Bethel, probably because that's as far as you can run. It would be politically incorrect to say she was a pretty girl; I should say she was a handsome woman. We might have gotten a lot more going, but Connie wanted a man who was home by six every evening. Her husband had been a long-haul truck driver who turned out to have a girlfriend in every town. My whereabouts at six depended entirely on Vickie's phone calls, and Connie wasn't ready for that.

Her blondish auburn hair was bobbed just above the shoulders and she always wore makeup. That may sound like a strange remark if you haven't spent a few years in the Bush, but if you have, you know that makeup is unusual and it's precious. Makeup on a woman is a beautiful thing, a high point of modern civilization. Women wear it to make themselves attractive, and it works. Also there's an element of, "It's the thought that counts."

I've felt a little miffed and resentful at the Wien Airline terminal when passengers are waiting for the jet to Anchorage. The women who have been wearing jeans and men's shirts, work boots and stocking caps in Bethel will be waiting for the jet in heels and hose, makeup and curls, and carrying purses instead of backpacks. We love and appreciate our women, and we want them to be practical, but darn it, it doesn't seem fair that all that beauty and femininity are being exported to Anchorage where they already have plenty.

Not that Connie needed makeup to be attractive. Her blue eyes were usually sparkling, and she had a pert little nose and a kissable mouth framed by a faint crinkle of laugh lines. She had all the curves and hollows a man could hope for, and she was one heck of a good dance partner.

Her trailer house has a patch of tiles between her kitchen and her living room carpet, and the thought that we just might spend the evening dancing on that brightened Christmas right up.

I dialed her number.

"Hello?" Soft Missouri accent, sweet as a muted cello.

"Hi, Connie, Alex. Are you busy?"

"Yeah, I'm pretty busy. I'm sitting on the couch sipping Tom and Jerrys, listening to Bing Crosby, and watching the Christmas tree lights blink."

"Need any help?"

"Sure. Bring your Captain Morgan with you. I've got plenty of mix but I'm running low on rum."

"Wonderful, be there in fifteen minutes."

I hung up the phone, reached for my parka, and the phone rang. It was Vickie.

Bushmaster was closed for Christmas, of course, but that didn't really mean anything. She didn't ask if I was busy; she told me to meet Trooper Perkins at the airport as soon as I could get there.

I threw on a snowsuit, zipped the parka, grabbed the bottle off the table, and slipped and slid my pickup across town to Connie's trailer. She lived next to the slough that was trying to make Bethel into an island, with a view of willows along the bank and a tundra hill with the high school on top. Her forty-foot trailer was on a gravel pad, so the bottom was nicely skirted and there was no worry about melting permafrost.

I stomped and squeaked across her arctic entry. Normally, I would have left my boots and parka there, but I tapped on the door instead. Connie was wearing a pink hostess gown with ruffles at the sleeve, a glorious smile, and just the amount of makeup that I would have loved to rub off. A whiff of Christmas tree, hot spiced rum, warmth, femininity, and Bing Crosby, enveloped me.

She saw I still had my boots on and was dressed for outside instead of a drive across town. Her smile faded. I handed her the bottle and couldn't begin to express my regrets for not staying. She gave me a sad little smile and a kiss that kept me tasting and dreaming all the way to the airport. It was her eyes that tore my heart out and her expression that explained her refusal to marry me.

"Merry Christmas, Connie."

"Merry Christmas, Alex."

❄ ❄ ❄ ❄

Trooper Perkins was a good man, spending his second winter on the Delta and still in awe of it all. He could have been Tom, parking his blue Land

Rover and stalking to the airplane. He was the same size as Tom and wearing the same uniform, but his walk was different, and there was a pink, boyish aura about his face. I was never sure whether he was perfectly shaved or didn't have to shave yet. We were headed for Sheldon Point, where the landing is on a frozen lake, so we took the Cessna 185, no seats in back.

A straight line from Bethel to Sheldon Point takes you close to the mud volcanoes. They're not really mud, actually lava rock, and look more like an exhibit than the real thing. The little group of six craters ranges from two to three hundred feet tall, a few hundred feet across. They grew all by themselves, fifty miles from the nearest pimple in any direction, a few hundred thousand years ago, I suppose. Perkins stared at the volcanoes, just as everyone else does.

We made Sheldon just before dark. It's the last outpost of last outposts, clinging by its toenails to a dry strip between lakes that go up and down with the tide. The Bering Sea batters one side, the Yukon allows the village to remain by making a sweeping turn around it where it meets the ocean.

The first thing you see is the suspiciously long thin lake where the Department of Transportation has been trying for years to build a runway. They cleared off the tundra and spread gravel one winter. The following spring, the gravel sank several feet into the mud and the tide rose into the resulting depression. You pass a couple more naturally shaped lakes with tufts of muskeg sticking through where the wind has blown away the snow.

Next comes the high ground, six feet or so above the tide line, and that supports the one-story store, school, and post office. Then the oval-shaped lake that provides a landing for ski planes in winter, floats in summer. Fifteen assorted cabins and HUD houses circle the lake on a shore that's three feet above the high water line. One of the new HUD-type buildings near the north end of the lake is the clinic. A boy could stand on the clinic steps and throw a rock into the Bering Sea, the Yukon River, or Sheldon Lake, except there aren't any rocks to throw.

We landed on the lake in the middle of the village. Several of the houses had Christmas lights in the windows, which meant that the village generator was running. Wassilie, the village cop, was out on the ice, guiding me to taxi up next to the clinic. Yes, same name as the cop in Kotlik. Wassilie is a very common name on the Delta. He wore a *sik-sik-puk* parka over matching fur pants that rested on the toes of his shoepacks.

The clinic at Sheldon is the same design as the one in Alakanuk, and a bare light bulb on a gooseneck was already illuminating the five wooden stairs and the porch. When we stepped inside, Wassilie threw his hood back. He was wearing a matching hat and his usual questioning expression. I still don't know whether the world was a little too fast for him or he was keeping it at bay by pretending to be dense. His outfit was not made by his wife because he didn't have a wife. His outfit was made by Mary Hunter. I recognized her style. It likely took Mary four months to stitch those little squirrel hides together so they looked like all one piece, and it probably cost Wassilie two months' wages. His job as the village cop was a paid position, subsidized by the state.

He had two passengers for us, stretched out on exam tables. I recognized the deceased, but I didn't really know them. Hooper and Hinkley: one had been the store operator, the other, the postmaster. Each had been shot in the head, apparently while entertaining a visitor in his home. I suddenly realized that like my two earlier deceased passengers, each of these victims was a bachelor who lived alone. These guys had obviously been shot with a .30-06 rifle, and as usual, there was a clue.

Several people had seen a man with a rifle slung across his back tear out of the village on a Polaris snowmachine and head upriver toward Alakanuk. Perkins, Wassilie, and I got the bodies bagged and stowed in the plane, but Perkins wasn't coming back with me. With the bodies out of the clinic, he could wipe off the blood and sleep on an exam table. He wanted to canvas the witnesses in the morning. Wassilie even thought they might be able to follow the snowmachine. It had the wide track for floating on deep snow, and it was unusual, if not distinctive. Instead of taking the main trail, the driver had headed across the tundra.

To me, that seemed another obvious ploy to implicate Ski. His wide-track Polaris wasn't unique, but it wasn't the norm. The murderer was obviously setting up Ski, but what connection could there possibly be between Ski and the murders in Sheldon? I decided to concentrate on flying and leave the detecting to Tom.

I knew that tracking the machine wouldn't get them far because by that time there was a hard-packed trail from village to village, pretty much the entire length of the Yukon. I suspected that Perkins was nervous about flying at night, but maybe he was just being conscientious.

Anyhow, the bodies were signed into the custody of Detective Price. I took the stiffs back by myself, shouldered them into the back of my pickup, and dropped them off with the doctor who had drawn Christmas duty at the Public Health Service hospital. The doctor looked sleepy and needed a shave.

He was the type who looks tall because he's overly thin. He had the general demeanor you expect to see in hospitals in a patient's robe, not wearing a doctor's white coat. I think Christmas duty consisted mostly of sleeping in the lounge, but he didn't look happy about being there and even less happy with the two Christmas presents I gave him.

I checked my watch; it was a quarter to ten, too late to call Connie. Not that I wouldn't have stayed that late, maybe even stayed over if we drank enough rum and danced enough, but showing up with regrets and excuses right at bedtime seemed a little pointed.

I tooled through the dark, past the various Christmas-lighted windows to my cabin. I turned the oil stove up high and peeled off four layers of clothes. That's parka, hat and mitts, snowmachine suit, pants and shirt, and thermal underwear. On my feet there were only three layers. The shoepacks came off after the parka. I peeled the felt booties out of their canvas cover so they could dry. Wool socks came off after the snowmachine suit, and the last thing, after the underwear, was the cotton socks.

I took a cold shower, but not by design. It was just that the stove had been on low for too many hours and the hot water tank had cooled off.

CHAPTER 14

KOTLIK

I met Tom at the Kuskokwim Inn for an early breakfast. A pretty young brunette waitress, who had the audacity to look wide awake at seven, poured coffee without asking and took our orders. It was pitch black outside, with a duplicate coffee shop reflected in the windows. Next to the glass on the outside sat a sharp trooper in uniform and a scruffy pilot who remembered to take his hat off when he saw his reflection.

This time our war council had some meat to it. I shared my insight about all the victims being bachelors and Tom pointed out that they were also the most prosperous members of their communities. The waitress brought ham and eggs, toast, and canned orange juice. We whiffed them down but managed to talk between bites.

Tom swallowed. "There has to be a connection between the victims, and we've got to find it."

"Yeah," I agreed with him, "and we need to know why someone is going to great lengths to frame Ski for the murders. Once again, the wide-track Polaris headed toward Alakanuk points a finger at Ski. There has to be a reason for that."

"Obviously." Tom wasn't overly impressed with my detecting abilities. Tom had a *proactive* idea, as the detective course would have described it. He sat back and spread grape jelly on his last piece of toast. "If I were the manager of the village store in Kotlik, I'd be getting nervous about now. Maybe we should pay him a visit."

"Good idea. I've got to run up to Sheldon this morning and get Perkins. Can you come up with a good reason for a charter to Kotlik by noon?"

"Is the Pope Catholic?" Tom asked. I took that to mean yes.

❊ ❊ ❊ ❊

Perkins came trotting across the lake from the direction of the school, and I swung the plane around to meet him. He was bursting with pride at his major breakthrough in the case. He was still climbing in when his spiel started.

"We followed that machine for ten miles upriver before we lost it. It finally busted out of the brush and joined the main trail, but the guy was sure trying not to be seen."

I had a different interpretation of that. I thought the guy stayed off the trail to give them plenty of time to identify the type of machine, and it had worked.

Perkins fastened his belt. "The perp was definitely riding a Polaris, and that narrows things right down. Arctic Cats and Yamahas are the most popular machines up here, so all we have to do is track down the Polaris owners. There were only three in Sheldon and I checked all their alibis."

Perkins was anxious to get back to Bethel and write his report, and I was anxious to get him there. I'd taxied back to the end of the lake during his spiel. The moment he shut up, I shoved the throttle against the firewall. The engine bellowed, so he didn't talk anymore. Sure enough, I had a charter to Kotlik, with Trooper Tom, waiting when we landed.

Vickie had scheduled Tom in a 206. She wanted the 185 with its skis for a trip to the Children's Home on the Kwethluk River. Walt was waiting for the 185, but he had been nice about it; he had warmed up the 206 for me. Walt was an ex-military jockey who had flown everything that had a power plant and an airfoil. He made up his own instrument approaches to villages that didn't have radios. I think he liked Bethel and flying charter, although in the ten years I'd known him, I'd never seen him smile.

Wheels were no problem at Kotlik. We landed on the river, right beside the village, and the snow was packed down like a highway. Bright afternoon sunshine reflected golden from the snow. Kotlik has two airports, the old one that is too short and rough, and a new one that's too far from the village. Neither gets used after the river freezes.

The village cop came out to meet us, and he was wearing his .38 outside a beaver parka, but he didn't meet us just because we were us. He was meeting all the planes, his expression a dangerous scowl, which was impressive because he was an Eskimo version of a pro linebacker. I noticed a deputy, also wearing a revolver, providing backup. Kotlik was in a state of siege. Apparently Tom's proactive idea had already occurred to them.

Now, I have to tell you that this cop was named Wassilie, and I'm sorry for the confusion because the cop at Sheldon was also named Wassilie. It's a worse problem than you are imagining. Eskimo names take some getting used to, and the reality is worse than the books where all Eskimos are named Nanook.

On the Delta, there isn't the usual distinction between first and last names. Some very common last names are George, Joe, Sam, and Charlie, not to be confused with the Charles family. Do not confuse the Evan family from up-river with the Evon family on the coast. This cop was named Marvin Wassilie, but if you called him Marvin, he just might use his .38 on you. Better to just call him Wassilie and swallow the confusion. Wassilie is one of the most common names, both first and last.

A new nurse who was hired by Public Health Service was almost in tears during her ride back to Bethel. She had been sent to Tuluksak with instructions to give an urgently needed injection to "Wassilie." Fortunately, she had a good supply of needles and penicillin with her, because when the call went out, the Wassilies lined up. There was Wassilie Joe, and Wassilie George, and Wassilie Charlie and Wassilie Kokrine. Then came Joe Wassilie and George Wassilie, and of course, Wassilie Wassilie. The plucky little nurse injected half the men in the village.

Maybe the Wassilies knew which one needed the injection, maybe they didn't. There is just enough language barrier that you can never be sure. What is sure is that no Eskimo would ever put another on the spot by pointing him out. Also, they probably figured that the shot was a good thing, so why not have one?

They may have been on full alert, but Marvin Wassilie and his deputy couldn't help us. We were too late to talk to the manager of the Kotlik store. He'd had proactive ideas of his own and left for Unalakleet when the Bush telegraph reported the Sheldon killings, probably before Perkins and I got there.

"Unalakleet" meant that he had gone to Nome. They're a hundred and fifty miles apart, but the only reason on earth for going to Unalakleet is to hop a plane to Nome. Tom and I tromped up the wooden sidewalk toward the store, past the two-story wooden water tank, now frozen solid, and between the houses. It wasn't comfortable. Almost every man we met was wearing a sidearm, and we were getting hostile stares. It didn't matter that one of us was in a trooper uniform and the other was a pilot that they all knew; we still didn't belong there.

Even Sammy, the assistant store manager, looked nervous when Tom asked to talk to him. If you happen to remember the WW II propaganda picture that showed a Japanese pilot as a soft little butterball with buck teeth and owl eyes behind round-rimmed glasses, that was Sammy. Guys who joined the army based on that picture got a rude surprise, but Sammy was as sweet and gentle as the picture suggested.

He led us past the mechanical cash register and down the wooden aisle to the office. He didn't close the door and stood as far as possible from me. That was not normal. I had flown Sammy and his very pregnant wife into Bethel one dark and stormy night, and we came within half an hour of having to name the baby for the pilot. That's the custom if a baby is born in an airplane, and there are several Alexes and an Alexia in the villages.

Anyhow, Sammy's normal reaction would have been to run home and come back with an armload of salmon strips for me, but today he seemed to be looking me over for a gun. He wasn't much better with Tom. Apparently he thought that Tom had come to accuse Sammy of the murders. Customers who had been milling in the aisles seemed to be disappearing, too.

Tom perched on the edge of a desk and gave Sammy a comradely smile.

"So, Sammy, how long have you worked for Muktuk?" (That's not a name, it's a nickname and means "blubber," but it was used affectionately.)

"I didn't do it," Sammy said. "I been right here the whole time."

"We know that, Sammy. That's why we asked for you. We need someone innocent that we can trust."

That seemed to help. Sammy stopped fidgeting and leaned against the other desk. Don't get the idea that Sammy wasn't bright. Sammy was sharp as a razor, but English was his second language, and even though he was speaking in English, his thought processes were in Yup'ik, so sometimes his answers appeared to be nonsequiturs.

"Yeah," he said, "what did you want to know?"

"Well, I just wondered how long you've been working here?" Tom did not have his notebook out; that would have been too frightening.

"I guess about sixteen years."

"So you and Muktuk go way back together?"

"Muktuk didn't do it, either. He was right here, too."

"We know that, too, Sammy. We're just here because we're worried about him and we want to protect him."

"Don't need to," Sammy figured. "He's gone to Nome."

"Well, sure, but he'll want to come back sometime, so he'll want us to catch the killer first."

That made sense to Sammy. He went to the big electric pot and poured us each a ritual cup of coffee.

"Did Muktuk say anything before he left, or have any idea who might be doing the killing?" Tom asked.

"He didn't say nothin'." Sammy went back to leaning against the desk, blowing on his coffee. "When he heard who was killed at Sheldon, he turned almost as white as you. One of them tourist planes from Unalakleet was here, and Muktuk went right out and got on it. The plane didn't leave for another hour, but he stayed right on it, anyway."

"Well, obviously he must have trusted you, if you've been working for him for sixteen years."

"No, I only been working for Muktuk for about ten years. See, I was already working here when Muktuk bought the store."

Tom frowned. "I thought Muktuk was born and raised right here."

"Well, sure he was, but he was a trapper. He used to go out on the ice for seals, and one time the ice broke off and floated away with him. He killed a walrus and lived on the fat for three weeks until the ice drifted clear to Scammon Bay. That's why we call him Muktuk."

"So, what happened ten years ago?" Tom wondered.

"Muktuk got one of them government loans in Anchorage, and he came back and bought the store. Said he was never goin' on the ice again, and he ain't."

"Sammy, being a trusted local man, and being on the inside of everything, you probably hear things that the police would never hear. Do you have any idea who is doing the killing?" Tom took a sip of coffee, but his eyebrows were up and he was watching Sammy's reaction.

"Sure," Sammy nodded. "We all know. It's that big gussak that lives across from Emmonak. He was in Vietnam, and it drove him plumb crazy, and he started killing people again. He probably thinks he's back in the jungle. Happens all the time."

"Who told you that?" Tom asked.

"I don't know, everybody. I guess we'll have to go down there and kill him. Emmonak should do it, because he's their problem, but they ain't done it yet."

"Don't you think he might be innocent, and maybe someone is setting him up?"

"'Course not." Sammy finished his coffee.

"Sammy, you know that Alaska is a civilized country now, and we have to let the law handle things?" Tom looked hopeful.

"Well, sure, but the Eskimo law was here first."

"Well," Tom said, "it's a good thing we have citizens like you, who will try to calm people down and call the troopers if things get out of hand."

"Yep," Sammy said.

Tom and I walked back to the airplane and Wassilie was there to see us off. Tom wavered, wondering whether to talk to Wassilie. He took a good look at Wassilie's eyes and decided not to.

I didn't wait for Tom's instructions. I took off north but wheeled us around south to head for Emmonak. Tom was preoccupied and frowned for a while. I could see plenty of good reasons for frowning, but he surprised me.

"I'll need to read my report again, if the captain is through with it, but it seems to me that Demientoff got a government loan and bought his store about ten years ago, too."

"Is this police business, like maybe we should stop in Emmonak and talk to Joe first, or shall we head straight to the cabin?"

"Maybe we should talk to Joe." Tom went back to frowning.

The Emmonak airport was hard-packed snow, no problem. I taxied onto the parking apron and threw the cover over the cowling. It was almost twenty above, so there was no need to button up the plane. We tromped across the bridge and took the main trail between cabins to the city building. Emmonak was way ahead of most villages on that score. It's three times the size of most villages, and because of the cannery, Emmonak is richer than most.

Anyhow, they have a two-story wooden building with city offices in front, and in back, a half-sized gymnasium that is used mostly for bingo games. Upstairs, they have the only hotel between Bethel and Nome. The hotel has eight rooms and you can wheel in as many beds as you like. There isn't any restaurant, but there are a couple of places in the village where you can buy hamburgers. Most people who stay at the hotel bring hotplates with them and cook in their rooms. I think that's what the city expects guests to do.

The sweet, quiet girl who was running the office wanted to be helpful. She called for Joe on the CB radio but got no response. She brought us coffee and offered us chairs while she kept trying to raise Joe. We sipped the coffee so slowly that it got cold, but Joe never responded. The receptionist was embarrassed, and offered more coffee, but Tom decided to let it go. We wandered back between the houses toward the airport.

Villages aren't laid out in squares the way towns are. The cabins get arranged by family groups, with sons building next to their parents, sometimes in semicircles, but usually with enough room for walking between houses. When the snow comes, people leave tracks in their usual visiting patterns, and then other people use those tracks for trails and make more. Pretty soon, you could probably tell who visits whom by following the trails, but you can also cross the village in almost any direction.

Tom angled left until we came to the slough between the village and the airport and then turned right to parallel the slough. That brought us past Jesse's house. The door was closed and snow was drifted up against it, so it probably hadn't been opened since we had lugged out Jesse's body.

The snowplow had been used by someone, and nestled between the plow and the cabin was Jesse's snowmachine. It was a Polaris, and it wasn't iced in as deeply as it should have been. Tom took a good look at that machine, nodded, and we continued on to the bridge and back to the airplane.

CHAPTER 15

THE FORTRESS

We took off and flew across the river. Ski was on the riverbank half a mile upstream from the cabin, cutting driftwood with a chain saw. I glided down right over him and gunned the engine. Even with a chain saw running, that got his attention. That 300 horse IO 540 (that's inline, opposed, like a V-6, only more so) is barely muffled, and when it really speaks, it shakes the trees and the ground. I looked back and Ski was tossing his chain saw and some wood into his sled.

I chopped the power, racked down flaps, and set us on the first smooth foot, but the snow was packed and crusted. It felt like a paved airport. We taxied up in front of the cabin, and by the time I had the engine covered, Ski was bumping along the edge of the river.

We each grabbed an armful of wood out of the sled and carried it up to the wood box on the porch. Punik met us at the door. Now that I knew why her sparkle was gone, she looked great: calmer, and maybe radiant. We shed parkas and unzipped. Punik brought coffee, and we settled into our usual spots, except this time Ski reached across and laid a hand on Punik's shoulder.

Tom didn't pull any punches. He reported the conversation at Kotlik, just the way it happened, and punctuated it with the in-progress search for Polaris snowmachines. Ski and Punik were grown-ups. Tom needed to give them the facts; they needed to decide what to do for themselves. Tom couldn't offer any pie-in-the-sky solutions, like police protection. That's iffy enough in a city, nonexistent in the Bush. Ski was, technically, a fugitive, and that made it even tougher.

Punik got up to pace, and it seemed to me that maybe she was in charge. As the keeper of the expected progeny, her decision would be final. I would have flown them anyplace they wanted to go, South America if they had asked, but her thoughts weren't running that way.

"It's not as bad as it sounds. Kotlik is not Emmonak. They're almost a different culture, more Inupiat than Yup'ik, because their natural ties are to Stebbins and St. Michael. The Yup'ik way is first to shun a person or a family. That's almost a death sentence, or at least it used to be. When you're being shunned, no one can see you or hear you. You could actually starve or freeze right in the village, but you also have the option of trying to get to another village."

I stuck in my two cents worth. "That was in the old days, before guns, and there were no gussaks involved. Nowadays, their heroes are John Wayne and Bruce Lee." I wasn't trying to be negative, but I did think they were in serious danger. What I wanted them to do was grab their coats, get in the airplane, and let me drop them in Anchorage in five hours. I wasn't getting very many votes.

"My baby is going to be born right here in the house that we built for him. Alex, if you bring my mother up when the time comes, that's fine, but I'm staying here. If we leave, and they really want to get rid of us, they'll burn the house."

I wondered how she knew the baby was a he, but I didn't doubt her, and I was sure she was right about the house. The house didn't seem that important to me, but then, I hadn't spent two years building it.

Ski took over. "Look, I've got my rifle, and Punik has hers. If a lynching party shows up, we'll stack their bodies along the riverbank for you. If we have some warning, it's me they're threatening. All I have to do is leave, and Punik is in no danger. If they want to kill me, they can try it in the woods." Ski fingered his scar, and I knew he was thinking that it wouldn't be the first time. For just a second there, I saw an expression on Ski that was frightening and not unlike what Sammy had been talking about.

Tom stood up. "You know, Ski, a little protective custody might be the best thing all around. The important thing is to live through this. The guilty party will be found, all of this will be over in a couple of months, and you can rebuild whatever has to be rebuilt."

"No thanks, Tom. You're probably right, but I couldn't survive in a jail, even for a night. If I'm not under a wide-open sky, it has to be by my choice, and it can't be for very long. I'd be much happier in a snowbank, if it comes to that."

"All right, Ski. I think you're wrong, but I respect your decision. If we hear you on the radio hollering Mayday, we'll be here with the cavalry in an hour and a half, but that's a long time. Remember they started running a check on registered owners of Polaris machines this morning, and there can't be very many. If an arrest warrant is issued, both Alex and I will try to get the 'house fire' message on the radio. Buddy, if they send me, don't you be here."

Tom grabbed Ski, gave him a hug, and charged out the door, trailing his parka behind him. I pulled Punik and Ski together for a three-way hug and followed Tom. There wasn't anything else to say.

Before he cut me off with his sleep act, Tom did make one more statement.

"Muktuk knows exactly who is doing the killing, and why. Maybe he even knows why Ski is being framed. He didn't run like that just as a precaution. There is a connection, a list, for Christ's sake. He knows he's on it, and he knows he's next. I wish to heck Nome was in our district. Maybe I can get the Nome office to pick him up for questioning, but it's going to sound pretty silly to them."

That gave me some ideas. Nome is a little out of my district too, because of the jet schedules. You can get a jet from Anchorage to Bethel, and from Anchorage to Nome. If you need to get from Bethel to Nome, it's a lot cheaper, and maybe even faster, to take a jet to Anchorage and another to Nome, rather than charter.

The idea that was dawning was that I should get off early New Year's Eve and be off New Year's Day. The Cessna 310 could make Nome in three hours. I wondered if Connie might like to ride up to Nome for the New Year's celebration.

I had another idea, too. Maybe my detective training was going to pay off.

"It might be a good idea to check out those government loans. You always hear that they're available, but you never hear of anyone getting one. Now we've heard of two and they must have been issued about the same time. Muktuk and Demientoff both bought stores approximately the same time. Wouldn't it be a hoot if the guys at Sheldon got loans, too?"

"Good idea," Tom conceded. "I'll check it out, but I don't see how it explains the connection to Ski." He thumbed his hat down so the trooper badge was almost sitting on his nose and did his sleep thing. I don't mean to give the impression that Tom had narcolepsy. The fact was that he worked a crazy schedule, got called out at night frequently, and really needed any sleep he could get.

The southwestern sky put on a brilliant orange and red show of sunset. Snow on the tundra picked up the colors, and we were flying through a kaleidoscope. The engine had a relaxing, satin-smooth sound, every valve in every cylinder and all twelve sparkplugs performing perfectly. The white flash of the Bethel beacon came over the horizon. A minute later the alternate green flash contrasted with the sunset colors, and the white lights that were Bethel grew up out of the tundra.

CHAPTER 16

THE FEAST

I spent the next day cleaning up all the dregs of leftover holiday mail for the nearby villages and hanging by the radio most of the time. I made a fifteen-minute run to Napaskiak, a twelve-minute run to Napakiak, a twenty-minute run to Kwethluk, and half an hour to Akiachuk, with a long cup of coffee by the radio after every run.

When I got back to the airport at 5:30, a familiar 206 was tied down next to the gas pumps. I tied up double-time and ran into the office to call Connie.

"Hank is in town; pick you up in ten minutes." I hung up; that's all she needed to know. She would call Bergie for reservations while I got my pickup started and be waiting by the road when I drove by. She was, and we got to Leen's Lodge at three minutes to six.

Hank is a pilot, and a good one, and sometimes he flies for one or another charter service for a season, but Hank's first love is to be a businessman. Hank and I shared the stories of our lives one evening when we were both weathered down by an ice storm in King Salmon. We did the thing that all of our years of experience and piloting skills dictated. We found a warm bar with a fireplace and tried to drink the bar out of Black Russians while the wind screamed in frustration because it couldn't blow down the bar.

We were doing a good job on the Black Russians, and the bartender brought a bottle of vodka and a bottle of Kahlua and left them on our table so that he could tend to other customers. That's why my memories of Hank's life story are a little vague, but I think he was an aircraft salesman somewhere in the Midwest and got tired of watching other guys have all the fun. He bought one of his planes himself and barnstormed his way to Alaska.

All the present haste and excitement was caused by Hank's latest business venture. He was buying a thousand pounds of king crab when the ships docked in Kodiak and flying them straight to Bethel the moment they were loaded. You may think you've had king crab, may even think you like it, but if the crab you had was out of the water for more than twelve hours, then you ain't never had king crab. Having Bergie Leen cook it for you frosts the cake.

Our scientists have done wonderful things with preserving food. You can eat strawberries in Point Barrow in December and spinach in McMurdo Sound in July, but some things are just not meant to be preserved. Pork chops should only be eaten on the farm the day after butchering, scallops should only be eaten on the docks in Seward, and crab should be eaten no more than one fast airplane ride from the ocean. I hope you've had the pleasure of knowing exactly what I mean; but then again, if you have, it will spoil all the preserved and frozen stuff for you.

We charged into Leen's Lodge to a game of musical chairs. The dining table at the lodge seats sixteen people on each side, and two on each end, for a theoretical thirty-six. Bergie had stuck two more chairs on the ends, but there were forty of us crowding into the dining room. Bergie might have turned Connie and me down, because we called way too late, except Bergie still figured that she owed me for flying her up to the Nyak mine for the birth of her first great-granddaughter.

Connie and I shared a chair, scooting and nudging, until she got up and sat on my lap. Hank was there, sitting at the head of the table, looking as proud as he had every right to be. I think he brings the crab to Bethel just so Bergie will cook it for him.

The other guests were the movers and shakers in Bethel, but you wouldn't know it to look at them. If you stumbled into that dining room in some other city, you would think you were in a Salvation Army soup kitchen, but glancing around the table, I could see at least six millionaires and several others whose worth I wouldn't want to guess. That's an Alaska thing. In an Anchorage bank, you'll see some three-piece suits, but those are the loan officers and the cashiers. If you see some old guy wearing a flannel shirt and overalls and needing a shave, he probably owns the bank.

Norm Goldberg, the fur buyer from Seattle, was sitting next to Hank, wearing an old gray Alaska tuxedo and looking like an understudy for Santa Claus. The garment we call an Alaska tuxedo is coveralls, like your mechanic wears, insulated in winter. This time of year we'd drop Norm off in a village, any village. He'd be carrying only his briefcase and his checkbook. Three days later, we'd move him to another village and haul a thousand pounds of fur back to Wien Air freight. In a good year, Norm would paper the bush with checks, two and a half or three million dollars' worth. The day a Goldberg check bounces will be the day that the Rainier National Bank in Seattle closes.

Next to Norm was the manager of the National Bank of Anchorage, Kuskokwim Branch, with his new lady, a stunning blonde straight from Vegas or Seattle. I never learned the names of his ladies, because they didn't stay that long; Bethel is not for everyone.

Then came the Swanson brothers who owned the general merchandise store, supplying everything from groceries to lumber, hardware to clothing, and beside them reigned Chief Eddy. Chief Eddy Hoffman was the traditional head of the Yup'ik nation. The Chief is on the homegrown side, with a few rough edges, and there were some awkward moments when he went to Washington, D.C., to lobby Congress during the Alaska Native Land Claims struggle. He had a tendency to introduce himself as "The Chief" and he never quite understood that there were people in Washington who didn't know, chief of *what?*

The Alaska delegates were properly obsequious, because an endorsement by Chief Eddy meant thirty or forty thousand votes from current and former residents of the Delta. Personally, I enjoyed calling him Chief and showing the respect he deserved. There was no artifice in him. He saw himself as the servant and the protector of his people.

We didn't have a problem with plates because the plates were just for shells. Between each two chairs sat a little pot of melted garlic butter and a pile of paper napkins. Forty wine glasses were squeezed onto the table and a bottle of chardonnay by every third chair. That was all that was on the table until Bergie started bringing in the platters of crab. She set a heaping, steaming platter of crab legs on one end of the table, ran back for another and set it a little farther down, and so on. By the time she got to the other end of the table, it was time to start over.

Dummy, one of the dozen permanent residents at the lodge, was the man missing his left hand. He'd grab a shell in his teeth, pulverize it with his right hand, hold the remains on a napkin with his stump and extract the meat. He was eating at least as fast as anyone else. Jack McGuire was on my left, making the crab extractions look neat and proper and swabbing his mustache after he devoured each morsel. Jack was a different type of man from the rest of us, wearing a white shirt, jacket, and string tie and cracking crab with nails that looked manicured.

Jack was always clean, one of the few Bethel residents who didn't have motor oil stains under his fingernails, and there was an aura of talcum powder about him; but don't think he was effeminate. If you called him that, he'd probably pull a Derringer out of his sock and shoot you dead. It takes a special kind of man to sit at the poker table with twenty or thirty thousand dollars in the pot, waiting for the cards to turn. Jack did that two or three times a week. His schedule was to pick up all the loose cash in Bethel, go to Vegas with a hundred thousand, and be back in a month, organizing a new game.

For half an hour we sounded like a popcorn popper with the cracking shells before we started to taper off. It's a terrible situation when you're stuffed miserably full but the food is so good you can't stop eating. Bergie brought out a final platter, set it in the middle of the table, and brought a stool from the kitchen. I shoved our chair tight up against Jack McGuire's to make room for Bergie.

Connie slid half off my lap and half onto Jack's. He didn't mind in the least, and Connie didn't seem to mind either. I think Jack was a professional ladykiller in his day, as well as being a professional gambler, and maybe you never lose the knack. He did look a little like Maurice Chevalier, and I could imagine him singing, "Sank heaven for leet-le girls."

If either of us had eaten another bite, we'd have had to stay over, but we forced ourselves away from the table and staggered out. We parked in front of Connie's trailer and enjoyed a long, leisurely, contented kiss with plenty of melted butter on it.

"Thanks, Alex, that was fantastic."

"Want me to come in and lick off the butter?"

That brought a dreamy smile, eyes closed, but then she slowly shook her head.

"How about tomorrow night? We could melt some more butter, and maybe some chocolate. Tomorrow morning I've got to go in early."

"DA running for office again already?"

"Nah, we've got to get an indictment out. Trooper Perkins just broke a big case up on the Yukon and he wants to go make the arrest as soon as it's light."

"Perkins broke a case?"

"Yep. Tom has been sleepwalking, and Perkins nailed this guy. He asked the Anchorage computer for the names of registered owners of Polaris snow-machines, and out pops the name Erwin Kawalski in Emmonak. That's the guy that the murder weapon belonged to, who's supposed to be in Chicago. Isn't that your friend, Ski?"

I didn't answer. I hope Connie thought I was just being solicitous. I practically carried her inside, pecked her once more, and ran. Halfway to the airport, I tried to slow down because I realized that it wouldn't do Ski any good if I ran off the road and killed myself, but the pickup wouldn't listen.

I charged into the office, grabbed the microphone and hollered, "The house is on fire." Then I calmed down a bit, took a deep breath, and tried again. "This is KL7DIT calling in the blind for Alakanuk or Emmonak. We are trying to check a rumor of a HOUSE FIRE in one of the villages. Does anyone have any information about a HOUSE FIRE in Emmonak? Did someone call a charter to respond because of a HOUSE FIRE?"

I stopped for breath and Punik came right back at me. "KL7DIT, this is KBZ30, we are receiving your message loud and clear, but there are no house fires in the villages."

"KBZ30, this is KL7DIT, are you absolutely sure you're receiving me? Are you sure there are no HOUSE FIRES up there?"

"I'm sure. I can see both villages from here, and everything is under control. Go home to bed, Alex."

I took Punik's advice, wondering how come I was so shook up and she was so calm when it was her problem.

I called Vickie at 7:30 in the morning to tell her I was feeling too sick to fly.

"Gee, that's tough, Alex. Too much crab last night?"

"What makes you think that?"

"We had our crab at the inn, but we passed your pickup at Leen's Lodge."

"Nah, I don't think it was the crab. I think I've got the Asian flu, and maybe a touch of croup."

"Yeah, you sound terrible, Alex. I'll send Mike to Emmonak with Trooper Perkins at eight-thirty. Do you suppose you'll be well enough to make Mike's run to Holy Cross at nine?"

"Sure, I'll climb out of my deathbed for that."

Maybe that's why I've never married; I've never been able to fool a woman for a minute. I really didn't want to take Perkins up, though; it wouldn't have looked right if Punik and I were crying on each other's shoulders while Perkins searched for Ski.

CHAPTER 17

THE INVASION

Mike is the youngster in our group of Bushmaster pilots: tall, dark, clean, and sharp, with his sights set on the major airlines, and he'll probably make it. The cutoff age for airline hire is 28, and you need ten thousand hours of flight time to qualify. He was on track, but still a little in awe of us old-timers. He was flattered to be taking a state trooper flight and couldn't wait to tell me all about it when he got back. According to Mike, this is what happened.

Three snowmachines raced across the river and slid to a stop in front of Ski's cabin. Joe, the village cop, and his deputy ran around to the back door. Mike had been riding behind the deputy, but Perkins was too macho to be a passenger. He had borrowed a machine. Trooper Perkins loosened the gun in his holster and marched up the stairs to the front door. Mike hesitated, then followed the trooper.

Punik threw the door open.

"Hi guys, come in. Excuse me a moment, there's someone at the back door."

She turned to stride down the hall and open the back door. "Hi, Joe, Alfred, come on in, coffee is on." She left the door open, detoured through the kitchen, and came back to the front room with five steaming mugs of coffee on a wooden tray.

Trooper Perkins stood in the front doorway, hand on his gun. Mike was peering over his shoulder.

"Where's Kawalski?" Perkins demanded.

"Oh, he's not here. Come in, come in, have some coffee." Punik stood pointedly holding the door, so Perkins and Mike stepped through and Punik closed the door behind them. She held out her tray and gestured toward the couch. Perkins took his coffee mug, but he strode over to look in the kitchen. He backed into the living room.

"Nice place you have here." He carried his coffee in his left hand, kept his right hand on his pistol, and checked the bedrooms and bath like maybe he was taking the grand tour, admiring the house.

Joe and Alfred came down the hall from the back. Joe shook his head at Perkins and shrugged his shoulders. Punik handed them mugs, took her own, and sat down on a wooden chair at the dining table, motioning Joe and Alfred toward the couch. They sat, and Mike wavered and took another wooden chair, leaving the easy chair for Perkins.

Perkins came back and stood beside the chair. "Where is Kawalski?"

"He's on his trapline. He left the day after Christmas; probably won't be back before the end of January." Punik sipped and smiled. Perkins sat down, but didn't smile. "Just where is this trapline?"

"Oh heavens, I don't know. Men don't tell women things like that. Upriver somewhere, I think."

Perkins rested the mug on the chair arm. "How was he traveling?"

"He took his snowmachine, of course. Traplines are usually thirty or forty miles long, and who knows how far upriver it might be."

"And that machine would be a wide-track Polaris?"

"Yes, it would, exactly like that one you're riding."

"That's Jesse's machine. I just borrowed it."

"I didn't mean it is Ski's machine, I just meant it is exactly like Ski's machine, same color, same wide track. Ski loves that wide track. I think most of the trappers use identical machines. They're good when the snow gets deep, you know."

"I know." Perkins still had his scowl, but Alfred was all smiles.

"Yeah, I borrowed one from my cousin after that big snow last year. They're great for deep snow."

Both Perkins and Joe turned scowls on Alfred, and he subsided to sip his coffee.

"I believe your husband owns a .45 automatic?" Perkins asked.

"Well, he did, but it was stolen. He reported it stolen to George because he went to Alakanuk the day he noticed it was missing. Didn't George file a report or something?" She looked the wide-eyed question from Perkins to Joe and back.

Perkins turned his scowl on Joe. Joe shrugged his apology.

"Was that before or after Jesse was shot?" Perkins asked.

"Gee, I don't know. It was quite a while ago. When was Jesse shot? Anyone for more coffee?"

Mike and Alfred held out cups; Punik jumped up and went into the kitchen, Perkins right behind her, hand on gun. He took a good look around the room, stomped over and jerked the broom closet open, then slammed it shut.

Punik didn't seem to notice his antics. She carried the pot into the living room and poured for Alfred and Mike. Joe hesitated, then extended his mug, and she topped it off. Perkins' mug sat on the chair arm, untouched. Punik dribbled in a few drops anyhow, filled her own cup, and took the pot back to the stove. Perkins tore himself away from the back window and followed Punik to the living room.

"Look, Mrs. Kawalski, this charade is not going to work. We have his hat, dropped at the scene of a crime."

Punik looked shocked. "You have Ski's hat?"

"Identified and locked up in the evidence locker in Bethel."

"Oh, I don't see how that is possible."

"Not only possible, a fact, Mrs. Kawalski."

"And you think the hat belongs to Ski?" Punik frowned.

"Half a dozen people have identified it, ma'am."

"Which hat do you mean?" Punik wondered, still frowning.

"The one made from timber wolf faces, and don't try to tell me that he left here wearing it."

"Oh no, he wouldn't wear that hat on the trapline. That was his wedding present. I'm sure he left here wearing his old beaver hat. I think his wolf hat is in the closet." Punik jumped up and strode into the bedroom, Perkins two steps behind her. She strained, but couldn't reach the top shelf. Perkins shoved the clothes aside to check the closet, turned around and dropped to look under the bed.

"Would you reach it down for me?" Punik was stretching, but barely reaching the shelf. "He keeps his hats on the top shelf."

Perkins reached up, ran his hand along the shelf, stopped, and pulled down the wolf fur hat. He stared in disbelief. He stomped back into the living room and handed the hat to Joe. Joe looked at it, turned it over, sniffed the lining, and gave Perkins his shrug. Alfred plucked the hat out of Joe's hand. "Yep, this is Ski's, all right."

Punik took the hat from Alfred and started back toward the bedroom.

"Hey, give me that hat." Perkins advanced; Punik retreated.

"Mrs. Kawalski, give me that hat."

"Oh, I don't think I should do that. Ski is very fond of this hat. He'd be terribly upset if I gave it away. I assume you have an arrest warrant, but does it include confiscating his personal property?"

Perkins spun around and stomped toward the door, then stopped himself. He deflated, sighed, and turned. He nodded his head politely.

"Thank you for the coffee, Mrs. Kawalski. I'll be back."

"Oh, it's Punik. Please call me Punik, Trooper Perkins." She gave him her dazzling smile.

CHAPTER 18

HAPPY NEW YEAR

H i, Connie, Alex here. Want to go up to Nome for the New Year's celebration tomorrow night?" I was calling from the office, ignoring Vickie's knowing smirk.

"Will they have melted butter there?"

"Connie, on New Year's Eve, everything in Nome will be melted. We can lick the whole town off each other." Vickie pretended to be scandalized.

"Sounds dreamy, Alex. What time shall we leave?"

"Three-ish, I hope. Only one flight scheduled tomorrow, so far. I just have to run Billy Fox down to Kipnuk at noon, then the day is all ours."

"Alex, that hath a familiar ring to it. Call me when you really get back and when we can really go. Is there anyone on the coast who hasn't been shot yet?"

"Not that I can think of. I'll call you around two-thirty."

❄❄❄❄

At two-thirty New Year's Eve, Billy and I landed the 206 on the ice of Baird Inlet. Billy went to work scraping ice off the windshield so that we could see out; I walked around the airplane, whacking with a rope to break up some of the ice on the control surfaces and the wings. We had been to Kipnuk twice. We just couldn't find it.

Kipnuk is on the southwest coast, forty-five minutes from Bethel and three hundred miles from Ski and Punik's problems. Bethel was overcast and the cloud touched the ground thirty minutes out. We held our heading, a hundred feet off the ground, for fifteen minutes, and we should have been over Kipnuk. We could see two or three hundred feet, most of the time, but we didn't even see the Kipnuk River go by.

I flew straight ahead for another five minutes, which is thirteen miles in a 206. We should have come to the coast, but we didn't. We turned around and headed back the way we came, still searching for the river and hoping to see the village, but by that time there was so much ice on the windshield that we were seeing only out the side windows, and nothing familiar went by.

I continued hedgehopping back toward Bethel until we got out of the cloud, and we were right where we should have been, Baird Inlet fifteen miles north of us, Kipnuk now forty miles behind us. We turned around and tried it again. I really wanted to get Billy home. He was a good customer because he was running a little store out of his home, but mostly he was just a nice guy. Maybe around forty years old, he'd been the maintenance man for the BIA school forever; he and his wife ran their little store on the side.

Billy had dreams. There were more kids running around his house than I ever managed to count, and while they were still in grade school he had already picked out which of his boys would become pilots and run the Kipnuk Air Service he planned to start and which of his boys would run a huge new store someday. Billy was the one who salvaged the old, one-lung Witte diesel generator when Nyak mine threw it out.

We hauled it to Kipnuk in the trimotor and tinkered with it until it ran. The next time I was in Kipnuk, there was Romex cable strung on the tundra between houses, and Billy was selling electricity to his neighbors. I've drunk a lot of ritual coffee in Billy's house, and he taught me most of the Yup'ik words I know.

We finished scraping ice and leaned against the wing strut. North and east of us it was just a gray, overcast day. We could see probably ten miles. South and west was white cotton. Directly west of us, invisible in the cotton, was Nelson Island, with mountains and muskoxen, Nightmute, Tuksuk, and Tununak. South along the coast, the village of Chefornak, and then the only terrain feature on that part of the Delta, Tern Mountain.

Tern Mountain is a red cinder cone four hundred feet tall sticking up out of the tundra. South of that, flat tundra and wandering sloughs spread for forty miles to Kwigillingok and the mouth of the Kuskokwim. In the middle of that bare flat stretch were thirty houses and a school called Kipnuk. All we had to do was find it. I pulled out the sectional chart, although we both could have drawn it with our eyes closed.

From where we sat on the Baird Inlet, ten minutes at 200 degrees would take us south of Tern Mountain, ten more minutes at 240 degrees would take us to Kipnuk. No problem. We took off and I set our course and marked the clock on the instrument panel. Five minutes later, we were in the cotton, indicating three hundred feet above sea level and seeing nothing. Five minutes more, I made the turn.

Ten minutes passed: nothing but cotton. Eleven minutes, *whoosh*, black buildings whiffed by fifty feet below us. I locked onto a two-minute turn, held our altitude and slowed us down. Thirty seconds, all white. I lowered the flaps and dropped us down ten feet.

"Over there," Billy shouted.

The runway snow berm was right beside us, and looked to be at the same height we were. I jerked us right, over the berm, then left to line up with the berm, and there were wheel tracks in the snow beneath us. I chopped the power.

❆ ❆ ❆ ❆

"Hi, Connie, remember me?"

"Sorry, I can't talk to you now. I have a hot date with a cold pilot two hours ago."

"Well, don't hang up. We can chat until dumb-dumb shows up. How about we two-time the schmuck and fly away into the sunset together?"

"What sunset? It looks like the inside of my mattress out there."

"Oh, I love that bedroom talk. Let me take you away from your sordid existence to where the lights are bright, the music is loud, and the men are all on time."

"Make me an offer."

"Thirty minutes. I just have to put the heat on the 310, run home, shower, shave, slip on a tux, pick up my toothbrush, and have the chauffeur bring the Rolls around."

"Why don't you stay dirty and disgusting, pick me up in your pumpkin, and we'll scrape the crud off of you in Nome?"

"Whatever you say, but I'm not very lickable at the moment."

"Might be fun to fix that. Don't hang up the phone; leave it off the hook and let's blow this pop stand before anyone catches us."

She hung up, so I did too and ran to throw my flight bag into the 310 and plug in the heaters. The temperature was above zero anyhow.

❄ ❄ ❄ ❄

Both engines bellowed equally; a good sign. The tarmac dropped away; I retracted the gear, eased off some flap, and kept the power on. We went up like a New Year's rocket and ripped into the belly of the clouds. Connie's mattress was a little bumpy but not bad. I stowed the rest of the flaps, backed off to eighty percent power, synchronized the engines, and continued to climb a thousand feet a minute at a hundred thirty knots. At five thousand feet, we rolled to a heading for Nome.

At ten thousand feet, the mattress had rips and tears in it; sky flashed past the holes above us. At twelve thousand feet, the mattress spread out below us as mattresses should, and pink sunset streaked the clear sky in the southwest behind us. DME, that's distance measuring equipment, part of the VOR system, said Bethel was forty-five miles behind us, and Loran said it was getting farther at a hundred seventy knots. The outside temperature stopped bouncing up and down like a yo-yo and settled at thirty below. That was good because Nome was reporting thirty below, so we were in the same air mass as Nome, and it was clear.

The mattress spread out for an hour. The moon came up to light it. Connie stayed glued to her window as if it were a view of the Grand Canyon. When the mattress tapered off and the edges crumbled, the Bering Sea ice was blue facets in black settings below us.

Punik and Ski were behind us now and probably not having a very good New Year's Eve. Muktuk was ahead of us, and I thought maybe I'd spoil his celebration. The Seward Peninsula poked up out of the ice, old round mountains that looked much smoother than the ocean ice below us.

Suddenly a brilliant flash like sheet lightning burned the sky on our right. A gigantic red wheel that covered a third of the northern sky emerged from the darkness, like a print appearing in a darkroom. Two blue floodlights blinked on to flank it, then gradually defocused, and a ghostly green spirit dance ripped across the sky.

The spirits danced in a line, sometimes dreamy, sometimes angrily whipping their line like an attacking snake. If they still taught penmanship by having you make rows and rows of push-pulls when you were in school, then you know what a spirit dance looks like. If not, picture a picket fence, pickets almost touching, brightening and dimming in waves, the whole fence liquid and moving like a conga line.

The scientists at the University of Alaska claim that the aurora borealis is a natural phenomenon. They tell us that the earth is a giant toroid coil; basically a circular magnet. Maybe in some high-school physics class you held a magnet under a sheet of paper and poured iron filings on top of the paper? The filings lined up to show the lines of force around and between the poles of the magnet.

If you didn't do that, picture just one of the infinite number of lines of magnetic force around the earth. It comes out of the ground at the South Pole, arcs gracefully up to a zenith a couple of hundred miles above the equator to form the ionosphere, and down to reenter the earth at the North Pole. It then travels through the core and comes out at the south again.

If you have that pictured, then visualize a bunch of lines, spaced apart over the equator but all coming together at the pole, and you will see that a lot of lines stack up at the pole, and the magnetism gets so strong that our compasses point to it. When the lines come down, they pass through the atmosphere, magnetism getting stronger as they converge, and clouds of elements that float in the atmosphere get ionized and light up like the gas in a neon sign.

The scientists even tell us that the different colors are different gases. They claim that solar flares get the gasses and the magnetosphere all agitated and are responsible for the colorful displays. That's what the scientists tell us.

Next time you happen to be flying over the Arctic on a dark night and see the spirits dancing, you will know that scientists are full of crap. The dancers in that bobbing, weaving, blinking line, snaking from the zenith to the horizon, are the spirits of every Eskimo who has ever died. Connie stared with eyes and enticingly lipsticked mouth wide open.

"Nome radio, are you having a Happy New Year?"

"Who wants to know?"

"Eight-Two Bravo, out of Bethel, estimating Nome in thirty minutes."

"Your flight plan says twenty-five minutes. What kept you?"

"Had to stop and admire your fireworks display."

"Yeah, not bad tonight. We try to make the tourists happy."

"We appreciate it. Any chance of getting a taxi to meet us?"

"I'll call around and see if I can find a sober one."

An ancient green Pontiac with a taxi sign on top was waiting for us. Connie huddled in the taxi while I tied down the plane, buttoned it up, and plugged in the heaters. We slipped and fishtailed down Seppala Drive, a narrow plowed road sketched across the open tundra toward the bubble of light that was Nome. The driver was apparently eager to get back to the party. We skidded around the curve onto West Third Avenue, but the snowbanks were higher than the cab, so no town was apparent. The turn onto Bering Street was ninety degrees. We took that in a four-wheel drift. The left rear slammed into a snow berm, but bounced off and the lights of Front Street were ahead of us. The driver made the final left turn—the other option was diving onto the frozen Bering Sea—and slid to a stop in front of the two-story white clapboard lodge.

❄ ❄ ❄ ❄

Fourth Avenue in Anchorage, Second Avenue in Fairbanks, and Front Street in Nome have a lot in common after dark. Bars are packed like dancers, cheek to cheek, all with strobing lights and blaring music. You can tell which bar you're in by the loudest music, but you can probably hear the bars on either side, too.

You can tell you're in Nome by the stack of antlers and by the chair-sized whale vertebrae along the street. I rented two adjoining rooms at the inn as a gentlemanly gesture, thinking that one just might be enough, but semantics are everything. The inn was a classy place with a big queen-sized bed, a dresser, a chair, and a sink with running water in every room. Down the hall were two bathrooms, unisex for fairness.

Connie dumped her bag in her room. I peeled off my snowsuit, washed all the skin that showed, and ran a comb through my hair. I put my parka back on and met Connie in the hall. She was wearing stretchy black slacks, high-heeled boots, and her sealskin parka over a heavy sweater that looked Norwegian.

We trooped down the wooden stairs, crossed the gravel road, and dived into the maelstrom of light, music, and booze. Picture feeding, or maybe watering, time at the zoo. Wolf parkas, beaver parkas, seal parkas, rabbit parkas, muskrat parkas, beads, tassels, and fancy work were all jammed together. Everyone looked too big, because parkas add inches, and they gave the wearers a strut, like a suited-up football team.

Most of the patrons wore hats pushed back on their heads. There were seal, beaver, fox, muskrat, marten, lynx, wolf, and probably others, but I forget which ones I've already mentioned. Oh yeah, several hats and some parkas were *sik-sik-puk*.

Half the patrons wore mukluks. A few were the traditional sealskin that tie just below the knee. Those have walrus-hide soles, flat, smooth, and slippery as glass. The insulation inside is dry grass and it works great because when you walk, the grass chafes and makes heat by friction, like rubbing two Boy Scouts together. When they cool off, you stuff in more grass.

Most mukluks end mid-calf with a fur ruff around the top and bands of needlework below the ruff. The fancy stuff is made of bits of short-haired black hide and white hide, cut and stitched together to make squares or scenes with figures. Fancy dressers have matching bands around the bottom of their parkas.

With the room packed tight, everyone sweating, and half the furs wet, the odor was just like you're imagining, but once you're part of it, you don't notice it. I don't mean to imply that Connie was the only woman in the crowd, but you had to look pretty closely to spot the others. There's nothing like thirty below zero to promote unisex dressing.

The obvious drink was hot buttered rum. Bartenders didn't even ask. I tried to keep it light, letting Connie get ahead, two to my one. Not that I had any despicable designs of getting her drunk, but I was looking for Muktuk. We started at the stack of antlers and hit every bar, working along the beach away from Bering Street toward the Nome–Council Highway. I was having one drink per bar, Connie two. If she noticed that I was restless, she didn't mention it until the fourth bar.

"Who are we looking for?" she asked.

"Just checking to see who's here."

"Uh-huh. Let me know when you find him, and it better not be a her." Did I tell you that I've never been able to fool a woman? She sucked her cinnamon stick (this was one of the classier bars). That was my cue to go fetch her another drink. If I'd tried to order, the bartender couldn't have heard me over the racket from a three-piece western band. I just waved a ten-dollar bill between two parkas on bar stools. The bill was snatched, replaced by two glass cups with handles. The cups brimmed with honey-brown liquid, and I fought my way through the forest of furs to the wall where Connie was leaning.

We worked our way down the strip and were getting close to the end. When we darted between bars on the cold wooden sidewalk, I could see past the last building where the road turns into a white ribbon through the white tundra toward the optimistically named Nome–Teller Highway, but still no Muktuk. All at once customers started pouring out of the bar, half of them carrying drinks, and I noticed that the big clock behind the bar said eleven-fifty-five. We drained our glasses and followed the crowd.

People surged across the street into a vacant lot and bunched up, standing in two feet of crusty snow. It was still thirty below, and that's one reason we were such steady bar customers. You didn't want to spend more than half a minute outside making the transfer. I stepped behind Connie and wrapped my arms around her. She snuggled against me for warmth, but in two minutes the whole crowd was packed so tight that it didn't matter who was with whom.

A beaver hat several spaces ahead of us turned profile, and there was Muktuk. I couldn't move, and anyway, I liked the place I was. The spirit dance had changed to random searchlights in the sky, still green, switching on and off, detaching and collapsing, but the crowd didn't notice.

The little sparklers rocketing up from earth and bursting into multicolored umbrellas were far more interesting to them. The crowd roared its approval, ripples of excitement running through the pack. Connie made a warm streak down my front, and I noticed how well we fit together. She was cheering with the best of them.

The climax came with a dozen rockets at once, lighting the whole town in brilliant neon for fleeting seconds. I spun Connie around for a kiss, the crowd shoving us together deliciously.

"Happy New Year, Connie."

"Happy New Year, Alex."

The crowd surged back to the bars while they cheered and applauded the fireworks. I locked onto Connie's hand and followed the beaver hat. That was a good trick, because there were thirty beaver hats in that crowd, but I got the right one and shoved our way into the first bar, ten people behind Muktuk.

"Wow," Connie protested. "Are you thirsty or did you just want to break our embrace?" People crowded against the bar four deep. I held a ten-dollar bill in my hand and reached over several heads toward the bar. The bill was snatched, two hot rums replaced it, and we went looking for a place to stand beside a hot radiator. Muktuk had been even faster; he had his rum and was leaning against the wall toward the back of the room.

I squeezed Connie's hand to show her that she really was important and whispered, "Stay here." I dodged parkas along the wall and sidled up next to Muktuk.

"Hi, enjoy the show?"

"Who the hell are you?" He was trying to focus his eyes on me, but they weren't working very well. They were bloodshot, almost red, and looked watery, maybe filmy. One eye refused to cooperate and wandered off by itself.

"I'm Alex, the pilot from Bethel. You know me from Kotlik." Muktuk looked as if he'd been slapped. He dropped his drink, spilling the hot rum down the front of his parka, and backed away until he hit the corner.

"Hey, easy does it, I'm just here for the fireworks."

"Keep away from me," he shouted. "You can have the money, take the whole ten million for all I care, just leave me be." He charged toward me, and I almost grabbed him, but at the last second he spun away, or maybe lurched, and ran through the crowd.

He slammed into several backs along the way, and various drinks went flying. At least two guys that I saw turned around and slugged the guy behind them. The third time, I was the guy behind and barely ducked in time to avoid decapitation.

Muktuk was ten yards ahead of me, and losing me because I was a little more inhibited about slamming into people. He ran straight out the door, full tilt. I got to the door just in time to hear the horrible bump, squishy, moist, but solid and definitive. No brakes had squealed because the street was ice. The taxi slid, turned sideways, bounced against the wooden sidewalk, and stopped. Muktuk rolled off the hood like a rag doll.

I ducked backward through the crowd. Connie came out of the bar. I grabbed her hand, hustled her two doors down, and swam against the current to get into that bar. I waved a ten at the bartender. The bar was suddenly empty; he brought our drinks.

"Hey, didn't you hear? Some guy just got iced outside."

"Yeah, I heard," I told him.

For the first time all night, there were empty chairs and tables in a bar, lots of them. We took a small round table with two iron chairs and sat down. Now you know how to get a seat in a Nome bar on New Year's, if you need one.

"My God, did you kill him?" Connie asked.

"No, I didn't. He killed himself."

"Because of something you told him?" Connie seemed more interested than shocked.

"Connie, all I did was ask him if he liked the show."

"Well, I've been meaning to tell you that your small talk could use some work."

"Actually I was hoping to get past the small talk. Muktuk was a tough old bird who survived ordeals that would have killed most. Doesn't seem right for him to go this way. Other than the mother lode of hot buttered rum, he was our excuse for coming to Nome. He apparently knew who is murdering people on the Delta and probably why it's happening. He may have had the answer to the most baffling question of all, why the attempts to frame Ski for the murders. Let's toast his memory, raise a few solemn glasses in his honor, and then a few to mask the disappointment of not getting to talk to him."

If we seem blasé about Muktuk's death, that is the arctic attitude. Deaths and births are part of daily life and they happen in the open, not institutionalized the way they are in the cities. Maybe you get immune to them; maybe it's a defense mechanism.

We heard a siren outside, and people started trooping back in. The second show of the night was over. The siren may have been an ambulance, but I knew it wouldn't do Muktuk any good. I'd seen the way his head lolled when he rolled off the taxi, as if it were attached to shoulders by a rubber band, and the reason it did that was that every vertebra in his neck was shattered.

The bar was about up to double its capacity. I pulled Connie out of that bar and started for the inn. In fifty feet, that is, passing the second bar, we were already too cold and ducked inside.

We worked our way steadily back to the inn, usually one, sometimes two bars at a time, and had a drink, sometimes two, in each. It was between three and four in the morning (my watch face had gone blurry) when we made the final dash across the street and helped each other up the stairs at the inn. Just as in my wildest dreams, Connie stumbled straight into my room. We fell across my bed with our clothes on, and I guess she went to sleep. I know I did.

It must have been noon when I felt the bed move and opened my eyes to watch the girl of my dreams upchuck in the sink. She rinsed her face, rinsed the sink, and stumbled off toward her own room. I struggled up, slipped off my parka, and held my head on with my hands while I staggered to the open bathroom door down the hall.

CHAPTER 19

A PLAN

We were heading home from Nightmute. Tom had taken depositions in an apparently accidental drowning. The body hadn't been found, of course, and never would be, and that makes lots of paperwork. Nightmute is technically on Nelson Island, although you have to look sharp to see that the narrow neck of the Baird Inlet isn't a river. Anyhow, when you go under the ice that close to the ocean, you move to the bottom of the food chain and that is that.

From a gussak point of view, Nightmute ranks high in the queue of most desolate places on earth. Cliffs rise behind it, seven or eight hundred feet tall, but across the Nightmute River, bare flat tundra stretches to the horizon. Even the name is desolate. I've heard it translated both as "the place where the wind stays" and "people pressed down by wind." The *mute* part is common and means where something stays or is habitual, like Sleetmute, Piamute, Ohagamute, and so on. The *night* part is pronounced *nikt* as if there were a German influence. Whatever the etymology, the reality is that a constant wind blows down the face of the cliffs, so the weather is always miserable.

A couple of winters earlier, I had been standing on the banks of their frozen river with Stanley, the cook at the BIA school. Both of us were hunched inside our parkas and shivering. I asked him why he stayed there.

"We stay because we are so rich. We have the river for fish, the ocean for seals, the tundra for birds and berries, and life is just so easy here."

Rich and *easy*, like *beauty*, must be in the eye of the beholder. That was a couple of months after Stanley's "medical emergency," and we had become good buddies that night, although I had been victimized by a scam. Bill Cole, the principal at the BIA school, called Vickie on the radio and declared a medical emergency at Nightmute. It was cold, it was dark, it was snowing and blowing and awful, but I fired up the 185 and headed for Nightmute.

Half the flight was on instruments. When the clock said I should be over Nightmute I spiraled down, slowly and carefully, expecting to hit a mountain at any moment. I was still a thousand feet up, but getting terrified, when I spotted the line of lights. All of the snowmachines in the village were lined up on the river, marking a runway. I plunked down on the ice and started ripping out rear seats, expecting a stretcher. Instead, it was Stanley who came strolling toward the airplane, dressed for town and carrying a little overnight case.

It developed that Stanley's wife was in the Native Hospital in Anchorage, expecting their first baby, and Stanley wanted to catch the evening jet. Bill knew very well that it was no fit weather for a normal charter, so he played the "medical emergency" trump. It was only a little stretch. Stanley *was* headed for a hospital.

When Tom had collected depositions from everyone who had seen the ice break and we started back toward Bethel, a white fluffy cloud was sitting on the ground, and it was only a hundred feet thick. Rather than hedgehop and dodge bushes all the way back to Bethel, I went on top for an easy comfortable flight under blue sky. The cloud slowly tapered up, so now we were at five thousand feet, twenty miles out of Bethel, and the cloud didn't look so fluffy anymore. Naturally I'd been hoping that the cloud would end, but it was going right on up and apparently reached clear to Canada. It had ugly black canyons and whirlpools in it, as well as occasional strobe lights.

"Hey, Alex, what's with lightning in January? I thought lightning storms were summer problems."

"Don't ask me, take it up with the weather gods. Might have something to do with the Bering Sea, the Arctic Ocean, and the Alaska Range confusing things. Bethel weather is hatched in a Mixmaster. Besides, that might not be lightning. It could be leftover New Year's rockets. You were asking more pertinent questions?"

"Well, I did wonder why you killed our star witness."

"Tom, I did not kill Muktuk. Maybe he committed suicide, or scared him-self to death, but I didn't kill him." I nudged us left a half-degree to follow the sixty-degree radial, inbound to Bethel.

"You just said, 'Hi, Muktuk, how's tricks?' and he killed himself?" Tom was trying to look at me, but the cloud kept distracting him.

"Yeah, that's about what happened. He was trying to figure out who I was, and when I said he knew me from Kotlik, he went off like a New Year's rocket."

"You're telling me that Muktuk didn't recognize you?"

"No, he didn't. I think *blind drunk* may be more than an expression."

"Him, or you?"

"Aw, come on, I was in good shape. I hadn't had more than a dozen drinks at that point, just enough to keep warm."

"Okay, you were as sober as Judge Gilmore. You really did a nice job of interrogation, Detective Price. Did you run a psychological profile on the sub-ject? Maybe get an idea of why he committed suicide?"

"Yes, as a matter of fact, I did, and if you'll stop being so damn superior, I may even tell you."

"Oh, be my guest. I'm dying to hear your analysis." Tom stared down at the black cloud below us, distracted by the strobe lights that were ripping around inside it. I waited until the cloud stopped flashing and I had Tom's attention.

"Fact is, he thought I was going to rob him. He may have thought I was someone else, because he couldn't focus his eyes, and they kept wandering off in different directions, but he said, 'Take the money, take the whole ten mil-lion.' Do you suppose he really has ten million stashed?"

"Well, if he has, it's not in his bank account. Ten thousand, maybe."

"You checked his bank account?"

"With a warrant. Turns out you were right about the government loans in Sheldon. Store owner bought with fifty thousand cash about ten years ago, and at the same time, Hinkley built that big new house with room for the post office and then rented it to the postal service. Jesse bought the snow plow for thirty thousand cash."

"So there really is a government agency that makes loans?"

"That's the catch, and that's why I checked all their bank accounts. I couldn't find an agency that admitted the deed, so I thought I'd check and see who they were making payments to."

"And?"

"No help. Not one of them has made any payments to anybody."

"Nice agency. When you find it, I'm going to apply. Better tighten your seat belt."

"Suicide isn't contagious, is it?" Tom pulled on the strap; the belt cut into his lap and across his shoulder.

I called for an instrument approach and dropped down into the cloud.

"At least," Tom said, "we know the killer is from Emmonak."

"We do?"

"Couple of reasons. In order to steal Ski's hat, he had to see Ski go upriver. Either he spent weeks shadowing Ski, or else he just looked across the river and saw Ski going out with his sled to cut firewood. In order to steal Ski's automatic, he had to stake out the cabin for a week, or just notice when both Ski and Punik came into the village."

The cloud was definitely not white and fluffy. We slammed into an invisible wall, dropped two hundred feet and hit the bottom of the air pocket with a bang.

"Okay, you're thinking real good, Inspector. Shall we go arrest everyone in Emmonak?"

Tom had that *thinking* look again. "Pretty soon. Something isn't right about Jesse's killing. I can't put my finger on it, but I wake up at night thinking that we both know who the killer is."

The light went out and the windshield turned black. Snow, or maybe hail, pounded us, sounding like gravel on a tin roof. We were sucked up a hundred feet, slammed back down. I slowed the plane to make it easier on the wings. We were down to 2,500 feet and Bethel was reporting a thousand-foot ceiling.

"Well, if I wake up at night and know the name of the killer, I'll give you a call. What do we do next?"

"What we should have done in the first place."

Something grabbed us by the tail and sucked us straight up. I killed the power and pointed us straight down. We were indicating one hundred fifty knots and still going up 500 feet per minute.

"What should we have done in the first place?" We were slamming back and forth across the 180-degree outbound radial. DME showed twelve miles. "Bethel Radio, 8-4 Zulu, initial approach fix."

"Searched their homes. There won't be any clues to the killings, per se, and that's why we didn't bother."

The monster released our tail and we dropped like a spent arrow.

Tom continued, "But now what we need is to find the connection between them, find out where they all got that mysterious loan, why all at the same time, and maybe even a link to Ski."

We fell right out of the cloud into smooth air at fifteen hundred feet, and Bethel was five miles ahead of us.

"Bethel Radio, 8-4 Zulu, canceling IFR and proceeding with a visual approach."

Tom's relief was obvious. I tried not to show mine. " Do you want to run up there this evening?"

"Are you kidding? I've got thirty depositions to file, and wouldn't it be a novel idea to get search warrants?"

"Wow, working with a professional sure is exciting. Search warrants, huh? I have so much left to learn about detecting. You can stop squeezing your seat now, we're not going to bump anymore, and I'm afraid you'll break the springs."

CHAPTER 20

THE PICTURE

It was snowing in Alakanuk, but the flakes weren't falling down. The snow was going sideways at thirty miles an hour. The sky was white; the runway was white. I tied the 206 to the log drag they used to smooth the runway and buttoned the nose up tight. The plane was rocking, tugging at the ropes like a skittish horse, but it wasn't going anywhere. A quarter mile of ragged, tumbling tundra on our right led to the Yukon, but we couldn't see that far.

We turned our parka hoods down to keep the snow out of our faces and trudged into the wind toward the village. With your hood down, you're looking out through a six-inch tunnel, and you keep that mostly pointed down at the road, but there was nothing to see anyway. The thirty-knot wind was a physical force that had to be overcome, so we were leaning into it and pushing, like swimming upstream.

I wondered about John Donne's statement, "No man is an island." He wasn't thinking about winters in the Arctic. I felt exactly like an island, a living thing surrounded by stark dead nothingness. Trudging along in my little circle of vision, with nothing changing, the world so alien and hostile to life, was isolating. The wind was a steady rush, more pressure than sound. You get a feeling of being a very small thing in a very large void and a suspicion that maybe you don't belong there. When I let myself think about where we really were, at the top of the world, a few miles from the frozen Bering Sea, with no civilization between us and the North Pole, I bordered on paranoid.

Sure, Tom was there, trudging along beside me, but I could neither see nor hear him. He, too, would be cocooned in his own little island of self-generated warmth. It was hard to believe that the wind fighting and tugging at us wasn't a live, malevolent thing. The fact that it is mindless, will wear you down and kill you without thought or notice, is its most frightening aspect.

Eventually the road turned, as all roads must. Black willows beside us showed that we were moving in a way that the unchanging white tundra had not. They also showed that the snow was pelting down and swirling in eddies, like a swarm of white bees zipping angrily around. We passed the willows and crossed the village toward Demientoff's cabin.

The houses we passed were like black ghosts, appearing out of the white murk and fading away. The wind was going crazy, blowing under the houses but swirling around where the houses blocked it. A whole band of horns and flutes were trumpeting and whistling, but with no organizing conductor. We'd be leaning into the wind, then in calm for a few feet, then slammed in the back. Snow was drifting up in patterns, long tapering ridges where the wind was blocked but rushing like a river of milk between houses.

Most of the houses were what we called HUD houses because they were built by the U.S. Department of Housing and Urban Development. Before there were government agencies, and after the Eskimos acquired a taste for more comfort than the sod houses like the one Evan built at St. Marys, a good many log homes were built.

Those log homes weren't the picturesque cabins like Lincoln Logs might make on a full scale, and not much related to the peeled-and-varnished edifice that Ski and Punik built. The old-timers were mostly built of driftwood that came down the rivers in the springtime. Logs of various sizes and mixed genres were hewn to fit together. The results were solid and weatherproof but seldom beautiful.

They were built on the ground and were steadily sinking, about a foot every five years. The unheated arctic entries remained at ground level, so you stepped down into the houses. When ground water became a problem, they added a new floor above the sinking one, so the ceilings kept getting lower. Demientoff's floor was one step down and the ceiling had shrunk from eight feet to seven feet, so the floor had been raised at least twice.

We paused in the arctic entry to shake the snow off and throw back our hoods. We were both wearing wolf mitts, but they hang on a leather strap around your neck so you just pull your hands out of them. The entry was rough-cut bare boards with a frozen dirt floor, and served as a walk-in freezer for game as well as keeping the wind out when the cabin door was opened. Tom gave a good loud knock as a matter of form. I think it's a requirement, like telling a fugitive to halt before you shoot him. We expected the house to be vacant so we were surprised when the door was opened by a young woman.

"*Wauka?*" she said, half question, half uncertainty. That's the Yup'ik equivalent of *hi*, or *hello*, but the casual, noncommittal one. If a Yup'ik says *chamai* that means he's glad to see you and wants to visit. She wasn't too sure since she certainly was not expecting strange gussaks to appear in a blizzard.

"May we come in?" Tom asked.

"*Eee-eee.*" She stepped back and held the door open. I think it was Tom's uniform that convinced her. *Eee-eee*, two syllables, accent on the second, is the Yup'ik *yes*, and that term would be understood across language groups, including the Inupiat to the north. Perhaps there's an element of onomatopoeia to it. It's not so different from the Spanish *si, si* or the French *oui, oui*.

The house was warm but dark. An electric lamp, gooseneck with a metal shade, sat on the kitchen table, but no overhead lights were on. A window a foot tall and two feet long on the far side of the room appeared to be frosted or snowed over. The whole house seemed to vibrate with the wind like a loose violin string.

The furniture was an eclectic mix of wooden cast-offs and bare boards. The only decoration in the room was a picture of the Virgin Mary. A narrow shelf under the picture was covered with a white cloth, and two inches of stubby candle flickered on the shelf to light the picture. A second room behind the stove had no door, and the foot of a wooden bed frame was visible.

Our hostess wore the traditional *kuspuk*, a one-piece, A-line affair made of cotton with a light hood attached. The *kuspuk* was elaborately embroidered with flowers, but dimmed by some years. Our hostess was dimmed, too, and it hadn't taken very many years. She was a pretty girl, I guessed not yet twenty, with straight black hair cascading down her back, but she was missing several strategic teeth. Maybe that's why she wasn't smiling.

A toddler, wearing cloth diapers, was crawling around the bare wooden floor. The little boy crawled happily over to check us out. He grabbed my pant leg to pull himself up and ran his little brown hand over my white one, checking to see if I was real.

His mother caught him around the waist and pointedly plunked him down on the floor beside the oil-burning cook stove.

"I'm sorry to intrude, ma'am," Tom was oozing charm and politeness. "We're looking for the Demientoff cabin."

"This is the Demientoff cabin. *Guffiak?*" our hostess asked. That was accompanied by the Yup'ik raised eyebrows that made it a question. She was offering coffee.

"*Quiana.*" (Kwee'ana, thank you) Tom ducked his head in assent.

When Billy Fox down in Kipnuk taught me to ask for *guffiak e suckaluk* he called them the ancient Yup'ik words for coffee and sugar. I did wonder why the ancient language had a word for coffee, but supposed that it was a catchall term, probably including the tundra tea that the Eskimos have made for several thousand years.

I got a different slant on that one dark and stormy night on Akutan Island, halfway down the Aleutian Chain. I had tied the Cessna 310 to two oil drums and the airport skid to keep it from blowing away and was settling in for a bleak night in the village clinic, listening to the wind howl. A lovely young Aleut girl came into the clinic carrying two steaming mugs and offered me *guffiak e suckaluk*.

"Wow," I said. I'm a thousand miles from Bethel and you're speaking to me in Yup'ik?"

"No," she said. "Russian." That cleared up a lot of linguistic mysteries.

Our hostess swept a white pile of needlework to the edge of the table and indicated two chairs. We did our field strip and sat. Neither of us much wanted coffee, but turning it down would have been the social gaffe of the century. Our hostess brought two mugs, mine with a serious crack in it, to the table and lifted the enamelware pot from the stove to pour.

We sipped. It was good, and the cups were clean. I made a show of warming my hands on the cup and savoring the coffee. "*Quianukfa.*" Meaning thank you very much. "*Ah sic took,*" it pleases me. The banter in Yup'ik wasn't because our hostess was short on English. She was checking our credentials. Apparently we passed because my soliloquy brought a bright smile for a moment before she closed her lips.

With the obligatory hostessing out of the way, she pulled the wooden stool she'd probably been using for a footrest to the end of the table and sat down. She didn't join us in drinking coffee, and I was pretty sure that was because she didn't have a third cup.

"You wanted to talk to me?" She seemed both surprised and a little pleased, as if maybe not many people wanted to do that.

"Yes, ma'am," Tom smiled, showing his Scandinavian ivory, then closed his lips. "We have a search warrant to look over Demientoff's belongings. We're working on the case of who killed him, hoping to find some clues."

"Oh, don't you know? He was killed by that big gussak who lives across the river."

"We know it looks like that, ma'am, but we don't think so. The gussak was home in bed with his wife when Demientoff was killed."

"Well, of course Punik backed up his story. She's not from here, you know; she's from upriver somewhere, so you really can't trust her."

"Well, all the same, we'd like to look around. Are these Demientoff's things?" Tom indicated the furniture around the room.

"Oh, no, these are mine. We had the traditional sharing out when he was killed, each person choosing something according to how they were related to him. I got the house, even though my husband was only a fourth cousin. That was the village elders just being nice because we lived in the soddy out back, and maybe no one else wanted the house anyway."

"Is your husband here, ma'am?"

"Paul was killed two summers ago in a barge accident. He never got to see his son because little Paul was born afterwards."

"I'm really sorry to hear that, ma'am. Are you going to be all right?"

"Oh, sure, we're fine. We have welfare and food stamps, and I'm selling my needlework. Now that we have this big beautiful house, there are no problems. We're going to be just fine."

That was a repeat, and I wondered if she was trying to convince us or herself. The little boy deserted his post by the stove and crawled over to me. He climbed right up my snowsuit, snuggled into my lap, and stuck his thumb in his mouth. I wondered if kids can tell when a guy is single and theoretically available. I hugged him; he smiled around the thumb and closed his eyes.

"Is there anything of Demientoff's left?" Tom wondered.

"There are a few things, real personal stuff, in a suitcase." She stood and stepped through the open doorway into the bedroom. She came back carrying an ancient steamer trunk that looked as big as she was and heaved it up onto the table. She opened the hasp and swung back the lid.

There were some clothes in the trunk, ratty stuff that Demientoff had probably intended to throw away. He was rich by village standards and probably lived very comfortably. The clothes he was wearing when we stuffed him into the body bag were new and expensive. The parade of furniture that left that cabin during the sharing out probably looked like bargain day at Macy's.

Tom didn't like it much, but he dug down through the trunk. On top was a bathrobe and a couple of pairs of slippers, underwear, and a torn shirt that no one had wanted. At the bottom was a high-school diploma from Mt. Edgecumbe, the Native boarding school by Sitka, and some National Guard mementos.

Next came photographs, old and faded. He had a class picture from Mt. Edgecumbe with the students all staring grimly at the camera and the teachers looking like prison wardens. The boarding school was on Japonsky Island, but from the expressions in the picture, it could have been Alcatraz. Why is it that old pictures are so obviously old? Maybe the hair is a little different, maybe the clothes, but when a picture is thirty years old or more, you know it.

There was a nice portrait of Demientoff looking like a high-school kid but wearing a National Guard uniform with sergeant's stripes, and another of six young men in uniform lounging beside a WW II cannon at some base with palm trees.

Tom came to the bottom of the trunk, stuffed the detritus back in, and closed the lid. "That's everything of Demientoff's?" he asked.

"Yes, I'm afraid that's all that's left. His good stuff is scattered all around this village and Emmonak, too. Would you like more coffee?" She sounded hopeful, but Tom shook his head.

"No, thanks, we have to be going. I really appreciate your cooperation, Mrs. . . . ?"

"Demientoff. My husband was only a fourth cousin, but he had the name, and maybe that's part of the reason they gave us the house." She almost smiled, the gaps in her teeth showing for a second, and she closed her lips self-consciously. My social conscience was screaming at me. I hoped that someone would marry the girl, get her teeth fixed, and be a father to the little boy who had gone to sleep in my arms.

Unfortunately, you can't save the whole world. I stood up, carried the little chap into the next room, and laid him gently on the bed. On an impulse, I bent and kissed his apple cheek. When I straightened up, Mrs. Demientoff was standing in the doorway watching me. I squeezed her hand when I stepped back into the front room. I think there was more human understanding in her look and our hand squeeze than there is in most half-hour conversations.

Tom and I zipped, pulled on parkas, waved our thanks, and stepped back out into the snowstorm. I noted a pair of snowshoe hares hanging from a nail on the porch, and wondered how many meals they represented.

The snow was still spitting down, but with our backs to the wind we seemed to float right along with it. I taxied back halfway toward the downwind end of the runway, very slowly and very carefully. With the wind behind you, you don't want to hit a berm because if the tail starts up it might keep right on going, up and over. You're holding the yoke forward, as if you were pushing the nose down and the tail up, but with the wind behind you the action of the elevator is reversed. What you don't want is the wind underneath your tail feathers.

We took off more like a kite than an airplane. The prop acted as the kite string and we were flying in a couple of hundred feet. I turned toward the river and we followed the snowmachine trail downwind to Sheldon's Point, weaving back and forth over the ice at treetop height. Locals had stuck small spruce trees in the snow every few hundred feet to mark the trail. That can be important when visibility is low. Even in the fabled and deadly whiteout conditions, the problem isn't that you *can't* see but that there is nothing *to* see. White on white under white just doesn't show. With no direct sunlight to make shadows, it might be hard to pick out a trail through the snow five feet ahead, but a dark tree sticking up may be visible for a couple of hundred feet.

At Sheldon Point, the trail ran between houses toward the lake. I swung to the right, slowed us down, and followed the river beside the houses to the end of the village. We made a tight turn back into the wind around the last house, landed on the lake like a parachute, and taxied up behind the clinic to get us out of the wind.

The calm spot was fifteen feet from the clinic, so I used two tiedown ropes to secure the bale above the left wing strut to the center pillar under the clinic. Snow was pouring under the clinic like a river and making drifts behind everything that wasn't moving, but above waist height there was a calm spot and the plane wasn't rocking.

We turned our backs to the wind and float-walked, along with the snow, across the lake to the post office. The post office had a long narrow arctic entry across the front with windows on both the outside and the inside and a door at each end, like an outside hallway. That was an unusual and very good idea. We let the wind carry us to the door on the downwind end.

The wind on the Delta is pretty reliable: north in winter, south in summer. Village houses are built with the doors on the south side. The village of Nightmute, for instance, has all its doors on the south side. When the wind changes in the springtime to blow in their doors, the whole village packs up and moves to their fish camp, where the doors are on the north side. I got quite a sermon on that subject from Bill Cole one dark and stormy night. Bill was the principal and teacher at the BIA school in Nightmute.

He was from North Dakota, medium-sized and in his thirties. He was a sharp dresser, dress shirts and slacks, wore a neat little mustache, and spoke Midwest-cowboy. We sat in the bright, warm kitchen of his apartment at the school and listened to the wind shriek while we shared his bottle of Chivas Regal.

His first year at Nightmute, Bill got up one spring morning to find that the wind had changed, and no kids showed up for classes. He climbed down the stairs from the BIA hill to the village and wandered from house to house, knocking on doors. He was the only resident left in the village, with a month of school left to teach. The next year he was ready and moved the school to a tent at the fish camp.

Tom and I tromped up into the post office porch. The wind screeched and protested, but we managed to pull the door shut behind us and did our shaking and stomping. Through the second door to the inside, there was a good-sized waiting room. A regulation postal window at the left end allowed a glance at the mysterious inner sanctum, and a young woman standing at the counter behind the window seemed to be on guard duty.

Several people were sitting around the room but apparently were not on postal business. The room was warm, and it was light because of the double windows in the entryway. It was just generally a good place to be on a cold, windy day.

The right end of the room had a door that led back into the living quarters, but there were two yellow tapes stretched across it. One proclaimed, "Crime Scene" over and over, the other said, "Police Line, do not cross." We both had to stop and stare at those tapes because that is not a usual Bush thing. I suppose most big cities are wrapped up in tape like that, but this was new to the area, and I wondered about the origin of that tape.

Tom reached between the tapes to try the door. It wasn't locked, so he shoved it open, ducked under the *Crime Scene*, and stepped over the *Police Line*. I followed him. The room we entered was opulent by Bush standards.

Directly across from us shone nice big windows, double paned so they weren't frosted, and defying the winter with hanging green plants inside. Under the right-hand window, a highly polished wooden dining set reflected the light. We were standing on a carpet between a couch and a big leather recliner. The recliner was kicked back and emitting soft snores.

We detoured around the snoring chair and checked out a big modern kitchen with dishes in the sink. A frying pan with fresh omelet traces sat on the stove. The house was definitely being lived in, and I should have realized that the plants in the living room were being watered. We passed the snoring chair again and glanced into the bedroom. A king-sized bed had been slept in; some dirty socks and underwear were clustered on the floor beside the clothes hamper.

Several pictures on the walls needed a closer look, but it was safer to wake the sleeper first and explore some more afterward. The sleeper was Wassilie, the village cop, and he was wearing his pistol, so it was not a good idea to surprise him. Tom went back and opened the entrance door, then gave a good loud knock on it. The patrons in the waiting room probably thought he was crazy, but when the chips are really down, all Eskimos believe that all gussaks are a little crazy, so we rarely surprise them.

Wassilie broke off in midsnore, slammed the recliner upright and jumped up. Tom was all smiles and bonhomie.

"Hi, Wassilie. Keeping a close eye on the place, I see."

Wassilie jumped into the opening Tom had given him. "Yeah, never know when a killer is going to return to the scene of the crime, and I'm ready for him."

We left that subject there. The fact that Wassilie had moved in, and apparently intended to spend the winter, was none of our business.

"We have a search warrant," Tom explained, "so it's okay to go through Hinkley's things."

"What are you looking for?" Wassilie wondered. "We found that big gussak's snowmachine tracks and followed him almost back to his cabin. Several people saw him ride out of town."

"Well, there are some problems with that." Tom said. "Kawalski was home when Demientoff was killed, and he was shopping in Emmonak while the killer was here."

I'm not sure where Tom got the part about Ski being in Emmonak. I think he just made it up, but he was trying to make a point and I wasn't going to argue with him. After all, Wassilie was exaggerating his snowmachine tracking by twenty miles, and last I heard, the witnesses saw a man, with no further description.

"What we're looking for," Tom explained, "is the connection between all the victims. Can you show us just where Hinkley was sitting when he was shot?"

"Sure." Wassilie walked over to the table and indicated the chair at the head. "He was sitting right here with a glass of whiskey in his hand."

"How about Hooper? Wasn't it about the same?"

"Yeah, he has living quarters attached to the store and he was just having a drink, too, when Kawalski broke in and shot him."

"Any signs of a break-in?" Tom asked.

"Nah, I don't mean he broke in, I just meant he walked in and caught Hooper unawares."

"Well, we think it was different. We think both Hooper and Hinkley were having drinks with someone they knew, and Kawalski has never been to Sheldon Point."

"Yeah?" Wassilie played his trump, "Then where are the other glasses?"

"Probably washed and put away in the cupboard. Let's look around." Tom headed for the bedroom with Wassilie right behind him, so I followed along.

Tom opened a couple of dresser drawers, but the clothes were obviously Wassilie's, blue uniform shirts on top, so he closed the drawers and looked at the pictures on the wall. There were a dozen pictures and Tom worked half-way around the room before he stopped to stare at one.

"Hey, Alex, take a look at this."

I saw what Tom meant. He was looking at a picture of six young men in National Guard uniforms, posing around a WW II cannon with palm trees in the background. I was sure that that picture was printed from the same negative as the picture in Demientoff's trunk.

Tom took the picture down and checked the back. No names. He carried it to the dining table where the light was better.

"Do you know who these guys are?" Tom asked Wassilie. Wassilie took the picture and studied it for a while.

"I think these two are Hooper and Hinkley when they were real young. See, you can tell by the eyes. I don't know the others."

I reached for the picture and scanned the faces, trying to see which men the boys had become, and there on the end, elbow draped across another guy's shoulder, stood Muktuk, looking twenty years younger than he did in Kotlik and maybe a hundred years younger than he did in Nome.

"Well, I'll be damned," Tom said. That was pretty strong language, because Tom was on duty, and troopers do not swear when they're on duty. "Look, the guy he's leaning on is Demientoff, sure as can be, and this one with the heavy eyebrows must be Jesse. Who the heck is the other guy?"

We all stared at the happily smiling face of the guy who was kneeling in front with his arm slung over the cannon barrel. Wassilie was shaking his head and Tom and I were kicking ourselves. We had no idea who he was. The more I stared at that smiling face, the more the smile looked like a sneer, and then a confident smirk. A picture of six men, and five of them dead, could not be a coincidence. That sixth man, whoever he was, was in serious danger.

Tom hung the picture back on the wall, which turned out to be his second mistake in the case. He looked at the rest of the pictures, checked the bookshelves, and inspected the hole in the wall where the .30-06 bullet had disappeared. He seemed to run out of ideas, checked his watch, which told him it would be dark long before we got back to Bethel, and we departed the crime scene.

CHAPTER 21

MAY DAY

Tom did the modern electronic sleuth bit and it didn't help a heck of a lot. He logged onto the state computer system and called up all the members of the National Guard from the Bethel district between fifteen and twenty years ago. That got him four hundred and forty-six names. Then he matched that list with the registered voters in Emmonak and got fifty-three matches, basically every man in Emmonak between forty and sixty years old.

The problem with that approach was that he was only guessing about the fifteen to twenty years part, so if he slid that five years either way he came up with every man in Emmonak between thirty-five and sixty-five. In other words, we were back to my original idea of arresting every man in Emmonak.

It was close to five, after civil twilight, which is a good excuse for a charter pilot to go home and check in with Captain Morgan on a cold dark night. I was thinking that would be a good idea and was just hefting my flight bag into my locker when I heard a voice on the radio that stopped me. The voice was very quiet and calm. It said, "KL7DIT this is KBZ30." I had already jerked my bag back out of the locker and was running through the ready room when the radio said, "Hi, Vickie, this is Punik. Will you please tell Alex that this is Mayday?"

I didn't hear what Vickie said because I was shouting at her to call Trooper Tom, and I wished he was with me, but I wasn't going to wait. Mike was just tying down the 185 when I ran up and threw my flight bag behind the seat. He shrugged and untied the wing he had just secured, then hit the dirt when I blasted him with the prop. I started down the taxiway toward the runway, said, "Screw it," poured on the coal and took off on the taxi strip. The moment I cleared the gas shack, I did a wing over and headed for Emmonak.

That was the end of the histrionics. An airplane is like a ship, in that it has a design speed, or hull speed. In the 185 that speed is one hundred and sixty knots, and you do that with sixty percent power. After that, you can add as much power as you like, burn the engine right off the nose, and go two percent faster. Adding power is like trying to make your car go faster by banging your head against the windshield. It doesn't help, but if you're frustrated, it feels good.

I stayed at four hundred feet, partly because there was a little headwind above me, and partly because the tundra ripping by at one-sixty right below me gave the illusion of speed. I reached back over the seat and unzipped the flight bag. The .357 was in a plastic wrapper on top. I got that unwrapped and in my pocket, along with a full box of shells. Since the bag was open anyway, I pulled out a Hershey bar and took out some of my frustration with the lack of speed on that.

I hit the Yukon right over the cabin, chopped the power, racked the flaps down too soon, did a split S to plunk down on the ice in front of the cabin, and jumped out while the skis were still sliding.

I ran up the trail, bounded up the stairs, and had my fist raised to pound on the door when the door opened and I sprawled right onto the carpet. The door slammed behind me. Punik was sitting on the floor behind the door, rifle in her hand, but howling with laughter at my undignified arrival.

I sat up, and at first glance everything was normal, then I noticed bullet holes in the big front window, and when I looked around, every window I could see had been shot out. Punik's laughter was tapering off, and there was a hint of hysteria along with her mirth.

"Punik, what happened?" Not a very astute question, but it suited my position, still sitting on the floor.

"Someone was shooting at me through the windows. I killed the lights, grabbed my rifle, and started shooting back."

"One someone, or lots of someones?"

"Only one, I think. He was riding around and around on a snowmachine, shooting through different windows. I was afraid to put my head up to look, so I just reached up to point the rifle, sort of where the sound was coming from, and shot at it. I thought maybe if I shot a lot, they would think that Ski was here too and that would scare them away."

It was dark inside the cabin, but there was enough light from the sky through the windows to let us see a little. The 12-gauge shotgun was lying on the floor by the kitchen door. "Did you shoot that, too?" I asked.

"Yeah, I thought if I shot the rifle and the shotgun at the same time, the guy would be sure there were two of us here. Maybe it worked, because he took off right after, but I forgot that the shotgun was going to kick. It went flying over my head and banged into the wall."

"How long ago did he leave?" I asked.

"About twenty minutes, I think. I called Vickie right after the first shot, and I think he kept shooting for about half an hour. Oh, Alex, it was awful."

"Okay, sweetheart, you did really well, and it's probably all over. There'll be a good moon tonight, so no one is going to sneak up on us. Can I borrow a five-gallon bucket?"

Punik got up from behind the door, but she carried her rifle with her out to the kitchen and came back with an empty five-gallon lard bucket. I took the bucket and then realized I didn't much want to go outside.

"Look," I decided, "I've got to go out to the airplane. How about you leave the door open, lie on the floor, and keep me covered?"

She nodded, I opened the door and no bullets came screaming in, so I took my .357 in hand and tried not to run down the trail. When I looked back, the barrel of Punik's .30-.30 was lying across the doorsill. I jumped into the airplane, fired it up, spun it around, and taxied it between my ropes that were still left from Christmas. I stuck Punik's bucket under the cowling vent, reached in and popped the quick-drain valve. The hot oil spurted out into the bucket while I tied down the plane and dug out the cowling cover.

When the gush of oil tapered off, I closed the valve and covered the engine. I carried the oil back up to the house and no bullets hit me in the back. Punik got up when I stepped onto the porch, and I made a dignified and upright entrance. The bucket of oil fit behind the stove, and I wandered over to stand by the kitchen window and stare out into the dark woods. Punik handed me a cup of coffee and took her own to the living room to watch the front.

For an hour nothing happened, except that Punik brought me another cup of coffee. Then a plane flew over low and circled to land beside the 185. It is a thrilling experience to watch a really good pilot set a 206 down. He drifted over the ice, right at stalling speed, keeping himself in the air with just a whisper of power. He cleared the final ridge of ice by four inches, chopped the power, and was rolling on the first smooth foot of ice.

The plane rolled for half the manufacturer's specified distance, spun around, and taxied back to park beside the 185. The door popped open and Tom and Mike came trotting up the trail. Punik opened the front door and snapped on a flashlight to show them it was okay to come in. I resisted a terrible urge to trip them.

With the cavalry there, it didn't seem so dangerous anymore. Punik turned on a couple of battery-operated lamps. I shoved the .357 in my belt and Punik leaned her .30-30 against the gun cabinet while she went to get the coffee. Punik repeated her tale and Tom listened attentively. He was obviously thinking in terms of profanity, but he was on duty so didn't voice it.

"Maybe we should have a look at those snowmachine tracks. I'll bet dollars to doughnuts it was a wide-track Polaris." Tom drew his revolver and Punik handed him the flashlight. I got the .357 in my hand, and Tom and I walked out the back door. Moonlight gave a bluish cast to the cleared circle behind the house and the old generator shack. Ski had kept a path tramped down from the porch to the shack, and no new tracks came from the woods. Tom gestured for me to circle the shack left while he turned right. Snow was two feet deep most of the way with a three-foot drift at the back. I waded through that and met Tom. No new tracks, so no one lurking. Tom snapped on the flashlight and we followed the beam into the shadows under the spruce trees.

From Punik's description, we did believe the attacker was gone, but that was far from a sure thing. Tom held the flashlight at arm's length in his left hand, following the beam with his pistol. I stayed one step behind him on his right side in case someone shot at the flashlight. Snow varied from a few inches to three-foot drifts where wind had swirled around the trees. We skirted the drifts, trying to see where a shot might come from, but all of the shadows were moving, and every one of them looked like a man with a rifle.

I tried to tell myself that we were okay unless the light glinted on steel, and that didn't happen. The snowmachine track was worn deep because the rider had used the same trail several times. It had been made by a wide-track Polaris. We turned and followed the trail to a spot where we had a view under trees to the back of the house. Tom stooped and picked up casings from three .30-06 shells. He pocketed those. All was quiet on the northern front. We crunched back to our original trail and returned to the house.

We stopped on the back porch to stomp and brush snow off our pants and boots. Tom was in his thinking mode, but I couldn't help bugging him. "Well, detective, any brilliant conclusions?"

"Maybe. At least I have a good idea of where the mystery machine is coming from."

Mike and Punik were standing at the kitchen window watching our excursion, and Punik was carrying her rifle again. The four of us wandered into the living room to look out over the river. Jets of cold air poured in through bullet holes in the big picture window. Punik set her rifle down and disappeared into the kitchen. She came back with a roll of two-inch-wide duct tape and started putting bandages over the bullet holes.

"You were about to identify the mystery machine?" I prompted.

"Has to be Jesse's. Mike and I will hop over to Emmonak, and I expect that machine will still be warm. We'll report the attack to Joe. We're out of his jurisdiction, but I'm betting that the machine isn't. Maybe someone saw who was riding it. At least Joe can keep an eye on it."

Punik looked the question at me, and I nodded. "I'm staying right here until morning. You did a good job of protecting yourself, but let's not try it again. Having an airplane outside should discourage attackers."

Tom was still thinking. "The enigma is getting worse. We've got to figure out why anyone would want to frame Ski, and now, why he was here shooting up the cabin when he must have known that Ski wasn't here."

Tom had a heck of a point there, but I didn't think it was conclusive. "Maybe whoever it was figured that shooting at Punik would bring Ski out of hiding?"

"Maybe," Tom conceded. "Do you know how to contact Ski?" He was asking me, and I nodded. Ski had told me where his hideout was on Christmas Day, and I hoped he'd still be there.

"Is it safe for Ski to come home?" I asked.

"Well, Perkins has cooled off considerably. Punik, you should have been a trial lawyer. You're a regular Portia. Perkins came home from your meeting wondering if maybe he was the killer himself." He turned to me. "Alex, you do realize there's going to be one more murder, and this one will be our fault."

I nodded. A picture of six men, with five of them dead, had to be a lot more than coincidence. I did not point out that Tom had had that picture in his hand while we were in Sheldon Point and had left it there. "I'll get Ski back here, and then hop down to Alakanuk and grab the picture from Demientoff's trunk. You'll be back in the morning?"

"I'll see if Jesse's machine happens to still be warm from tonight's attack. Maybe someone saw who was driving it. If I can find a witness, I'll arrest whoever was here tonight for terroristic threatening, if not for the murders. If that doesn't work we'll take the picture to Auntie Vi in the morning. She'll know who that sixth guardsman is."

Tom had a good idea there. Auntie Vi was the matriarch of Emmonak. No one knew how old she was. She had no idea herself. I doubt that anyone knew exactly how many great-grandchildren and great-great grandchildren she had in the village; there were just too many to keep track. Auntie Vi was a walking canon of Emmonak history, and the history of Kwiguk before there was an Emmonak.

She lived alone in a driftwood cabin that sat next to the riverbank at the far end of the village. The *alone* part was her choice, her statement of independence, but it was a figurative thing. There were seldom fewer than twenty people jammed into her cabin, most of them toddlers, and it was assumed that all of them were her progeny.

Tom zipped his snowsuit, so Mike reluctantly put down his coffee cup and followed.

"When you see us take off from Emmonak, fire up your airplane radio. We'll tell you what's happening on 122.5. In any case, you find Ski in the morning and get him back here. If people are going to shoot at the son and heir, Ski will want to be here, to protect mama, too, of course." Tom patted Punik's belly. Punik stood on tiptoes to kiss his cheek, and Tom and Mike stepped out into the darkness.

Punik turned off the lamp so that it was dark inside, just on general principles. I stood in the doorway with Punik's rifle while we watched the cavalry walk down the trail, fire up the 206, and hop across the river to Emmonak. The moon was doing a good job, reflecting off the snow, but it was inky black under the trees. I walked to the back door every few minutes, peering around the edge of the broken window, but I really couldn't see anything beyond the cleared back yard.

For a while, we listened to utter quiet until I heard the 206 start up two miles away at the Emmonak airport. I slipped out and stayed in the dark alley under the trees beside the trail. I turned on the master switch and the radio, no lights. The 206 lifted off, rotating beacon on the tail showed over the cannery, then the clearance lights. Tom was on the radio as soon as they left the ground.

"Bingo, Jesse's machine is still warm, and it looks like someone shot the windshield off with a shotgun. There's blood on the seat, but not much. No one saw the machine come or go, and Joe doesn't seem to be in the village, at least we couldn't find him. Are you guys going to be all right?"

"Roger, and roger. You'll be back in the morning?"

"Yep, bright and early. We need to find that sixth guy before the killer does."

"Have a good trip," I said. I clicked off the switches and climbed back up the trail. If you're wondering why I had to go down to the airplane to talk to them when there was a radio in the house, it's because the frequencies are different. Listening to an airplane on the single sideband radio would be like trying to tune in an FM station on your TV.

The problem Tom had in the village with witnesses and the snowmachine was that people in the villages don't hear machines, and they don't hear dogs. It's like if you live in LA or Manhattan, you don't hear cars. You automatically tune them out so that you can hear other things. If a machine started in the middle of the night, it would be heard for miles, but in the evening it's just part of the background noise.

"How shall we work it?" Punik asked.

"Sleep in shifts?" I suggested.

"Sounds reasonable. I'm not sleepy at the moment, so why don't you sleep first?"

"Are you kidding? I'm wired like a Christmas tree. I'll take the back."

I guess we spent an hour or more, me wandering from the kitchen window to the back door and returning, Punik in the easy chair, looking out over the river with the rifle in her lap. I really figured we were safe. No one could get within a mile of us on a machine, and if anyone tried to walk over from one of the villages, Punik would see him on the river, unless he took a three-mile hike upriver first.

I tried to psych out just what the killer's plan had been and whether he had accomplished his objective. If the whole thing was a charade to get Ski back to the house, that had worked. I'd go after Ski at first light, but maybe he was after Punik as well. Whoever was trying to frame Ski had to be thinking with loose screws, so why not kill Punik, too?

I tried to visualize a raving maniac, killing indiscriminately, but that didn't work. This killer had specific targets and reasons and was really pretty clever in his attempts to frame Ski. That brought me back to the dead end of any reason to harm Ski and/or Punik.

If I was going to assume a rational killer, then there had to be a rational reason for removing Ski. The word *removing* struck a new chord.

The killer had every reason to suppose that Ski would be removed immediately, straight to jail, and Tom's refusal to arrest Ski must have been frustrating. Following that line of reasoning, if Ski had been arrested, it was reasonable to suppose that Punik would move, at least back to her cousin's home in Emmonak. I was starting to wonder if someone had designs on the house itself, when Punik came into the kitchen.

"I'm going to bed, Alex. I think the show is over, and I really am tired."

"Good idea. I'll just hang out here a while longer."

"Thanks for everything, Alex." She gave me her ritual cheek kiss, handed me her rifle, and glided away toward the bedroom.

I stuck the .357 in my belt. I did feel a little silly waving it around toward a menace that wasn't coming, but I carried the rifle with me and expanded my beat to include the front window.

More time went by. The moon passed the house and was shining in the front windows. I was staring out over the frozen river, watching the way the moon turned the scene into blue-tinted wedding cake frosting, when a shadow slipped out of the trees downriver. At first I saw only the shadow from the moonlight, a black spider crawling along the edge of the ice. It could have been a man crawling, but the shadow was way too fast and much too graceful.

The shadow stopped on the edge of the ice fifty feet from the airplane and remained motionless for a couple of long minutes. When it moved again, I could make out the coloring of a gray wolf, just darker than the snow. He crouched and stalked toward the plane, maybe thinking of killing it, until he got close enough to smell it. He marched over, raised a leg and thoroughly claimed the ski, then trotted on up the river.

I was grateful to the wolf because his trek proved beyond any doubt that no one was lurking in the woods. I sat down in the easy chair, rifle across the arms, and let my eyes close until sunrise colors tweaked the horizon. When it was light enough to see under the trees, I struggled into my snowsuit, pulled on parka and mitts, and carried the rifle out the back door to look around.

The snow was piled helter-skelter through the trees, some places four feet deep, many places almost bare. I followed our tracks from the night before to the snowmachine trail and turned to follow it again. Tom's information about the shattered windshield was intriguing. The place where the windshield had been shot was obvious with little bits of plastic scattered over the snow, shining like tiny mirrors in the morning light. I picked up two more .30-06 shells.

When I got back to the cabin, Punik handed me coffee.

"Find anything?"

"Looks like Annie Oakley was practicing with a shotgun. You shot his windshield off at almost fifty yards."

"Is that good?"

"Might be a world record with a shotgun. I can certainly see why he left."

"Want some breakfast?"

"Not just yet. Why don't I go find Ski and you can cook for three . . . or four. I guess you're eating for two now?"

I carried the warm oil down to the river, took the cowling cover off, popped the Zeus fasteners with my pocketknife and removed half the cowling. That let me pour the oil straight down into the filler pipe. I snapped the cowling back on, pulled the prop a few turns, and the engine started. I let it warm, then did my trick of covering it while I untied the plane and tried to clean out the lard bucket with snow. That didn't work very well because the minute the oil residue cooled, it turned to molasses.

I carried the bucket back up to the cabin and collected a thermos of coffee and two cups. That brightened Punik up considerably because she finally let herself believe that Ski was coming home.

You kick the skis loose from the snow before you climb in, and the ski the wolf had claimed required some serious whacks. I took off and stayed low, right up the river, around the bend, and found the second slough. I circled twice, per instructions, landed on the smooth ice, and climbed out to lean against the strut and pour myself a cup of steaming hot coffee from the thermos. The area was pristine, just my ski tracks and unmarked nature, cold but scintillating in the morning light. Snow and birch trees had a pastel gleam, reflecting back the sunrise colors. I got that feeling of being the only inhabitant of an alien planet, only this planet wasn't trying to kill me; it was spreading its graceful charms for my enjoyment.

I'd sipped half a cup when what could have been a bear burst out of the trees and jumped over the snowbank at the edge of the slough. This bear was walking upright and was piebald: beaver hat, wolf parka, brown snowsuit, blue shoepacks. I poured a second cup and handed it to Ski. He looked pretty good, except for a three-day beard, and he didn't smell too bad, considering.

We decided that since he was moving home to stay, he should bring his gear and his snowmachine. Ski kept the thermos; I made more ski tracks on the slough. I climbed up to a couple thousand feet and checked the area, flew back and circled the cabin, then back upriver again. Ski's machine busted out onto the main river and shot down the trail toward the cabin. He appeared to be the only thing moving, so I drifted over and landed at Emmonak.

Tom had been right about Jesse's machine. The windshield looked as if it had been chewed up by a wolverine. I didn't see any blood, but heck, I'm still a novice detective. I wandered down to the village store and waited for it to open. The store in Emmonak is a monster affair operated by the Alaska Commercial Company, capable of meeting the demands of five hundred extra cannery workers during the summer.

When Archie finally came to open, still carrying a cup of coffee with him, I followed him in. I'd been thinking about Mrs. Demientoff's selling her needlework for cash, probably working all day for a ten-dollar bill, and I was hatching a plan. Five large-size blue blazers, summer weight, were on a rack. Archie helped me find embroidery thread. He fixed me up with a box of gold and a box of white, probably enough thread to reach to Bethel, but neither of us had a handle on estimating.

In the toy department, a volleyball and a truck with wheels that turned and a bed that dumped jumped into my cart. Archie wrote up the credit card slip for the merchandise and added "$500 for photographic equipment." He opened the safe and gave me the $500 in twenty-dollar bills. I rolled the bills, stuffed them in my pocket, and lugged two shopping bags back to the airplane.

Tom would be coming back, but he probably wouldn't leave Bethel until after eight, so I still had an hour before I should expect him.

Since the 185 was on skis, it could land on the river behind the store at Alakanuk and taxi up behind Demientoff's cabin. Mrs. Demientoff opened the door, but looked skeptical about letting me in by myself.

"Hi, I want to discuss some business with you, and I need one of the photographs out of Demientoff's trunk." She opened the door and stepped back, but she looked like a deer ready to bolt at the first provocation. I picked up the shopping bags and stepped inside. Being Irish has its advantages. I've never kissed the Blarney stone myself, but plenty of my ancestors have. I lied like the silver-tongued snake that I am.

"I saw your needlework when we were here the other night. You do really nice work, and I wonder if you can help me out. I need some jackets embroidered, or appliquéd, or whatever the term is, and I'd really appreciate it if you could do them for me." I pulled the jackets out of the sack and spread one on the table.

"What I need is for them to say 'Bushmaster Air' in the top half of a circle and 'Alaska' underneath, then a picture of Mt. Denali in the center of the circle." Using Mt. Denali for jackets from Bethel was a bit of a stretch, but a straight line of green or white tundra wouldn't look very good. I had her interest all right. She brought paper and pencil and sketched exactly what I wanted, and I was glad to see that she really was an artist.

Her son wobbled out of the bedroom, wiping sleep from his eyes with tiny fists. I scooped him up and hugged him, then sat him down and handed him the bag with the ball and the truck in it. He was fascinated by the bag and towed it around the room as if he was leading a puppy. I set the boxes of thread on the table and asked to see the trunk again. She dragged it out and I glommed onto the picture of the smiling sextet around the cannon. Definitely the same picture we had found in Sheldon Point.

I backed toward the door. "Oh, by the way," I said, "let me pay you in advance for the jackets. That way you can just mail them to Bushmaster in Bethel when they're done, in case I don't get back up here at the right time." I handed her the tightly rolled bundle of twenty-dollar bills and fled.

Maybe $500 was too much for that job, maybe it wasn't. What I kept thinking about was that night in Nome with Connie. I had $500 in my pocket that night, too, and all we really got for it was helacious hangovers and a miserable flight back to Bethel. From a purely selfish point of view, I had already enjoyed this $500 more than I had that one, and the jackets for the pilots were a pure bonus.

Tom and Mike landed just ahead of me at Emmonak. I handed Tom the picture and we marched through the village to confront Auntie Vi. She was enthroned in a wooden chair at her kitchen table, wearing a bright blue *kuspuk* and thick white braids wound around on top of her head. Four or five generations of women were chatting away when we stepped through the door but ceased instantly and sort of faded back into the corners. Auntie Vi invited us in with a regal wave of her hand and offered *guffiak*.

The way she cleared the toddlers and crawlers off the table reminded me of that scene in the movie *The Egg and I*, where Ma Kettle shoos the chickens off the table. We sat, two young women rushed to serve us, and the ritual began. Tom asked about her health, then about as many of her kids as he could remember. When he bogged down, I added a couple more names. Auntie Vi solemnly assured us that all were well.

She set our minds at ease about each of her grandchildren, then started on the great-grandchildren, until she got lost and a couple of voices from the corners added more names. She stopped with that generation, the social obligation apparently satisfied, and launched into an abbreviated family history, starting with the day they fought their way in skin boats through floating ice cakes to land on this shore and start Emmonak. We sipped and listened, and the truth is, it was pretty interesting. You want to hear those stories, at least once.

We looked at a picture of one of her granddaughters in cap and gown graduating from Berkeley. That was Tom's cue to produce the picture of the six National Guardsmen. Auntie Vi caught the granny glasses that hung from a chain around her neck and perched them on her tiny nose. She ticked off the names of the guardsmen just the way we had figured. She paused at the impishly smiling kneeler.

"And this scamp here grew up to be our very own village policeman, Joe."

CHAPTER 22

JOE IS MISSING

Joe was not in the village, and neither was the big black Arctic Cat that the village provided as the official police vehicle.

"What do you think?" I asked. "Did he realize he's on the list and run, or is he already dead?"

"Good questions, and the answer might be 'none of the above'. Let's check his house."

We tromped up the stairs into his arctic entry; the door wasn't locked. The HUD houses come with locks and keys, but the villagers probably don't know what they're for. In the Arctic, your life may depend on getting inside a house. Even knocking on a closed door is not part of the Eskimo culture. If you want to go into a house, you just open the door and go in. No one is surprised, and no one minds.

One night in Bethel, a sudden blizzard caught me at the airport. I made it about a mile before the pickup bogged down, and I waded through drifts the last quarter mile to the first house. No one was there, but I made myself at home. The next day, after Bethel dug itself out, we discovered that a half dozen people had spent the night in the nearest house, sometimes with no idea whose home they had invaded. Someone spent the night in my cabin, washed the dishes, and left a note that just said, "Thanks."

Several years ago, when I was embroiled in the relatively urban miasma of Anchorage, still innocent of the mores of the Bush, I was surprised to wake up in the middle of the night to find a young Eskimo woman shaking me. She had found the front door unlocked, wandered through the house, found me asleep and woke me. She asked directions to the Native hospital. I stammered them out, and before I was awake enough to dress and give her a ride, she had vanished into the night. What she did made perfect sense. I was happy to give directions, and I've always been sorry that I didn't give her a ride because she had over a mile to go. Still, to a city boy, it was disconcerting.

Joe's HUD house had a front room, spacious by Eskimo standards, with a gold-flecked white linoleum floor, an oil-fired space heater, table, chairs, and a couch. The room was clean except for boot tracks on the linoleum that led into the kitchen. I wondered if Joe ever actually stopped in the living room or knew what it was for.

The kitchen had light blue linoleum, an oil-fired cook stove, a table, two wooden chairs, and a sink. Since there is no running water in Emmonak, there was a dip barrel beside the sink with ice cakes floating in it. The cupboard doors were all open, and in the bedroom closets were open, covers ripped off the bed, but these were the tracks of a hasty departure, not a slovenly lifestyle.

"Why the devil did he take off?" I wondered. "When he knew he was in danger, why not ask for help, protective custody or something?"

"Maybe he doesn't trust us, but I think it's more than that. Whatever those guys were involved in, it was heavy stuff and you can bet it was illegal. Remember, Muktuk took off too. Seems like they're more afraid of their secret coming out than of being killed. We're not dealing with choir boys caught cheating at Bingo."

Joe had apparently taken the big quilted comforter that comes with every HUD bed, but he undoubtedly had a sleeping bag, too. Most ominously, a gun cabinet hung open and empty. We didn't find any pictures or any notepads with impressions fortuitously left on them.

Tom had stopped to inspect the empty gun cabinet. "He left in a hurry, but under his own steam. Looks to me like he's planning to hide out in the bush." He closed the cabinet and we checked out the bathroom.

The bathroom had a tub, a sink, and a commode, but of course, there was no plumbing. Beside the commode sat the arctic equivalent, a wooden box with a toilet seat on top, a honey bucket inside, and a bottle of Pine-Sol beside it. The medicine cabinet over the sink was open and a metal Band-Aid box was spilled into the sink, an open bottle of hydrogen peroxide perched on the edge.

It appeared to me that the large bandages were all missing. "Looks like a little first aid was administered. To Joe, or someone else?"

"I'm not taking any bets on who." Tom did a quick check of the open cabinet. "What I will bet is that the bandages have something to do with the snowmachine being shot up. Let's check the village."

I wondered who would be living in that house if we came back in a week.

We wandered through the village and hung around the store for a while, asking about Joe. No one had seen him since the previous afternoon. Tom and Mike headed back to Bethel, via the river and any likely looking tracks they found. I took off and flew down the Emmonak River toward the coast, both of us listening to 122.5 in case we spotted Joe.

A regular snowmachine highway led down that river, with branches off here and there. Fish camps were scattered along the river where Eskimo families spend their summers. Most camps had shacks or sheds, and many had machine tracks leading into them, but none of the tracks was recent. The river petered out, the willows disappeared from the banks, but the ice and the tracks continued.

The sea ice was tossed and stacked like a miniature version of the Dakota Badlands. Many chunks were the size of small houses. One monster sheet, almost big enough to land on, was tilted up ten degrees because it had plowed right over the pack ice beside it.

The trail wound around the largest cakes, over hummocks and past cracks, heading out to sea. Tracks left the main trail, going their separate ways where Emmonak hunters had split up in their never-ending quest for seals. I spotted a couple of kill sites where the snow was littered with splotches of black blood. Then I saw a whole family of seals, scrambling off their sun porches and diving into holes through the ice. That told me that no one was lurking in the vicinity.

I turned around, buzzed the fish camps along the way, then turned down the Yukon and checked the camps and trails toward Sheldon Point, but it wasn't going to do any good. All Joe had to do was pull under a tree or throw a white tarp over his machine, and I could fly over him all day without seeing him. It's tough enough to find someone you're searching for who wants to be found, impossible to find someone who doesn't. I went back to Ski's cabin to see if there was any breakfast left.

It was too late for breakfast, but Punik fried me a moose steak that had been marinated in something like an Italian dressing (heavy on the lemon extract), with a couple of scrambled eggs beside it and a big hunk of toasted homemade bread. The steak was wonderful, much like German sauerbraten.

The toast was "buttered" with salted lard, not very different from margarine, and don't knock it until you've tried it . . . well, maybe tried it and gotten used to it. It's the usual spread in the Arctic, maybe because you can't buy margarine in five-gallon buckets.

Ski had patched most of the windows. He had used a wide roll of transparent tape over the holes in the front picture window, but the seal between the double panes was broken so the window was starting to frost. Thermopane windows work because there are two layers of glass with vacuum in between. The inside glass never gets cold, the outside glass never gets warm, and since there is no moisture in the vacuum between them, they don't frost over; at least, they don't if they don't have bullet holes.

Ski had covered the smaller windows with clear Visqueen. He had shaved, too, so our gathering at the table looked normal. I swallowed steak so that I could talk.

"We're pretty sure that our man is from Emmonak. He's almost certainly the one that Annie Oakley gunned down with the shotgun, and that means he's been using Jesse's machine. Now, we're very much afraid that he's after Joe."

"But why?" Ski wanted to know. "Why all the killing, and why pick on us?"

I had to chew some steak before I could answer, not that I had an answer. "Did you ever hear or see an old Sherlock Holmes story called *Crucifer of Blood*?"

"Sure," Punik piped up. "It was a play, and I read it at the mission. A bunch of old guys in England were being bumped off, I think, and the reason was from when they were all young soldiers in Africa."

"Yeah, that's about the way I remember it." This time my mouth was empty for a change. "We're thinking that the reason for the killings has to do with something that happened when all these guys were in the National Guard together. We just haven't figured out how you fit into it."

"Just how nervous should we be?" Ski asked.

"Well, I think you'll be safe, so long as you keep a rifle pointed out every window. Joe left the village but probably didn't go far. Remember, you dropped off the face of the earth less than three miles from here, and Joe could do the same. Maybe the killer is after Joe now and will forget about you. You weren't ever in the Alaska National Guard?"

"Hardly," Ski said.

"Well, guys, I hate to eat and run, but I guess I will. We'll stay glued to the single-sideband. Maybe you or Tom will get some good ideas."

On the way home, I circled over Ski's hideout on the slough and didn't see a thing after the track a mile away where Ski left the main river. If Ski could do that, Joe could do it too. Maybe he'd be safe. The killer had been shooting people in their houses, not tracking them through the wilderness.

CHAPTER 23

FINAL VISIT

He sat on the running board of the big Arctic Cat, feeling the warmth of the engine against his shoulder. He had the comforter from his bed, the plain white side up, covering the machine and himself so that only his head poked out, just one black spot among the willows on the riverbank. He watched the 185 lift off the ice in front of the cabin two miles downstream and scoot upriver toward him.

The airplane disappeared around the bend half a mile upstream; then he heard it circle and land, so now he knew where the big gussak had been hiding. He knew that the trapline story was crap, and he'd been half afraid that the gussak was close enough to hear the ruckus when he shot up the cabin, but that damn little hellcat inside had been problem enough. He felt the Band-Aids on his cheek and temple where the shotgun pellets had grazed him. *Why couldn't she have been a normal girl and run home to mama when her man deserted her?*

He had places to go and things to do, but first he had to get into that cabin for a few hours. *Just a couple of hours by myself in that cabin, then downriver and across the tundra to Cape Romanzoff. My National Guard training will get me on a military flight to Fort Richardson in Anchorage, and then I can head for Guam and find my father.*

He scooped up a handful of snow and ate it. *Maybe my father did stumble into the river in a drunken stupor and drown. That's what the other villagers assumed, but I was never able to accept that.* His recurring dream since

179

childhood had been of his father on a tropical beach under palm trees. He liked to think that his father was gazing longingly across the ocean, yearning for the wife and son he had left behind.

Sometimes he dreamed of a happy reunion with hugs and tears, sometimes he pictured himself finding his father and killing him for deserting the family. *That part I will play by ear when the time comes. First I have to get to Guam and find the truth.*

The 185 climbed back into the air and circled. *Dumb gussak pilot probably thought that I'd be sitting in the middle of the river waving a sign that says, "Come and get me."*

The plane patrolled up and down the river, circling the cabin then coming back to turn directly over him. He waved at the airplane, but kept his waving arm under the white comforter. Ski's blue Polaris burst out of the scrub across the river and flew toward the cabin. The airplane settled down at Emmonak, and he was alone on the river.

He rolled up his comforter, held it in his lap, and turned the key to start the Cat. He nosed around through the willows, used his original track back to the main trail on the river, and followed the tracks on the other side where the gussak had come down off the riverbank.

The tracks led him up the bank, wound through willows, and took him into a stand of spindly black spruce. There wasn't much snow on the ground under the evergreens, but he followed the trail, sometimes over bare spruce needles, occasionally over drifts. The wholesome, pungent smell of spruce was calming, comforting. The trail led him back down the river, around the end of the first slough, and across a bare patch of ice behind the beaver dam that had cut off the slough.

Spruce grew thicker after the beaver pond. He bumped and twisted between the trees, feeling confident because he could not be seen from the air. The trail led him upstream, back toward the main river, and finally to the head of the peninsula where the spring floods had piled logs and mud fifteen feet high. He shut off his machine and threw the comforter over it, but there was really no need; he was still invisible from the air.

One of Bushmaster's 206s came upriver and circled over the second slough. He climbed up on a log so he could see the slough and what had attracted the pilot's attention. There were the ski tracks from the 185, and footprints through the snow leading from this grove to where the plane had parked and back. The 206 jogged back toward the river and continued toward Bethel.

That told him quite a lot. *The passenger in that plane must be Trooper Tom, and Tom would have seen the shot-out windshield on Jesse's machine. Damn that hellcat woman. If Ski went home while Tom was there, then that meant Ski was no longer wanted for the murders. Maybe he shouldn't have run, because if they hadn't suspected him before, they would now, but the marks on his face from the shotgun, matching what had happened to the snowmachine windshield, would have been hard to explain. That shotgun was lousy luck. The load was completely spent, mostly just falling, but it had hit the windshield dead center.*

He wondered if they really had suspected him. There had to be a reason why the trooper hadn't arrested the gussak, but what was it? *I didn't make any mistakes. Every one of the murders was smooth as silk. Each of the victims trusted me, and was panting for the anniversary next month when they would share out the ten million dollars. They all agreed to the ten-year wait and that worked. No one was even interested in the case. Those idiots in Sheldon Point believed that Demientoff and Jesse had been killed by a robber. They didn't say so, but you could see that they were pleased. They thought it meant a bigger share for them. The only partner who might have been a problem was Muktuk in Kotlik, and that dumb jerk had got himself killed right on schedule with no help.*

He followed the footprints through the spruce needles, climbed over a log, and found himself in Ski's hideout, a natural cave-like room in a pile of driftwood. The hole between logs was right at the edge of the trees, almost sticking out into the main river, so it had a good snow cover over the top. He went back to his machine and lugged his gear and groceries into the driftwood cave.

Ski had made a mattress of spruce boughs beside a tiny mud fire ring. He sat on his sleeping bag but didn't unroll it. *Not bad. This cave is roomier than the soddy I was raised in at the edge of Emmonak.* He used some dry spruce boughs to make a minuscule smokeless fire in Ski's fire ring. He opened a can of beef stew, leaving the lid attached for a handle, and propped it next to the fire to heat.

The smell of the heating stew, and the clean woodsy smell of the burning spruce, took him back to the soddy of his childhood. It was a rare and precious night when his mother was cooking a dinner. Many nights he had waited, his stomach rumbling with hunger, hoping that his father would bring home food. Sometimes his father brought home a chunk of seal or a fish. Those times the family feasted, and his mother looked young and happy.

Other nights, his father came home empty-handed, or worse, drunk. He went to sleep hungry those nights and used dreams of being rich to mask the pain in his stomach. His father came home drunk more and more often, then stopped coming home. He was twelve years old when he became the family breadwinner. He hustled, fished, trapped, and hunted, but there were many hungry nights. He had spent those nights plotting how to get rich and how to find his missing father.

He stirred the stew and remembered those years. By the time he was fifteen, it wasn't a dream anymore, it was becoming a plan. He wanted to see his mother happy every night and wanted to buy her gussak dresses like the other women wore. That didn't happen. His mother began to cough up blood and got thinner and thinner. She shivered with cold, even when he had built a driftwood fire and the soddy was so warm he could barely breathe. She died when he was sixteen, and he was on his own, his only legacy his dreams of wealth. Now it was going to happen.

He unwrapped his arsenal from the oilcloth he'd stripped off his kitchen table. He selected his .30-06 rifle, his .38 revolver, and a box of shells for each. He wrapped the shotgun, the .300 Savage, and the rest of his ammunition back in the waterproof oilcloth.

The stew was steaming. He opened a package of pilot crackers to go with it and ate his breakfast while he thought over his plan. *The sure way to get the gussak and his hellcat out of the cabin was to burn the place, but do I dare risk it? Would the fire also burn the old, tinder-dry log cabin that was almost attached to the new one?*

He was going to have to walk back to the cabin. The machine would make too much noise. Didn't dare use the river either; too much chance of meeting someone on the trail. Wading through brush for three miles would take until almost dark, but if he didn't get lucky tonight, he'd rough it in the woods and get lucky tomorrow. All he needed was one clear shot at the gussak. Outside would be best. The hellcat would come running out and he'd shoot her, too.

He slung his sleeping bag and his rifle on his back, hung the holstered .38 on his belt, and filled his pockets with trail mix and candy bars. He struck out southwest under the spruce trees to parallel the river. He thought it might be a good omen that he was also walking in the direction of Guam.

If the guys had continued to follow his instructions, the entire plan, right through the sharing on the tenth anniversary, would have worked. Instead, they seemed to have forgotten that he was the mastermind. They were treating him with the same disrespect he had received when he was a skinny kid trying to survive in Emmonak. Worse, they were already flaunting their wealth in ways that might draw attention.

Those two simpletons in Sheldon Point had accepted his explanation for bringing a rifle in and leaning it against their tables. He told them he was looking for moose on the way down, and they believed it, although there hadn't been a moose south of Alakanuk for twenty years. All of them were dumb. It still rankled that the Guard had made Demientoff a sergeant while he remained a lowly specialist first class. The Guard, like everyone else, judged men only by their size.

Well, all that was over now. He would have the rest of the ten million, which he certainly deserved. After the robbery, he had given each of the others $60,000 and that story about government loans. He had only taken $5,000 for himself, enough to pay for a few trips into Anchorage but not enough to attract anyone's attention. The rest he had hidden in that old cabin, and it was safer than a bank, at least until that damn gussak came along.

He passed the final beaver pond and the last of the snowmachine trail. Spruce growth was a little thinner to his left, away from the river. He angled that way, skirting the deepest drifts.

The very fact that the other guys thought I was going to share the money meant they were too dumb to deserve any. They had been well paid for two hours' work; that was enough. If they wanted a share of the money, they shouldn't have kept calling me "Shrimp" and "Shorty." My plan worked perfectly and changed their lives. If they had acknowledged me as their leader and been willing to do exactly what I told them to do, we could have proceeded with the plan, but I can see that they wouldn't have done that.

His own plan was to find his father and maybe move to the other side of the world, possibly taking his father with him. For the sharing-out to have worked, the partners would all have had to disappear quietly, one at a time, with plausible excuses. He would have set that up, told them when and where to go, and provided the excuses, but he had come to see that they wouldn't follow his instructions. Once they had their hands on almost two million dollars each, they would flaunt it around, try to drink it up, and draw attention until someone figured out the source of the money.

He shook his head in disgust. When they were busted, he would become a fugitive, and even if he were in Bali, there would be people looking for him. That was not acceptable. So: The partners had to die. His plan would have been on track if that stupid trooper had arrested Ski for the murders. Well, his plans were ruined now. He was a fugitive and wanted for murder, not just bank robbery, but if he got the money and moved away far enough fast enough, it might still work out all right.

When the gussak moved into the old derelict cabin, he hadn't been too worried. Lots of newcomers had big ideas about building cabins in the woods and getting away from it all. Most of them lasted a couple of months, almost none of them made it a full year, and especially not those who married Eskimo wives. When the gussaks found out that they had married the entire Eskimo family, most of them were on the next plane to Seattle. It was just bad luck that Ski and his hellcat hadn't given up yet.

He had given them every opportunity to move out of the cabin. If they had been sensible, if the gussak cop had arrested Ski, if Punik had moved back to her cousin's place, they could have gone on living, but they were stubborn. Now they had to die, and that certainly was not his fault.

He found the moose trail that paralleled the river. Walking was easier; the moose had eaten the brush and broken through the drifts. He hadn't seen or heard of any moose around, so the gussak had probably poached it. It was unusual for a moose to come as far downriver as Emmonak, and when one did it was invariably shot long before it reached Sheldon Point. *Wouldn't it be a hoot if Fish and Game had busted the gussak for shooting moose out of season, when that dumb cop wouldn't arrest him for obviously committing four murders?*

The moose trail left the spruce, away from the river into a stand of scrub alders. The tops were chewed off half an acre of young trees. He opted to stay under the evergreens for their cover from the air, but busting his own trail was slow. In a couple of hours the gussak would come out his back door to start his generator, and he still had a mile to go. He wondered how the moose meat had been. Moose meat was good and fat during the early season when the moose had been eating grass and leaves. By this time of year, the moose were eating wood, chewing up the alder, and rarely had any fat at all.

❄ ❄ ❄ ❄

I'd moved a salmon steak from the freezer down to the crisper in the morning, and when I stuck a fork in it it went through, so it was thawed. That steak was special and came with a story. The patriarch of Bethel is known by his Native name of Datu. He's also known as John R. Samuelson, but this is Native business. The first fish to come up the river in the spring are king salmon, and the legend is that they have a leader, the biggest, strongest fish in the school.

Every year, Datu catches that leader and shares him out. That establishes man's domination over the fish and sets the tone for the coming season. Just how Datu knows when and where to catch that fish is between him and the

River God, and I don't know about that. What I do know is that every year for the past maybe fifty years, Datu catches one whopping big salmon before anyone else, and I was about to enjoy a share of the spoils. There was enough fat in that steak to lubricate the pan, so I set it on a cookie sheet, spread a layer of mayonnaise over it, sprinkled on some capers and shoved it into the oven.

The day Datu brought my steak I didn't have time for a proper dinner, so I stuck it in the freezer. When I got back to town two days later, everyone was giving away salmon. Those who fish for their own consumption aren't restricted by the commercial periods, and they invariably catch more than they can use. People are knocking on your door at two in the morning, begging you to take a few fish.

By midsummer, fresh salmon steaks are no longer the treat they should be, but now in midwinter it had been a while, and I was looking forward to this one. I leaned back in my chair, getting the first whiffs of ecstasy from the salmon, relaxed and letting my mind go blank.

I found myself standing in Jesse's cabin, Jessie still in his chair, a trickle of blood from the bullet hole running down toward his nose. Joe stepped into my dream and set Ski's automatic on the oilcloth. It lay there, glowing its dull, well-oiled metallic sheen.

The implication was like a slap in the face. I leapt up, grabbed the phone, and dialed Tom's number. I was trying to hold the phone in one hand and struggle into my snowsuit with the other. Tom answered on the second ring.

"Tom, wake up! I know who the murderer is."

"About time, Detective Price, and I'm not sleeping. I just picked up a fax of a newspaper article that explains the motive. I have to check the passenger list for one jet flight, and we'll go make the arrest."

"Damn it, Tom, he's on his way to kill Ski and Punik right now, and you're playing Sherlock Holmes games."

"And he is?"

"Remember when Joe put Ski's automatic on the table? It was wrapped in a dishtowel, but it was clean and dry. Joe said he found it in the snow, and I guess we thought he'd wiped it clean, but then it had Ski's prints all over it. Therefore, it had never been wiped, ergo it had never been in the snow."

"Then why are you yammering on the phone? I'll be at the airport in twenty minutes."

"I'll be waiting for you." I was halfway out the door when I remembered the salmon. Dear Lord, it did smell good. I used a dishtowel to grab the cookie sheet and shoved the whole thing into the refrigerator. I did beat Tom to the airport. I ran into the office, almost pulled the microphone off the radio, hollered for KBZ30 a couple of times but got no answer. I ran outside and started the first 206 on the line.

CHAPTER 24

UNDER SIEGE

Punik shivered, but she wasn't cold. "He's out there watching us. I can feel him. He's planning to kill both of us, Ski, all three of us."

"Take it easy, hon. We're in here, and we're planning to stay alive, all three of us. We just have to plan better than he does."

"Oh, Lord, Ski, he's so cold. He doesn't mind killing us at all; he's excited, looking forward to it."

"You can feel all that? Have I married a mind reader?" Ski crossed the kitchen and pulled Punik against his chest to stop her shivering.

"I'm not reading his mind. I think it's what's meant by 'feeling vibes.' You know, when someone stares at you, and you can feel it? It's like that, only he's excited and he wants to kill us."

Ski hugged her tight and bent to kiss the top of her head, loving the feel of her, loving the fragrance of her hair, but feeling, maybe smelling, her fear, too.

"I wish I'd had you with me in 'Nam. You could have saved a lot of lives. I don't suppose you can feel just where he is?"

"No, not really . . . yes, I can. He's in the woods out back right where he was when I fired the shotgun at him."

"Okay, here's what we do. First, we never do anything that might be expected, anything we normally do. In 'Nam there were well-traveled trails, easy places to walk, but if you ever walked on one of them you were dead. You were doing what you were expected to do. He obviously knows us pretty well. He knew where I kept my automatic, so he knows what to expect, and right now he's expecting me to go out the back door and start the generator. Maybe we can use that against him."

"Don't go out there, Ski. Oh Lord, he feels so awful."

"Hey, I just told you, we don't do anything that's expected, but let's see if he does what we expect him to do."

Ski peeled Punik loose and stood beside the kitchen window, reaching out to pull the taped Visqueen away. It was getting dark, dark enough that he was sure no one outside could see into the unlit kitchen. He strode out to the gun cabinet in the living room and came back jacking a shell into the chamber of Punik's .30-.30. He eased the hammer down, leaned the rifle against the kitchen counter, and took Punik by the shoulders to look into her eyes. What he saw there was not the gentle girl he had married.

"Punik, if you get the chance, can you kill him?"

"Ski, I can kill anybody or anything that threatens the three of us."

Her eyes told Ski that she spoke the truth. "Here's what we're going to do. You take your rifle and stand on this chair so you can see out the window. I'm going to open the back door, but don't worry, I'll keep behind the logs. If he's out there, he'll shoot. If his rifle flashes, you shoot at it, then jump down off the chair, okay?"

Punik nodded, picked up her rifle and stood on the chair. She could see a good slice of the back yard and woods, already dark under the trees. Ski grabbed a broom from the closet, slipped into the bedroom and came back with his old raincoat on a hanger. He twisted the hanger's hook tightly around the end of his broomstick.

"Ready?" he called.

"Ready." Punik thumbed back the hammer, shouldered her rifle, and watched the yard.

At least this will be a good test of the vibes theory, Ski thought. He opened the door and reached out with the broomstick to hold his raincoat in the opening. Punik's shot could have been an echo. The raincoat ripped off the broom handle and Ski slammed the door.

The visitor's thought was, *Damn, damn, damn*. The birch he'd been resting the rifle against was split; chunks of frozen bark had hit him in the face. Had to be the hellcat, because he'd gutshot the gussak and seen him fall. He rolled down into the frozen snowmachine trail and scrambled away in case she shot again. Where the hell had that shot come from?

He crawled until he could see the end of the cabin where the whip antenna for the single sideband was mounted. The element of surprise was gone; no need to be quiet now. *Huh, some surprise*, he thought, *but at least this time they won't be calling the troopers.* The antenna was silhouetted against the sky. He rested his rifle on another birch, keeping his face right in the snow, just in case, and shot the base of the antenna. He saw the coaxial cable drop and swing against the side of the house.

Ski carried his raincoat to the kitchen, his thumb through the bullet hole. Punik stood calmly against the wall, well away from the window. Ski was about to ask if she'd hit the shooter when the next shot came from the end of the house, and they heard the severed coax cable scrape against the logs.

"Well, my next idea was to call for help. Guess we can forget that." They walked together out to the living room and Ski turned up the volume on the strangely quiet receiver. The static and general music of the spheres that should have been there were missing. Ski looked out the window toward the east. He didn't see any rising moon. "It's going to be a long, dark night," he muttered.

The visitor crawled along the snowmachine trail past the back of the house. The trail was deep enough to keep him hidden, and it was almost completely dark under the trees. He wondered if the hellcat might be crouched inside the back door, probably crying over the gussak's body. He knew the gussak was dead or dying. He had gutshot him dead center, and men don't stop .30-06 bullets. Surely he had shattered the spine as well as ripping up the guts.

He fired three shots at the heavy plank door, wondering if they would penetrate. No one shot back, so he dug the box of shells out of his pocket and reloaded the rifle. Just to prove to himself that he was in control, he leaned against the edge of the trail to eat a fun-sized Snickers bar. *Take your time, stay relaxed. This won't be a problem.*

Ski knelt to check the back door. Splinters were sticking out, but the bullets had not come through. This was no ordinary door, and Ski had bought it because it went with the rustic design, not because it was practical. Apparently, the three-inch-thick oak planks were bulletproof, but the standard hardcore front door wouldn't be. Ski wondered how long it would be before someone started shooting through that.

Bullets ripped through the Visqueen window on the back door. Ski ducked, but realized it would have been too late if he'd been standing. Punik, standing behind him but six inches shorter, felt the shock waves from the bullets almost grazing her head. Glass shattered on a picture down the hall, and the solid thwock of the bullet burying itself in the log was chilling.

The visitor crawled farther down his trail, put a bullet through each of the back bedroom windows, and reloaded. The house was dark and silent and he wondered if both occupants were dead. Could he have been lucky enough to hit the hellcat through the back door? He thought he should crawl on around the house and shoot through the front a few times. If the hellcat was still alive, that might panic her into running and make her an easy target.

Punik shivered against Ski's chest. "What do we do now?"

"We do what he doesn't expect, whatever that is." They were crouching in the hallway inside the back door with solid log walls on either side of them. Bullets ripped through the bedroom windows at the far end of the house. Ski ran to the gun rack and grabbed his .30-06.

"He's crawling around the house," Ski hissed. "He'll shoot the front bedroom windows next." Two shots shattered the front bedroom windows. "Quick, into the bedroom." Ski grabbed Punik's hand and ducked past the big living room window into the front bedroom. Ski's patches were torn from both windows. He jerked Punik down to the floor and waited until the next shot spewed glass out of the front room window.

"Take the right-hand window." Ski released Punik's hand and they each jumped to a window, rifles raised, waiting for a muzzle flash. The flash came; they both fired at it and dropped to the floor.

The visitor shot at the bedroom window before he rolled down the hill and scrambled under the trees. His hat was gone, and his rifle stock was shattered. Two shots, so they were both still alive? He emptied his splintered rifle through the bedroom windows and reloaded.

Bits of wood and shards of glass from the overhead light fixture rained down on Ski and Punik. "Next idea?" Punik shook glass out of her hair.

Ski had been too slow, or the visitor too fast. As he dropped, Ski felt the streak of fire across his back and warm blood sticky on his shirt. Punik didn't see him wince in the darkness, and he didn't want to scare her more than necessary. "What was that term that Alex learned in those detective books that he's so proud of?" Ski asked.

"Proactive?" Punik asked.

"Yeah, that's it. Time to get proactive. I want you to keep shooting, just like you did the last time he shot at you. Keep down behind the logs; never look up. Wherever he seems to be, shoot back at him, but shoot low, almost at the ground, and for heaven's sake, no shotgun."

Ski saw Punik's nod in the near darkness. The weight of his love for her threatened to burst his chest. He felt tears spring to his eyes. He grabbed her and kissed her. Punik felt his tears and understood exactly what they meant. Ski handed her his .30-06. He crawled across the living room floor to the gun cabinet and grabbed a box of shells for each rifle.

He called to Punik. "This might be a good time to start shooting." Punik raised Ski's rifle above the windowsill and pulled the trigger. Ski set the two boxes of shells on the floor in the bedroom doorway and ran for the back door. An answering shot zinged through the window above Punik, then shots were ripping through the front door. Punik recoiled in horror, but surely, Ski had gone out the back? Was the shooter making an association with doors? Was he feeling danger, a premonition, as Punik had felt? She had to keep him distracted, had to convince him that Ski was still inside.

With a rifle in each hand, Punik used them like cross-country skis to crawl. She stopped in the doorway to reload both rifles and slid her way to the living room. Large chunks of the front window were gone. She kept herself and her baby well down behind the thick logs under the window, reached up to point Ski's rifle in the general direction of the trees beside the trail. She pulled the trigger. Half a second later, an answering shot tore the rifle out of her hands and sent it skittering across the floor.

Her right hand went numb from the shock; the trigger guard had cut a slice from her thumb and blood welled into her hand. No time for that now. Punik raised her own rifle and shot, but jerked it down before the next shot crashed through the window and a shower of glass erupted.

Punik hugged the floor and crawled back to the bedroom. Glass and wood splinters littered the floor and white dust from the ceiling was thick in the air. She fired and immediately crawled back to the living room to fire again while shots ricocheted through the bedroom.

The visitor congratulated himself on his new cover. Apparently the trees were thick or dark enough to hide him; the shots from the house were missing him now. He stopped to peel some of the splinters off the fractured rifle stock and reloaded.

He scanned the front windows, willing himself to see in the dark, watching for any movement at the windows. He fired a shot into the living room, saw a flicker of movement at the bedroom window, shot at that. Another shot came from the living room and slammed into a tree twenty feet in front of him. He put a bullet where that rifle had been.

Punik's path back to the bedroom was slippery with her own blood. She crawled to the bed, used her teeth to tear a strip from the sheet. A pillow pushed up above the windowsill and instantly exploded, adding feathers to the debris in the room. Punik bound her thumb with the strip of sheet. She knelt on the floor, raised the rifle high over her head and used her bandaged thumb to pull the trigger.

With the windows gone, the house was getting cold, and Punik was shivering from the chill, as well as fatigue. Her parka was hanging in the closet, only feet away, but to reach it she would have to stand up. She couldn't do that, not with the risk to Ski's baby.

She wondered if the shooter could tell which rifle was being fired. She crawled across the glass and retrieved Ski's '-06 from the corner in the living room. It had a nasty gouge in the barrel, but it wasn't bent. She held the rifle high, closed her eyes and fired. The shock was normal, the rifle still worked, but it seemed to be heavier. She realized that she had set up a pattern, firing from one room, then the other. She mustn't be predictable. She tried to raise Ski's rifle again, but her arms trembled; she couldn't raise it high enough.

She understood Ski's instructions to shoot low, because he was out there, and she might shoot him, but shooting low meant the rifle had to be raised high . . . but maybe . . . She rested the rifle butt on the floor and shot up through the trees. Surely that was safe, but what if the shooter could tell where the gun was pointing? What if he realized she was just creating a diversion?

A bullet clattered through the spruce trees above his head and snow slid down to slam him in the back. With his hat gone, cold powder stung his neck and bunched under his collar. He swiped the snow away and flopped his parka hood up to cover his neck and ears. He had to stop this nonsense, stop wasting ammunition. He couldn't hit what he couldn't see. He thought maybe if he screamed right after a shot was fired they would think he was hit and come out to check.

A shot from the hellcat's .30-30 came from the bedroom. It had been the gussak's .30-06 that hit the trees overhead. He didn't realize that the shot had been twenty feet above him, so thought the gussak knew exactly where he was. He could not understand why he wasn't hitting them. Each time a muzzle flashed from a window he put a bullet where the shooter should have been, but they kept shooting.

Punik was getting frantic. She was shivering uncontrollably now, feeling faint, not sure how much longer she could keep this up. She remembered the shot that ripped the pillow. She thought that if she got the other pillow, stood up behind the logs and tossed the pillow past the far window, she could shoot the muzzle flash, and this time she wouldn't miss. She reached up onto the bed and jerked the pillow down. She pulled herself up beside the left-hand window, but her knees were shaking. She leaned against the logs for a moment to steady herself.

The visitor scanned the windows over his sight, rifle ready to fire, waiting for a movement. Punik got her shaking legs under control, rifle cocked and ready, and drew back the pillow to toss it, ready to leap out and fire. When she swung the pillow, he shot it right out of her hand. The shock jerked her away from the wall. She sank to her knees, gave herself up to sobbing openly with fatigue, cold, anger and frustration. She raised her rifle over her head and fired right at the ground.

The visitor saw the flicker of movement and fired. Punik's rifle spun across the room, the stock split completely in two. She screamed her frustration and crawled through the glass to retrieve her rifle.

Suddenly the visitor's head was jerked back by a steel grip in his hair and a knife blade pricked his throat.

"Good evening, Joe," Ski said quietly. "Would you mind dropping that rifle, please?"

Joe dropped the rifle, but sneaked a hand down for his pistol. His holster was empty.

"Looking for this?" Ski asked. He flicked the knife closed and Joe felt his own revolver pressed against the back of his head.

"Punik," Ski called, "would you put the coffee on, sweetheart? Joe doesn't want to play this game anymore."

❄ ❄ ❄ ❄

I slammed the 206 onto the ice in front of the cabin. We didn't hear gunshots, but were we in time or too late? I tossed the cover over the engine—it was still twenty-five below. We followed our pistols up the slope. If the battle was over—if Joe had won—we'd make fat targets.

Tom stepped off the trail under the trees into a bunch of scuff marks and came back dragging a rifle by the barrel. The stock was splintered and bloody. He carried it along with us. A bit of fur lay on the snow. I picked up a beaver hat with a bullet hole through an earflap. We were too late, but who had won? We half crouched to the porch.

Punik swung the door open with her usual smile and gave us each our cheek peck, just like old times, except that Punik had Band-Aids scattered over her face and arms and her right thumb was wrapped in gauze. Half a dozen bullet holes pocked the door, and the big front window had no glass; it was covered by a blanket. Punik hurried to bring us coffee. A wooden Blazo box full of broken glass and feathers sat on the floor behind the door. Blazo comes in square five-gallon cans, two to the box, and the empty boxes make a lot of furniture in the Bush. Ski sat on the couch, coffee in his left hand, idly playing with a revolver in his right. His shirt was open and a three-inch-wide bandage was wound around his chest.

Joe sat in the easy chair, his ankles tied together and lashed to the chair legs. His right hand was pulled up behind his back and held there by a rope around his neck, but he had a cup of coffee in his left hand. Tom and I accepted our coffees from Punik. Tom sat on the couch beside Ski; Punik and I took wooden chairs.

"So, what's new?" Tom asked. I hate it when Tom tries to be funny.

Ski apparently thought it was cute. "As far as we can tell, Joe had a bad case of insomnia last night, so he dropped by for a visit."

"He didn't talk about why?" Tom asked.

"Just wanted a cup of coffee, apparently. He hasn't said a word all evening."

"Well," Tom said, "in this marvelous new age of computers, if you want a reason, all you have to do is ask." I glared at him. If he had the answer, he could have shared it on the way up. He was grandstanding, like Hercule Poirot when he calls all the suspects together at the end of a story to reveal the killer.

"Actually," Tom continued, "it was Detective Price who explained it all. He supplied the magic number, *ten million*, I just entered it into the troopers' computer system. Did you guys realize there are an estimated ten million swans that nest in the tundra every year?" Tom paused for coffee. I proved that looks cannot kill.

"Did you know that in 1942, the Nyack mine pulled ten million dollars' worth of gold out of the ground in a month?" Tom apparently noticed that I was about to give up killing him with looks and try more physical means, so he got to the point.

"Did you know that ten years ago next month, ten million dollars were stolen from an armored car in Anchorage, and the National Guard was in town at the time? In fact, all four murder victims, Muktuk, and Joe were registered at the Sheffield Hotel and caught the evening jet back to Bethel Friday night without waiting for the rest of the Fur Rendezvous festivities. Why was that, Joe? Don't you guys like dog races?" Tom stopped for another sip of coffee. Joe seemed to sag in his bonds.

Tom pulled a sheet of paper out of his pocket and unfolded it. "Here's an article I just got faxed from the *Anchorage Times*, February 26, ten years ago next month." He paused for another sip of coffee and cleared his throat. He was milking his moment.

"A well-organized gang of at least six members waylaid and robbed an armored car just after ten yesterday morning. According to police, two members of the gang were waiting inside the First National Bank for the morning delivery. They held the guards from the truck at gunpoint, made them strip off their uniforms, and tied them with duct tape. The gang members put on the uniforms and carried the delivered money bags back to the truck. The truck driver, who asked not to be identified, reports that he was stopped for several minutes on D Street while a wrecker picked up a car. Police speculate that the wrecker was driven by a member of the gang, and the money was transferred to waiting cars while the truck was blocked. When the truck arrived at First Federal Savings, the money and guards were missing from the back.

"Bank officials told this reporter that because of the Fur Rendezvous celebration and the number of trappers in town to cash checks, this was the largest cash movement of the year."

Tom looked up. "Do I need to go on, or would you like to take over, Detective Price?"

"I sure as heck would." I stood and bowed to satirize Tom's performance. "They shared out enough money to set each of them up in business, dreamed up the government loan story, and Joe hid the rest." I needed one more sentence, and I reached for it. "Joe wanted Ski and Punik out of the house because the remaining money is hidden right here."

Tom gave a couple of insincere sounding handclaps, like applauding a really bad nightclub act. "Well done, Sherlock. If you really want to be a hero, you should now reach into your bag of tricks and pull out the money."

Ski jumped up and tossed the pistol to Punik. "The cache," he said, and we all trooped out the back door . . . except Joe and Punik. Joe could only move his coffee hand and Punik settled on the couch in front of him to toy with the pistol.

Ski grabbed a single-bitted ax off the back porch and attacked the cache, ready to chop it down, but first banging the floor and walls with the blunt side, looking for the magic trap door. No luck. He systematically banged the floor logs and found a weak spot. We stepped back and Ski reversed the axe and whacked a six-foot sliver off the split log, but it was solid wood, just a thin spot and dirt underneath.

"Maybe the ceiling?" Tom suggested.

The ceiling was a Celotex material nailed up to poles. Ski slammed the axe into the middle of a panel and it collapsed. A rain of twigs from squirrel's nests, bird droppings, and dried leaves poured down on us. Ski shook the dirt out of his eyes and kept right on chopping. In a few minutes, we were ankle deep in Celotex chunks and detritus and were looking up at the naked slope of the roof.

Two tiers of logs supported the roof above the ceiling level. Ski noticed a large plaster patch on one wall, stood on tiptoe, and whanged it with his ax. The ax went right through. We jerked the workbench over next to the wall to stand on. Tom and Ski jumped up onto the bench; I tried to keep it from collapsing. They pawed at plaster until a brown plastic garbage bag came out and bundles of hundred-dollar bills fell onto the floor. We carried armloads of money back into the house and Punik brought new bags.

Ski slipped off the rope that had bound Joe's wrists and Tom replaced it with conventional handcuffs.

"You have the right to remain silent," Tom said, "but apparently you know that."

Joe had to sit on the bags of money in back for the ride to Bethel. I had forgotten that sometimes Tom brought live passengers home, so I hadn't stuck in any seats.

EPILOGUE

S everal legends were born the following July. The elders still sing about them, and dances have been choreographed. Eskimo dancing, like the Hawaiian hula, tells a story. The chanting and the drums set the rhythm and the mood. The dancers tell of miracles and heroic deeds with hand gestures and body movements, like acting out clues in charades.

The most remarkable accomplishment, to my mind, went almost without notice. When Punik was two weeks from due day, Ski packed a suitcase, picked Punik up bodily and stuck her on a twin Otter that was headed for Bethel. Punik went without an argument and checked into the prenatal boarding facility at the Bethel Hospital with other ladies-in-waiting. To me, that was a miracle, but remains unsung.

The dance of Evan and Ella visiting heaven is a favorite all up and down the river. It originated in St. Marys and spread from village to village. The dancers mime exploration, tiptoeing into danger, then discovery and surprise, eyes and mouths wide open, hands flung up with fingers splayed. They do it over and over, faster each time, with all sorts of nuances that a gussak will never catch. You see, Evan and Ella had achieved immortality. Since the day that the little family walked into St. Marys, neither Evan nor Ella had ever again been cold or hungry.

One of the results of the new lifestyle in St. Marys was that Evan and Ella got heavier and stronger, but had less body fat. The other result was that when I picked them up to go to Bethel for the blessed event, fifty-six-year-old Evan and forty-eight-year-old Ella still had teeth, and Ella wasn't tired anymore.

Evan had built a wooden house with windows and doors and screens. He heated it with a stove that had a stovepipe and a chimney, so they no longer breathed the smoke of their cooking and heating fires. They had a bed with many caribou blankets and a warm house, so they didn't sleep with their dogs in winter. That meant no more fleas burrowing into them for warmth. In summer, the screens kept out the clouds of mosquitoes, so they were no longer blood donors while they slept. They had given up washing in seal oil way back when Punik was a toddler and had learned to prefer soap and water.

Some young Natives who were born in hospitals, raised on Pablum, and educated in schools mourn the passing of their Native culture. Evan had no such regrets.

With immortality achieved, Evan was anxious to get a look at heaven. When I drove them from the Bethel airport to the Kuskokwim Inn, Ella sat bolt upright and silent, fists clenched, but Evan loved it. There were pickups in St. Marys, newer than mine, but the only road was a one-lane track from the village to the airport, so even the newest St. Marys pickups rarely got out of first gear in the summer. They skimmed along at a good clip on the ice in winter, but Evan knew about ice. It was the paved road he was marveling at.

I got them a room at the Kuskokwim Inn and asked the manager to charge their meals. No problem. Evan explored, struck speechless by the size and opulence of the buildings. He spent whole days in the Swanson Brothers' store, wandering from the lumberyard to the hardware, to the groceries, to the clothing, and finding new miracles in every aisle. Someone told me that Evan spent four hours in the butcher shop watching the butchers cut up a side of beef and a hog.

Ella went straight to the hospital every morning. She and Punik spent their days while they waited for Ella's ninth grandchild in the labyrinth of corridors, going from room to room and visiting with each occupant. It didn't matter from which corner of the Delta the patients came. If they spoke Yup'ik, Ella would trace back through their verbal genealogy until she discovered in what way they were related. Many of the patients thought that Ella was an angel, and with Punik there to translate, many needs were met that language barriers had kept hidden from the hospital staff.

Another legend and dance that young Evan Kawalski grew up with was the story of how his father had summoned a lightning bolt to Emmonak and ridden it to Bethel for his birth. That was the summer that Bushmaster bought the Beech B-50. The smell of petroleum was in the Alaska air. Geologists from Atlantic Richfield and British Petroleum were calling from all corners of the state, wanting to be moved immediately to some other corner, and the Beech was our solution to that.

Unless you're a real airplane buff, you've probably never heard of the B-50. Beechcraft built it for the U.S. Navy as the last trainer their pilots flew before advancing to jets. Later, Beech scaled it down and tamed it to make the popular Beech Baron for civilian consumption, but there was nothing tame about the B-50.

It was around eleven at night but Bushmaster was keeping summer hours. The sun was down behind the northern horizon making that twilight that passes for summer nights. I had just hefted my flight bag into my locker when Vickie burst into the room. She had made guns out of both fists and was shooting me with alternate ruby nails, "Khee, khee, khee, khee. Punik just called. Tonight is the night."

I got the picture. I jerked the flight bag back out of the locker and ran outside. The B-50 was the first plane in the line and it suited my state of mind. I may have known that this night was coming for the last seven months, but I wasn't nearly ready. I want to make it clear that I did not panic, because bush pilots do not panic. I was just very concerned. Births, some of them right in the airplane, were not new, but this was little Punik, and I felt brotherly, avuncular; aw hell, I loved the girl. I guess I expected Ski's kid to show up weighing forty pounds, and that's what Punik had looked like for the last month. To a bachelor, it appeared mechanically impossible.

There's also that male dilemma. On this night, when you most want to help, would love to take charge and solve the problem, there's not a thing you can do. Fathers pace the halls of hospitals. I had the B-50 flat out doing two hundred and forty when I screamed down in a dive over the cabin, down the river past the cannery and through the village.

I didn't know where Ski might be, and I wanted him to see and hear me, so I had all the lights on, rotating beacon, strobes, anticollision lights, clearance lights, landing lights, taxi lights, and enough power on to wake up anyone who might be sleeping in Emmonak or Alakanuk.

At the end of the village I chopped the power, pulled straight up twelve hundred feet to lose some speed, did an inside loop and reefed on the yoke to lose more speed, dropped the flaps as soon as I dared, lowered the gear at a hundred and fifty knots and sideslipped straight down to the end of the runway farthest from the village.

I was still standing on the brakes too hard at the end of the runway, ready to slide into the parking apron, when Ski came sprinting across the gravel from the cannery. I locked up the left brake, spun around to put the right wing toward him. He bounded up the steps, fell into the passenger seat, and the moment the door closed, I lit the fire and took off downwind.

I suppose we did look and sound quite a bit like a lightning bolt with thunder.

The next afternoon we formed our tableaux. Ski and Punik lounged on the bed with little nine-pound Evan Kawalski between them. Old Evan and Ella stood at the foot of the bed with Tom and Minnie on their right, Connie and me on their left.

Punik had just finished nursing little Evan, and I've got to tell you that a happy mother suckling a healthy baby is the most thrilling sight that the human experience has to offer. It's too bad that some cultures keep that hidden, as though it were shameful. Punik was proud of the activity, and her pride sure seemed justified to me.

She reached to remove a damp diaper, and she didn't rush to replace it. A healthy set of genitals was also a point of pride, the key to the survival of a culture where not so long ago two of four babies died before they were two and life expectancy was forty. Little Evan was cooing, sporting an erect little member as big around as a pencil and an inch long.

With a sigh of satisfaction, he launched a golden stream toward the ceiling. It wavered back and forth like a snake while he happily wriggled his hips. The stream went up and up, then arced down to cover the six spectators standing at the foot of the bed.

The End

OTHER BOOKS BY DON G. PORTER

Deadly Detail
An exciting adventure suspense story covering Alaska during the time the pipeline was being built. September 2005, published by Poisoned Pen Press.

Happy Hour
A suspense about the attempt of the Russian Mafia to set up a protection scheme in Alaska. September 2005, published by McRoy & Blackburn.

For complete information about Porter's books, visit **www.dongporter.com**.

OTHER BOOKS FROM MCROY & BLACKBURN

MYSTERIES ❋ THRILLERS ❋ TALES OF THE BUSH ❋ TALES OF THE SEA
ADVENTURE ❋ TALL TALES ❋ SATIRE ❋ CHILDREN'S BOOKS
HUMOR ❋ FICTION FROM THE NORTH ❋ BOOKS FOR YOUNG AND OLD

Accessories are Everything in the Wild, by Nita Nettleton
Alaskans Die Young, by Susan Hudson Johnson
Battling Against Success, by Neil Davis
The Birthday Party, by Ann Chandonnet
Bucket, by Eric Forrer
Caught in the Sluice: Tales from Alaska's Gold Camps, by Neil Davis
Cut Bait, by C. M. Winterhouse
The Great Alaska Zingwater Caper, by Neil Davis
Happy Hour, by Don G. Porter
In Dutch, by C. M. Winterhouse
The Great Alaska Zingwater Caper, by Neil Davis
Keep the Round Side Down, by Tim Jones
The Long Dark: An Alaska Winter's Tale, by Slim Randles
Raven's Prey, by Slim Randles
The Red Mitten, by Sarah Jane Birdsall
The Wake-Up Call of the Wild, by Nita Nettleton

www.alaskafiction.com

WHAT REVIEWERS SAY ABOUT M&B BOOKS

Sarah Birdsall has been awarded a bronze medal in the 2007 Independent Publishers annual competition (IPPY) for her novel, *The Red Mitten*.

"*Alaskans Die Young*... is perfect for a relaxing read in an easy chair with a mug of steaming coffee on the side."—Shana Loshbaugh, *Fairbanks Daily News-Miner*

"Randles' descriptive skills [in *Raven's Prey*] do credit to his deep knowledge of Alaska, the people, and the way of life, as he takes you along on the hunt of a lifetime in the far north."—Gail Skinner, *On the Scene* magazine

In this often humorous, but mostly matter-of-fact autobiographical novel [*Battlling Against Success*], Neil Davis tells the compelling story of growing up on a homestead near Fairbanks in the 1940s.... Davis does an outstanding job of bringing all the characters to life."—Melissa DeVaughn, *Alaska* magazine

"[*Bucket*] is a tale parents won't mind reading again and again.... Eric Forrer's writing is as rich as an old-time fairy tale.... Eloise Forrer's unique, whimsical illustrations were done with colored carbon paper and an iron. The effect is something like woodblock printing, textured and lovely. Refreshingly, the book has no moral or lesson, except that sometimes you should let a story just take you away."—Donna Freedman, *Alaska* magazine

"C. M. Winterhouse ... has created a meandering and irresistible sometime sleuth in her debut novel, *Cut Bait*. ... Unlike some Alaska mysteries in which the only local color is the landscape, *Cut Bait* is filled with characters and situations that seem convincingly Alaskan."—Sandra Boatwright, *Fairbanks Daily News-Miner*

"[In *The Birthday Party*], Chandonnet's use of rhyme and meter keeps the story moving along toward the punch line...."—Nancy Brown, *Peninsula Clarion*

"Slim Randles can set one heck of a scene [in *The Long Dark*]....A quiet undercurrent of humor keeps the reader contentedly turning pages, looking forward to the next clever plot development. He has a good hand with a yarn." —Ann Chandonnet, *Juneau Empire*